PHYLMECS

Don't Let Looks Deceive You.
They're Here To Kill You

E.R. AYON

AYON PUBLISHING

Contents

Chapter 1
THE FEELING

Breakfast is one of my favorite parts of the day, and I really don't know why. Maybe it's the pure simplicity of it? I always place my frozen meat and egg burrito in the microwave for two minutes, and while that heats up, I pull up the current show that I am binge-watching (Futurama). Plain and simple but so calming. I wouldn't have changed this for anything in the world. But life, being life, always has a way of throwing curveballs. For better or for worse. In my case, it was not for the better. If I had known that this would be the last "normal breakfast" of my life, I would have surely savored it more. A lot more.

But I shouldn't get ahead of myself, and I'll start my story from the beginning. As I was saying, having breakfast is simply one of my favorite parts of my day, but this specific morning was strange. As I was about to hit play on my show an odd sensation swept through my mind. I started to feel like I was forgetting or missing something. A sensation that there was something I had to do, somewhere that I had to be. Everything just felt off. I began to feel bothered, and a bit uneasy. I felt goosebumps begin to form on my arms as I thought of what was making me feel this way.

"What did I forget?" I asked myself. Did I have to attend a meeting somewhere? Was there an exam that I forgot to study for, or a project I didn't do? My body started to feel warm as I felt my adrenaline start to flow through me. I began to feel jumpy. Not a good way to start my morning. Shake it off, I told myself and I gently tapped the sides of my head. Good grief, I mumbled to myself while the microwave alarm went off. I took my burrito out of the microwave, and as I sat my plate down my fingers began throbbing. The plate slipped from my hand and shattered everywhere. What is going on with me today? I yelled in frustration. There is no reason why my fingers should be throbbing like that. I gently rubbed my hands together.

One problem at a time, I told myself. It is just a plate. I went to the garage and pulled out a broom, and swept up the broken pieces. The broom handle felt wet as I finished sweeping. I stared at my hands. My palms were sweating, and my pulse was rising. I needed to do something to calm myself down. Okay, breathe, Daniel, I told myself. Focus and control your breathing. Retrace your steps from this week and last week, and think back if anything odd happened. Was there somewhere that I had to be, or someone that I had to speak to?

I went through a list of everything that I had to do for this week, and everything that I had done last week. There was absolutely nothing out of the ordinary, and I didn't recall having had anything upset me recently either. All I had going on were normal things like studying for my upcoming midterms, going to the gym, and hanging out with my friends. Okay, I told myself I must have had a bad dream or slept on the wrong side of the bed. There is nothing wrong. Yeah, that must be it. I must have had a bad dream last night, a very bad dream. As I said the words out loud I didn't sound too convincing to myself, but I kept repeating them. Slowly but surely I was starting to believe them. As the old saying goes, "If you repeat something enough you'll believe it." Thankfully, I felt my pulse going back to normal and my hands stopped sweating. Bad dreams are the worst, I reassured myself. Especially when you can't remember them.

Feeling better I heated up another burrito and quickly ate while watching the remainder of the episode. At least the last part of my morning is going well I thought. When I was done with my episode and breakfast I glanced at the clock on the stove and noticed that if I didn't start getting ready for class I would be late.

I quickly put my plate in the sink and went to get dressed. I yanked the first outfit I could find and dressed in a rush as I brushed my teeth. I was out the door shortly after. I had no time to comb my hair so I guess I would look like someone who just rolled out of bed. Not a good look Daniel, not a good look at all, oh well.

I had bigger things to worry about like actually passing my exams. I decided to study for my exams while on my way to class. By the time I got to school, I had all but forgotten the strange morning that I had, until I stepped onto campus. Slowly the strange sensation re-emerged as a lingering thought in the back of my mind. Don't focus on it, I told myself, just ignore it, focus on your studying. I still had thirty minutes before my first class started, so I put on some light music and tried to fade the thoughts away.

I don't understand why we need to learn this. I mean, who cares if the quadratic formula equals the square root of y/2, how would this even help me? I muttered to myself, and why is every song about love nowadays? I stared at my phone and switched the playlist that was playing. Where are all the songs about just having fun with your friends? By this point, I was asking myself pointless questions to distract my mind, from the weird feeling lingering in the back of my mind.

That entire day at school was even stranger than the first half of my morning had been. On top of having that strange feeling of forgetfulness lingering in the back of my mind, I now was having these strange and very intensive deja vu-vision episodes. Like I had done or been somewhere already but couldn't remember doing that thing or being in that spot. While in history class I had a strong vision. One minute I was in class and the next, *I was in an open plain and all I could see was destruction all around me. Buildings that I had never seen before were burning down. Buildings so oddly shaped that they did not look like they were from this planet. Yells and cries all around me. People ran around in circles wearing clothing that were almost like robes. It felt so real as if I was actually there. I could feel the heat from the burning buildings on my face. I felt the sweat on my forehead and heard the tremendous popping sounds that happen when a fire gets too big to control. I started to freak out because it was feeling too real to just be a vision or deja vu. I reached out to tap a person who was crying when I snapped back to reality.* I guess I must have looked anxious or distracted because all of a sudden I was "back in class," taken away from visions that I was having by the snapping fingers of Professor Brookes.

"Daniel, Daniel, are you there, or are you going to pretend that we are in drama class?" Huh? Excuse me. "I've asked the same question twice now, "Why do you think human technology has advanced so rapidly over the last 100 years?" Uhh, I think because people focus less on surviving and more on advancing. "Nice answer Daniel, but next time make sure you pay attention in class." I felt my face turn red as the entire class looked at me. I felt my shirt getting wet from my warm sweat. My classmate who also happens to be my best friend Javier looked at me and made a smirking face. He probably thought I had fallen asleep in class. If he only knew how wrong he was. As he smirked, all I could do was roll my eyes at him. What is going on with me today I wondered. I am not liking this whatsoever.

After my classes were over I knew that I desperately needed to go to the gym. The gym is my haven. I needed to go bad after the day I was having. Javier, do you want to come with me to the gym? <Daniel, look at me does it look like I have ever been to the gym?> I started to laugh because of course, it didn't look like he went to the gym. <Please, I am going home to rest and play some video games and have something to eat.>

I smiled at him, but then gave him a disappointed look. Javier I'll get you to come to the gym one day if it's the last thing I do. <Yeah, yeah Daniel you keep thinking that, please.> <In fact why are you going to the gym?> <It looks like you need to go get some rest, and some food in you I may add.> <Especially after all the daydreaming you were doing in class.>

Maybe Javier was right and I should just skip the gym and go home and rest, but I decided against it. Instead, I patted his tummy and said, "Javier, some of us believe it or not like to be active." Javier gave me the middle finger, but he knew I was joking. Javier is on the bigger side. He is around 6'2 and a good 300 pounds, but he is surprisingly very active and carries his weight well. I think he's been the same height and weight since we were in middle school.

Javier is the type of person who stands out when he steps into a room. His hair is always buzzed almost completely off, and he wears some giant Harry Potter glasses. When you look at him you may think he has an attitude, but once he flashes his smile your entire perspective of him changes. He has dark skin with a hint of small freckles. He looks like a big ole teddy bear. Sometimes we both laugh because we are both total opposites, yet he's my best friend. I've known him since we were both in elementary, and to this day I do not know how we get along so well since we have no common hobbies.

Anyway after saying bye to him, I headed to the gym with hopes that it would help me refocus my mind, and save the remainder of my day. When I got to the gym I did start to feel a little better. Just the environment felt like home to me. I don't strive to be super muscular or anything. I just like to be fit, and I like the feeling that working out gives me. I first started to work out about two years ago to build my confidence. I was very short, and I would get teased occasionally about my height, and about how skinny I was. After a couple of months at the gym, my confidence in myself grew, and I started to feel good about myself. Funny enough, to my surprise and the surprise of my parents a year after going to the gym, aka last summer I had a huge growth spurt. I went from 5'2 to 5'8. In only 3 months! I guess I was a late bloomer.

I am glad that I grew, but I was already happy before the growth spurt, thanks to the gym. One thing that I was secretly over the moon about was that my face matured a tad during my growth spurt. I was happy about this because I knew that I would be heading to college the following year. I already looked super young to be in high school, and since I knew I was graduating high school a year early I did not want to look like a ten-year-old freshman. Fast forward, I am now 17 and in my freshman year of college. I still feel like I look 15, but to my surprise, I have had a few people ask for my phone number, and frankly, I don't know why. I have plain brown hair and tanned skin. Very plain if you ask me, but I guess some people like plain.

It is funny though when they find out that I am only 17 they immediately leave. I don't mind. I am too busy to date anyway, and it would distract me like I am being distracted right now daydreaming about the last two years of my life. Okay, Daniel focus and start your workout, on second thought I need to go stretch out first. I needed my body to get loose after the day that I had. I did a 15-minute yoga stretch, and after stretching I went over to the curling station and that's when the strongest vision struck me.

I was suddenly looking at people running for their lives. They were yelling something, but I couldn't understand what it was. "I can't understand what you are yelling, please slow down and tell me!" They were speaking a language that I was not familiar with. It sounded like a mixture of Hebrew and ancient Greek. I glanced and saw some weird creature with its head attached to a person's head. I saw a child trying to pull this creature's head from what I assumed to be his mother's head. Suddenly I was back in the gym next to the curling station. I looked at myself in the mirror and I was covered with sweat, was it from the workout or my vision? What is going on with me today? Has the stress of school finally gotten to me? I knew college would be stressful, but this was ridiculous.

Suddenly I felt a hand on my shoulder, <Daniel are you okay?> I jumped about two feet into the air and snapped back into reality. It was Valerie, my other best friend. Valerie, Javier, and I all met in elementary school and we have been inseparable ever since. We all graduated a year early from high school as well. Valerie was looking at me with concerned eyes, <Are you okay>, she repeated. I felt my face turn red again. Of course, I am okay. Why wouldn't I be? Valerie looked at me and said, <Well you were just yelling,> I was yelling? <Yes, you were practically screaming, "Don't hurt them, leave me alone!"> What is happening to me, I thought silently. I tried to mask my concern for Valerie and smiled at her. Don't worry Valerie, I guess my wild imagination got the best of me. I guess I just need to stop over-excelling myself.

Valerie just kept looking at me. She was observing me. She didn't believe me, but she didn't want me to become more stressed by asking me more questions. She knew I was already embarrassed. Valerie is the type of person who can read a person like a book. She knows when someone is lying and she does not have a mean bone in her body. She is the type of girl who is beautiful but people do not see it since her shyness masks it. She has long red hair with big green eyes. She is slim and tall.

Valerie, I think I may head out early. I have a lot of studying to do, and I guess the stress of my midterms are taking a toll on me. Valeria looked at me and said, <Daniel I am always here for you.> <If you ever have an issue you can count on me okay?>

Thanks Valerie the same goes for you, and I want you to know that I genuinely mean it too. She smiled at me and gave me a big hug. <Text me when you get home okay?> I will, don't worry at all! My workout may have been short, but I was feeling better overall. The stretching did help me relax my body, and I was actually feeling pretty good. I was glad that I had friends like Javier and Valerie. It has always been us three since second grade. We are an odd little group with no real passions in common, but we click somehow.

I was really glad to be heading home. I hadn't realized how exhausted I felt until I started driving back home. All I could think about was my face hitting my pillow and just taking a good long nap. Those kinds of naps where, when you wake up you do not remember who you are, or where you're at. The best kind. My head was still slightly spinning from the chaotic day that I had. A good nap would take care of all of that.

Thankfully, I wasn't too worried about my crazy day anymore. I'm sure that everything that I experienced today stems from the stress of school, and the everyday life of a college freshman who really doesn't know what is going on in his life. Honestly, I just need to learn better time and stress management. I'm a smart kid, and I need to start believing in myself more. Once I do that, I am sure I will not have another chaotic day like today again. Yeah, I am sure that's it.

At last, I pulled up to the driveway of my house. I quickly parked the car and I went straight to the fridge to grab a soda. Before I could open the fridge I noticed the note pinned to it. "Daniel, we love you, and we hope you have an amazing week without us, love Mom and Dad." "P.S., we will try to call as often as we can, have fun, love Mom and Dad." Oh wow yes! I had forgotten that this week my parents would be gone for the week for their annual "before Spring Break vacation." It is the vacation that they take before everyone goes on their Spring Break vacation.

It is funny in a way that they do that, and this was the first year that they left me alone! A whole week without my parents I was ecstatic. I love my parents, don't get me wrong, and they have been the best parents that I could ask for, but who isn't happy when they have the house to themselves for an entire week? I was supposed to move out for college but decided last minute against it. Maybe I felt that I was too young, or maybe I just chickened out. Who knows, but at least for a week it meant that I would be home alone. Yay, I thought, now I can relax in peace.

I headed toward my room. I stripped down my clothes, and put on some comfortable pajamas. Now it was nap time. I set the alarm for just one hour. Just a normal nap, and after this nap I will feel refreshed, and hopefully ready to start studying for my midterms. I'll feed my dog after, and maybe even call up Javier and Valerie to see if they want to study a bit. I am planning to pass my first year as a college student with all As, and yes I know I am a total nerd, but who doesn't love nerds, right?

Chapter 2
THE APPEARANCE

"Tap, tap, tap, tap." I awoke suddenly; feeling dazed and confused. I wondered if I had heard a noise or if it was just a dream. I opened my eyes, and it was pitch black in my room. I grabbed my phone and checked the time. I was shocked that my nap had turned into full-fledged sleep. It was 1:37 in the morning. Great I thought, I just wasted my entire evening sleeping instead of studying for my upcoming midterm exams. On top of that, my parents must be worried sick that I haven't called them as the note had asked. Oh no! I also forgot to text Valerie to let her know that I had gotten home. Oh well, I sighed.

I had 4 missed calls and several unread texts from my parents, Valerie, and Javier, but I would text them later. First, I had to feed my poor dog who must be super hungry by now. He was probably the one tapping on my window. Cowboy sometimes taps on my window when he wants attention or food. One of the cons of having a big dog. Time to get up, I muttered to myself.

As I was about to get off my bed to go feed Cowboy my eyes slowly closed. They were heavy with sleep and shut. The next thing I remember is waking up again to the, "Tap, tap, tap, tap" sound. I am coming, Cowboy. I yelled with a half-asleep voice, but still, the tapping continued and this time it sounded more like a bang than a tap.

I felt a wave of fear run through my body. I quickly got up. That couldn't be my dog, someone was definitely pounding on my window now. Bang, bang, bang! The window and the walls shook. It must be someone trying to break in. Someone must have caught wind that my parents would be gone for the week. They probably thought I was with them, and that the house was alone. I felt my heart begin to pound, and I quickly scanned my room for my 20-pound dumbbell. I may be needing this, I thought.

If this robber was able to get through Cowboy, who is a Great Dane and weighs well over 100 pounds then this intruder must mean trouble. "Thump, thump, thump! The pounding was growing rapidly. What should I do? I told myself. Should I hide, run, fight, or call the police?

Okay, first thing first I need to assess the situation. I quietly tiptoed off my bed toward my window. There was no way this person would see me because I always kept my blinds shut. I like having a dark room.

Also, I have light protective curtains over my blinds so there was no way they could see into my room. That made me feel better as I quickly quietly made my way toward the window. I carefully opened the curtains, and I gently lifted the bottom blind every so slightly. What I saw made my blood run cold. I felt like time stopped instantly. I almost yelled but quieted myself by putting my hand across my mouth. What I was seeing was something out of this world.

Looming tall by my window was a being not from this world. I couldn't believe what I was seeing, and the thought that popped into my head of what it could be truly scared me. This had to be an alien! An extraterrestrial creature, a being from another world! A UFO as the conspiracy nuts say. I rubbed my eyes again to make sure I was just not being tricked by the shadows of the night. It was still there after I blinked several times. It was like no animal or human that I had ever seen. This "alien" was standing against the wall looking at me.

It had enormous eyes, huge really. Think about how big an owl's eyes are, and times that by two. Then you'll get a sense of how big this creature's eyes were. It probably sees perfectly in the dark. What caught my eye next was this purple jewel that it had right on the top of its head. It wasn't big, but it was bright purple. I couldn't tell if it was a piece of jewelry or a true part of its anatomy. As I stared at the jewel on its head I noticed the odd shape of the alien's head.

Its head was shaped very human-like, but it did not have a human face. Its face was doglike in appearance. It had a snout exactly like a Doberman. Triangular, long, and muscular looking. On the tip of the snout was its nose, and it was a bright purple. It seemed to almost glow in the darkness.

On a second glance, the nose did glow in an off hue. The moon's light reflected off of it. What my eyes gravitated to next were its two long ears on top of its head. Its ears were shaped oddly enough like a kangorous's ears. Ears that probably heard my heart beating in my chest. Those ears were thick and triangular. They were bright purple like its nose too.

It had a thick humanlike neck which connected it to a muscular body. Its torso resembled the body of a human mixed with the body of any four-legged animal. Think of the movie Tarzan and how his body was human, but also animal in structure. This is how this creature's body looked. This led me to believe this "alien," or whatever it was could walk upright, and also run on all fours.

Next, its two back legs were long and its back feet resembled the feet of a bear, not at all human, but more animal-like. Its two front legs were a bit shorter and those legs resembled human arms. Its front "feet" were not feet at all. They resembled an ape's hands. This creature could use those hands as well as any human. I was sure of it.

The creature was covered in gray-like soft sleek fur. Kind of like the fur on a well-groomed horse. It did not have any sort of tail that

I could see, but who knows since its night time. Lastly, what truly caught my eye were the creature's two massive wings. These wings were probably 10 feet in length on the back of its back. Its wings were purple and massive. On the top of its wings, it had golden blades that looked like they could slice anyone up like bologna. On the bottom of its wings, it had two additional golden-like blades that looked equally as sharp. I knew that these wings could do serious damage.

What surprised me most is that I believe the "alien's" wings were prehensile. They looked like they could bend this way and that way, and even pick up things if need be. This was not a creature you wanted to have as an enemy, and this was the being that was standing just a window away from me.

A deadly creature within inches of a kid with nothing but a twenty-pound weight. I felt my stomach drop to my feet. I had to be dreaming. This couldn't be true. I stepped away from my window and ran to turn on the light switch, but before I could turn on the light I suddenly heard a voice in my head. [Do not fear me, I am not an enemy.] I stood frozen. Instantaneously I felt goosebumps throughout my body.

[My name is Sevashkish, and I am here to deliver an urgent message to you Daniel.] [Please I ask may I come inside your house to speak with you?] I told myself, "Wake up Daniel, wake up," but I knew deep down that I was not dreaming. I knew in my heart that this was reality. The beating and pounding of my chest could not be a dream, yet I pinched and slapped myself to be sure. "Do I run outside and get help, or do I call someone, I thought?"

What do I do? I had to grab my phone and record this being, and then call for help. I was not going to be one of those people who say they saw an alien, and present no proof. I went and grabbed my phone, and when I looked at my cell phone it froze. The screen was completely white. Could this creature have done something to my phone? The "alien" spoke again, [Please I ask may I come inside your house to speak with you?]

How could I say no to this being of such power and strength I thought. I was scared beyond belief but I knew this much. This creature had swords on its wings, it had the power to kill me if it wanted to, and if it was asking for my permission it meant that for whatever reason it needed something from me, so it couldn't hurt me right at that moment. For some reason that ended up making me feel more anxious than before. Anyway, what choice did I have?

I responded, "Of course, I am coming to open the garage door, but please be careful with my dog Cowboy." [Do not worry about Cowboy, he senses the reasoning behind my presence and won't be an issue.] That was just weird I thought, but made me feel safer. I trust my dog when it comes to who he senses is a good vs a bad person. That's if he is still alive.

Chapter 3
THE REVEAL

I ran to the garage door, still in my sleeping clothes, and Sevashkish was there by the time I opened the door. He did not stand like a human, as I'm sure he had the possibility of doing. Instead, he stood on all fours, but with his head poised very highly and upright. His massive wings held high above his back. [Daniel it is a pleasure to meet you, and I am sorry for causing any fear.] [I do not know how much time I have to explain what I need to tell you, so I must be quick.] [I know what I will tell you now will seem so incredible that it may seem unbelievable, but I ask you to let me finish telling my story before you ask any questions.]

I felt like I could pee my pants. There was an alien or whatever it was, speaking with me and asking me for permission. All I could say was yes. What choice did I have? Besides, I was genuinely curious at this point as to what he wanted to tell me. Yes, please go on, I said through chattering teeth, and while holding my head.

It felt weird to hear someone else's voice in my head. It felt kind of like an invasion of privacy in a way because we are only used to hearing our own thoughts in our minds. Weird in a way.

[As I said my name is Sevashkish and I consider myself to be a defender of the free, a lover of life, and a carer for the weak.] [I come from a species called the Lukens.] [We Lukens are a species of the 7th dimension.] The 7th dimension I repeated? What do you mean by that? [I mean that in this universe there is more than one dimension Daniel, and I am from the 7th.] [You humans are now right in the middle of the third dimension.]

Suddenly I remembered a lecture I had in one of my physics classes. It was about the possibility of different dimensions in the universe, and the possibility of life existing in other dimensions. I also remembered something to the extent of how interactions between dimensions would never be possible without each one possibly getting affected. I couldn't remember the entire lesson clearly because it was a lesson on "borderline fictional physics," as my teacher had called it, so I did not take it seriously.

According to my physics teacher, or what I remember him saying, it was not possible for inter-dimensional beings to communicate with each other. So how is Seva or whatever his name is talking to me? I silently thought. Sir, mister, your name is Seva, or? [My name is Sevashish.] Okay, so you are a being of the 7 dimension. How are you able to talk to me? Isn't it harmful to talk to someone from another dimension? His big eyes lit up when I asked my questions. He seemed pleased by what I asked.

[I see humans are advancing in the sciences.] [Beings from higher dimensions may visit the worlds of lower dimensional beings, as visitors.] [No damage will happen if no contact in any way is made, with the lower dimensional beings.] How do beings from lower dimensions not see the visitors then?

[They are not in the same frequency level yet, though on rare occasions some do, but briefly.] [If contact is made with two inter-dimensional beings then extreme chaos may occur affecting both worlds.] Sevashkish, why are you talking to me then? Why put others in danger? I asked him in a stern voice. What do you want from me? I am just a regular person.

I am not the president. If you are from a different world, dimension, universe, or whatever, shouldn't you make contact with someone more important? [You were the only one who heard my call.] [A call made in the 7th dimension but on your planet.] [You are an exception to the rule of chaos, and nothing will happen from us having contact.]

[You see you are one of the rare ones that can see and hear other dimensional beings.] What? I started to feel lightheaded. I am officially going crazy. I had to laugh out loud. Am I really speaking with an alien, or am I just turning crazy? [I will explain all that I can Daniel, but please listen to what I have to tell you.] I couldn't say anything other than okay.

[My species, the Lukens, are 20 million years older than homo sapiens, but I believe one day that your species will be able to evolve to the same dimension as us, or maybe even pass us.] [This is one of the reasons as to why I took the risk to come to Earth and speak with you.] [Another reason is that the beauty and life of your planet are unmatched in the known universe.] [I cannot see it go to waste.] What do you mean by, "to go to waste?"

[Please know what I am about to tell you will seem unbelievable, but you must believe me.] I was starting to get really scared, and my palms started to sweat. [All of the population of Earth will be wiped out in about 8 weeks.] I simply stared at him blankly. Had I heard that correctly? Did he really say that all of the population of Earth will be wiped out in eight weeks? I felt chills run through my body.

What do you mean that all of the population of Earth will be wiped out in eight weeks? [I mean that in two Earth months, billions of people will die.] [Their bodies will live on, but belong to someone else.] [Who they are and their actual "self-being or soul," however you want to call it will be terminated and consumed.] [Every building, every tree, and every animal will be completely wiped out.] [Earth as a planet will become a place of hell.] [Earth will die, and become nothing more than a satellite, like your moon.]

I couldn't believe what I was hearing. Images of my mom and dad ran through my head. Images of all the animals that I had ever seen, and all the buildings I ever saw came flooding to my mind. This has to be some weird dream. I pinched myself, I slapped my face. Still, Sesvashkish stood in front of me. You are not real! I yelled to Sevashkish, and I ran back to the house and locked the doors. I went back into my bed and pulled the covers over me. Yes, I was sleeping. All I had to do was wake from this nightmare. Wake up Daniel, wake up, this is all a dream. I pounded my head lightly.

Suddenly, Sevashkish's voice boomed in my head. [Daniel, please listen.] [This is not a dream.] Before I could get out of bed Sevashkish was in my room. How did you get into my room? [Daniel, please listen to me.] [Everything that I have told you is true, and it is not a dream.] [You are the only one who can help your planet now.] I don't know why, but when he said that, it got me off my bed. I stood up and looked into his massive eyes. Okay, I am listening. He folded down his wings near his flank. I am assuming as a sign of relief.

[I know this is hard, but I must go into more detail on what is going on.] [This way you will understand.] At this point I didn't know what to say, all I could do was nod my head and say please go on. [Every 15,000 years on Earth for the past 112,000 years humans and everything they have accomplished in the span of 15,000 years are wiped out by a species of beings called the Phylmecs.] [This has gone on for 6 cycles now.] Out of nowhere, a vision came to my head.

I was near the ocean in a city filled with gold and old-looking buildings. Spaceships floated in the sky and people yelled in synch, "We Atlantians will not be taken, we would rather die than be taken." Suddenly I was in a forest and there were pyramids in every direction. I saw indigenous people with their heads connected to what looked like the Atlanteans to me. Both were frozen in time. Suddenly there was fire all around and everything went dark. Just like during the day the visions felt so real, and I do not know how I knew, but I knew that they were real.

I now believed what Sevashkish was saying. He must have been the one transmitting the visions to me. The people in my vision were of people of Earth, but of a different era who no longer existed. These ancient people were ancient civilizations said to live long ago, but no real evidence was ever found of them. The people that were said to be "myth" like the Atlantians. I guess all those conspiracy theory wackos were not so wacko after all. [Daniel you are seeing the reality of things now.]

[The Phylmecs are the alien race responsible for this destruction.] [They are an ancient alien race that is 10 million years older than homo sapiens.] [They are vastly advanced technologically speaking, but they are still in the same dimension as humans (3rd).] [The Phylmecs quit evolving 950,000 years ago, and normally when a species ceases to evolve they die out.] [They no longer can reproduce.] [They are stuck in their dimension and eventually, the universe naturally wipes them out.] [The Phylmecs knew this was happening to them when they quit evolving, so they created a technology to try and become immortal, or at least until their technology was perfected to a point where they could artificially advance to the next dimension.]

[They created a way that allows them to transfer their "self-be-ing-soul,"] you can say either of those three words. It's the same for us, I briefly interrupted. [Very well, so they transfer their "self" to another sentient being's body and completely take over that sentient's being's body.] [This means that they absorb and consume the actual consciousness or soul of the being that they have taken.] [The body of the victim lives on, but with the Phylmec "self" in it.] [The person to whom that body belonged is wiped out of existence.] [Their soul is consumed, so it was like the person never existed, to begin with.] [They will never get a chance to see another life or be reborn again.]

All this information was like someone was splashing me with cold water. I was never a religious person, but I have always believed in having a soul. What Sevashkish was saying did make some sort of sense to me, but still, I was confused. How is that possible Sevashkish? Our soul is who we are, isn't it? [Yes, but your soul is pure energy that is hosted by a physical body.] [Think of your body as the house for the soul.] [The Phylmecs developed a way to consume a being's soul and keep their body for them.] [They developed a way that allows them to enter a sentient being's body and take over that person's body.] [This of course means that the Phylmecs no longer look how they once looked.]

[Their appearances change depending on the current species that they are taking over.] [This means they never die, and they keep transferring their consciousness into a new body and absorbing the person's being-soul in the process.] [They grow stronger every time that they do this.] [They have caused immense genocide across the galaxy.] [39 known species have been eradicated thanks to them.] I couldn't process what Sevashkish was telling me. Honestly, I didn't quite understand what he meant. Are the Phylmecs a virus species? [Not originally, they evolved all they could, until they started to die out.]

[Naturally, they were a species about the size of an earth male chimpanzee.] [They had a similar body, but the Phylmecs had a long, firm tail.] [They had three eyes instead of two, and four hands instead of two.] [Their hands were shaped like an octopus's tentacles.] [Their entire body was yellow.] [As yellow as the Earth's sun looks on a warm cloudless day.] [The only thing that was not yellow was their dark blue eyes.]

[They procreated in what you would consider a normal way.] [The reason as to why they ceased to enter the 4th dimension is unknown.] [But some say their home planet lost its core consciousness, but we do not know if that is true.] [What is known is that they have always been technologically advanced, and an aggressive species of beings.] [They have always felt superior to other species of life in the galaxy.] [They used to hunt defenseless beings just for sport every year in a huge celebration that they called the harvest.]

I tried to take everything in, but it was difficult. Everything that Sevashkish was telling me was flat-out insane, but I knew he was telling the truth. I felt it. I did my best to absorb and comprehend. Sevashkish, if the Phylmecs have been coming to earth for over 112,000 years, why haven't they completely wiped out humans yet? Why do they keep coming back every 15,000 years? [They keep coming back because Earth still has a life force-energy to give to its children.]

What do you mean? [I mean your planet, or should I say planet Earth is alive, and gives every single organism part of its energy.] [Earth is what gives humans your sentientism or souls.] [In fact, it gives all organisms a form of soul, but only humans and possibly a few select other animals' sentientism.] Do you mean that Earth has chosen us to be aware? [Yes, Earth has chosen that.] Does this mean Earth thinks like humans do? [Earth has a mind and soul far beyond any person, or even any Luken.] [All planets who have sustained life in this universe are alive.] [They are alive in a way that not even we Lukens can understand.] [Daniel I am sorry that I am overloading you with information, but I must tell you all that I can.]

[The first time the Phylmecs ever met humans was when your species was learning how to control fire.] [They saw the potential in humans to become sentient beings, and sure enough, you humans were blessed by your planet to become the prominent sentient form on Earth.] [The Phylmecs observed and came to the conclusion that humans would be their next targets.] [The Phylmecs returned 200 thousand years later, and sure enough, humans were aware and sentient.] [At that time Earth had around 3 million humans, and the Phylmecs "harvested" all but 5000.] [I want you to listen to this part closely Daniel.]

[Before they left back to their planet, they chose 10 loyal humans to be the first kings and queens of the human race.] [These humans and their descendants have been in constant communication with the Phylmecs since they first arrived, and they are known as the informants.] [Believe it or not Daniel, they are the rich families secretly "running" your planet.] [The Phylmecs instructed them to make the planet fertile so that every fifteen thousand years they can come back and harvest as many humans as possible.] [They were instructed to dumb humanity down, so humans would never be able to evolve further again.] [Before their arrival humans lived in harmony with each other.] [There was no "ruler," but multiple people who worked together for the greater good of the people.]

[The Phylmecs destroyed the peaceful society that humans had.] [They have done all in their power to make human society mirror Phylmec society.] [A terrible non-spiritual and war-filled world.] [Humans were a peaceful species before, and that is why we

Lukens believe that humans should have already been in the fourth dimension.] [Sadly, the Phylmecs have not allowed that.]

[We Lukens estimate that there are about 4.5 billion to 5 billion Phylmecs, and as you know there are now currently 9 billion humans on earth.] [This will be their biggest harvesting of humans ever, and sadly their last.] [Earth won't last another harvest.] Wow, so to them, we are nothing but cattle. I was feeling tense with anger. [Phlymecs do not take a body older than 35 or younger than 4 years of age.] [Four years is around the time a child truly develops self-awareness and sentientism.] [Earth has around 4.5 billion to 5 billion people between the ages of 4 to 35.] What about the other 4 or so billion people? What happens to them? [When the Phylmecs harvest what they need they simply kill off the other humans.]

As Sevashkish was telling me this my eyes were starting to get blurry with tears. I was mad beyond belief. [I am truly sorry to be telling you this, but it will be a deadly massacre if they are not stopped.] [Like I said before, your planet will not survive another round of harvesting.] So many questions were running around in my head, and one really stood out. Sevashkish, why do they come every 15,000 years? I am not understanding that part very well.

[Daniel 15,000 earth years is the equivalent of 100 Phylmec years.] [If humans are kept from diseases and treated well the human body can live to about 140 years, and then it dies.] [They know the proper foods to give the human body to let it last around 140 years.] Oh, so 15,000 years for us is only 100 years on their home planet? Is that what you mean? [Yes, they live in a different galaxy where time flows differently.] [They live over a billion light years away, but they have set up a wormhole that lets them travel directly from their home galaxy to Earth.] [It only takes about 4 earth weeks to reach Earth from their home planet; give or take a day or two.]

[Since a human body can only withstand at least 140 years they don't take a risk, and they come back to Earth at about 100 years to start the entire process again.] [Of course, 15,000 years have passed on Earth by that point, even though only one hundred or so on their planet.] I suddenly felt a pit in my stomach. This couldn't have been happening for over 112,000 years, could it? [They also destroy all human-made structures to keep the people of Earth stupid.] [With the help of their informants you are led to believe that Earth is just starting off with human civilization.]

Why me? I yelled at Sevashkish! Why come and tell me Sevashkish? What can I do? Why not tell the military? The world powers? What can I do? I yelled at Sevashkish even though he had already answered me, indirectly, but had answered. [Daniel I came to you because you answered me.] [I believe that you are the one destined to help save your planet and all its beautiful life.] [I promise I will explain more, but please let me finish telling you about the Phylmecs.] "The one destined to help Earth survive?" What in the world was he talking about? I am definitely not a fighter or a leader in any terms. I am just a confused kid who is trying to figure out what he wants in life.

Chapter 4
THE PROCESS

[Daniel, when the Phylmecs devour and take over the body of a being, it is a time of great harmony for them.] [While they were still evolving, they would kill other species in huge sport-like competitions every couple of years as I mentioned earlier.] [Those awful sports-like competitions were great times for the Phylmecs as they brought the entire society together.] [Unfortunately, for us, it has now become a religious celebration for the Phylmecs.] [Their competitions evolved from the "simple" killing of other sentient creatures, to what it is now.] [The ceremonial harvesting of an individual's soul and the robbery of that individual's body.] [It is no longer a sports competition to them, but an actual ceremony for Phylmec society.]

[It is a time for celebration and intellectual growth.] [To the Phylmecs this is when they get to be "reborn and regenerate" in a new body.] [They learn more and get stronger with each ceremonial harvest that they participate in.] I was starting to feel sick to my stomach imagining how these celebrations hurt the victims. Sevashkish looked at me with worried eyes, but I just nodded my head for him to continue speaking.

[We Lukens believe that they have gone up half a dimension already by the eradication of all the species that they have taken.] [Also, we Lukens theorized that after this last human genocide, the Phylmecs will jump directly to the 7th dimension because of the vast number of humans that they will take and consume.]

[Never in all of Phylmec history has there been enough of an alien race to give each Phylmec a "new body" at the same time as everyone else.] [We believe that this energy level, and with the destruction of planet Earth they will be moved into the 7th dimension.] [They will cause massive harm if they are allowed to do this.] Honestly, I did not know what to say. I heard Sevashkish talk, but I was not understanding anything anymore. It was all too much.

I was tired, and all I could think about was how my life was changing. Last night I went to bed thinking aliens were fake and now there is one talking to me. To make matters worse, it was telling me that planet Earth was on the brink of destruction. Sevashkish stopped again and looked at me. I nodded for him to continue speaking since he had stopped, but my head was completely somewhere else now.

[The Phylmecs call the killing of other alien races *the Great Harvest Ceremony*.] [*The Great Harvest Ceremony* is performed in a series of steps, and the first step is to make contact and gain trust.] [When they arrive on earth they will lie to humanity saying how they "come in peace," and they will seduce humanity with; gifts, presents, and advanced technology.] [They want an easy takeover, and for Earth, it is much easier since they have been doing this for six cycles now.]

[The informants that they have on Earth, who are unfortunately many world leaders, will do their best to convince the masses that the Phylmecs are a great race who are here to help Earth.] [Some will even try to convince you that the Phylmecs are Gods.] [Building trust in humans is their first and most important step.] There is no way humans will fall for this! I yelled suddenly at Sevashkish. [Daniel, humanity will fall for this, and they have fallen for this.] [Do not forget that the Phylmecs who are coming look exactly human.] [They are older humans, but in human bodies nonetheless.]

At that moment I knew he was right because as a society we see older humans as more trustworthy and mature. I am sorry for interrupting Sevashkish, please go on. [After two weeks of gaining the trust of humanity, and after having had enough time to infiltrate the rest of the leaders who aren't informants; they will start the second and most destructive phase of the *Great Harvest.*] [They call this step "the Transfer."]

[The Phylmecs will land in every single country around the world. They will spread a message of peace, and send scouts to help all those in need.] [During this detrimental time, each Phylmec will scout out the person that they want to "take over."] [By the third week the Phylmecs have already chosen the person that they want to harvest.] [That person will more than likely trust them.] Wow, they want everything easy. These creatures are vile. [Yes, they do, and yes they are.] [That is why they do a secret infiltration because no one suspects.]

[The transfer of the Phylmec's "self" into a being's body is the most important step of the ceremony for the Phylmecs.] How so? [Well, they are transferring themselves from an old body to a new body, and are consuming the soul of that person.] They are eating the soul to have the energy to transfer their consciousness into the new body, right? [Yes, now you understand Daniel.] I was beginning to understand, and I felt scared. Even though I felt scared I needed to learn as much as I could. Only with more information would I lose my fear of the invaders.

[Our bodies are homes for our souls, and when the Phylmecs take our bodies they kill our souls.] "Our bodies are homes for our souls," Sevaskish's words flowed through my mind. How many humans had they taken in 112,000 years I thought. How many innocent species had become eradicated? How many people lost the chance to have an afterlife or be reincarnated? Sevashkish! I yelled. [Yes?]

Sevashkish, you said the Phylmecs have been coming to earth for 112,000 years and they stopped evolving almost 950k years ago, so does this mean that the same Phylmecs from almost a million years ago are still alive? [Yes, Daniel, as I told you they ceased to evolve, so this is the only way that they can continue to live on, by stealing bodies and transferring their consciousness into new bodies.] [These specific Phylmecs have been alive for almost a million years.] [They are ruthless and highly intelligent.] I was clenching my fists tightly together. I was beyond mad. These parasites have been using us for over 100,000 years! How could they do this? How can someone or something be so selfish as to take the life of someone else because they are afraid of dying?

Sevashkish what happens when they transfer themselves into a new body? [After the transfer is complete they must rest for 48 hours without doing anything that can cause the body to reject the new "mind."] [Daniel, only a third of the Phylmecs take over people at a time, so the transfer stage lasts about a week.] [They do this so people will not be aware that a mass number of normally healthy people cannot walk out of the blue, and so people do not start to notice all the random "dead alien bodies on earth."] I am confused. Why wouldn't they be able to walk, and why the dead alien bodies? [The first 48 hours after a Phylmec has taken over a body, the body cannot really move.]

[They are vulnerable at this point, and will not risk having all their society vulnerable.] [Also, once their essence leaves a body, their old body dies.] [They do not want humans to notice a bunch of dead bodies showing up everywhere.] [They need time to hide their mess, so that is why only a third of them participate in the ritual at a time.] That makes sense. They are smart. [Daniel, not only will they take Earth's people, but they will take all that Earth has to offer.] [The Phylmecs have always taken Earth's resources, but this time will be different.] [This time they will leave Earth dry.] [They are cruel and love to destroy.]

How is the transfer ritual done, Sevashkish? Is it painful, and do people fight back? [The Phylmecs must be physically touching forehead to forehead when the transfer starts.] [Once the Phylmec physically touches its forehead to its victim, then the being that is being taken over loses all consciousness instantaneously and dies.] [It is very hard to fight someone you don't know is there to cause you harm, and once they slightly touch your forehead to theirs, it is finished for the victim.] [The transfer lasts a total of 5 earth minutes, so this means the Phylmec must stay connected to the victim for that time duration.] [As you already know, the Phylmec must take 48 hours of rest.]

[Daniel, it is important that you know this piece of information.] [If the Phylmec and the victim are disconnected at any point during the 5-minute transfer, the Phylmec will die automatically.] [I want to reiterate to you Daniel, once a Phylmec touches their foreheads with another being the other being dies instantaneously.] [It is always best to disconnect a Phylmec during this process.] [By doing this we can avenge the victim, and it will mean one less dangerous Phylmec in the galaxy.] [This is the only time that they are vulnerable, Daniel.] [I repeat that with urgency because I do not want you to forget this.]

Sevashkish, how are we going to stop this? I mean they have been coming to Earth for over one hundred thousand years. They will come to Earth with human bodies, and they will be preaching to bring the heavens to humans. I know some people will be weary, and some even hostile, but the majority of humans will welcome them with open hands like you said, so what do we do? Do we warn people, or will they not even believe us? I am drawing blanks here. [What do you mean by drawing blanks?] Oh sorry, it just means I am confused!

Sevashkish how will the Phylmecs make their presence known on earth? [Daniel, they will make an announcement to every country in the world.] [This announcement will be seen in every format possible.] [They will of course land and meet with every leader of Earth, and we Lukens believe 70-75% of Earth's leaders are under their control.] [Everyone will hear this announcement of how they are coming in peace, and how they are solely here to learn from humans and share technology.]

How will they control the people who will freak out? I mean I know people will freak out. This is crazy! This feels like it is straight out of a movie. My head was hurting from the anger that I felt. This is just very overwhelming for me! I yelled at Sevashkish. I instantly felt bad. I am sorry for yelling at you Sevashkish. [Do not apologize, you have all the right to be mad.] For some reason hearing him tell me that helped me cool down a bit.

My pajama shirt was drenched in sweat with how nervous I felt. [Shall I continue, Daniel?] Yes, please. [Okay, I also believe that they will try to land at night.] [This will be so they can meet with the leaders before they announce their arrival.] [To cause less of a panic.] [Of course, this is just speculation, and they can change everything up.] How long do we have, Sevashkish?

[I believe we have 2-4 weeks before their arrival, and 6-8 weeks before Earth is destroyed.] Hearing all of this was making my blood boil. They will not get away with this. I do not know how, and I don't know why, but at that moment I knew I would do everything in my power to not let them get away with this. They might have been coming for over one hundred thousand years, but they had never met me before. I will fight with all my might, Sevashkish. He looked at me with a bright smile from his eyes. Sevashkish, I have a serious question. I know you kind of mentioned that they stopped evolving, but what was the real reason? If they are so advanced, why are humans still in the same dimension as them?

[It could be a million different things, Daniel.] [It could be as simple as it was just their time to die as a species, or as complicated as maybe Phylmec society was just not in the same frequency as species in the fourth dimension.] Sevashkish, please do not take this the wrong way, but are you telling me that not even the highly advanced Lukens know the reason why the Phylmecs quit evolving? Sevashkish looked at me, and his eyes got wider once again.

My stupid comment had made him smile. [Yes, you are right Daniel, not every question has an answer.] [If I had to guess as to what the reason was, it is because they are a dangerous species whose entire evolution has been the murder of the weak for their own gain.] Sevashkish didn't have an answer to my question, but his response did give me hope.

I was feeling a bit better now, because if species like the Lukens do not have all the answers that means species like the Phylmecs are not all-powerful. Maybe we humans do have a chance against them, especially with advice from beings like the Lukens. Sevashkish, I know that species from other dimensions should not interact with each other, but is there a way that you can tell me how to build weapons to help humanity fight these Phlymecs?

[Daniel, as much as I would love to help in that aspect, even just telling you about how to build weapons from a different dimension will lead to a dangerous ripple effect for both humans and Lukens.] [It throws off the balance of the universe.] [I cannot explain every detail as to why because even I do not know the reasoning, but just know this.] [Have you ever wondered why there is an asteroid belt in your galaxy?]

Honestly, no I haven't. I thought that was just the remains of when the galaxy formed. [No Daniel, that is not what happened]. [What happened was that a species of the 4th dimension tried to help a species of the second dimension evolve to the third.] [This interaction was like throwing oil into a fire.] [It caused severe damage that killed both species.] [It caused mayhem for your galaxy and many planets in your galaxy were harmed because of it.] [Luckily, Earth was shielded by most of these asteroids by your moon.] [This is why your planet was able to survive.] I don't know why I know the answer, but I quietly muttered, "Mars."

[Yes, Mars was once a thriving planet with amazing life, but now it is dead.] [I hope you now understand why I can't give advice from the 7th dimension, or weapons from the 7th dimension.] Yes, I understand now. [All I can do is give you ideas that may help you from your own third dimension.] [As much as I love Earth and its creatures, even simple advice not from the 3rd dimension will have a horrific effect.] I understand Sevashkish and any advice that you can give me based on what you know of the third dimension will be amazing.

Chapter 5
THE EXPLANATION

[Daniel, now that I have explained and revealed to you all the truth, I will now tell you why I came to you.] [Your purpose in all of this is truly undeniable.] For being an alien Sevashkish sure knew how to be suspenseful. I thought to myself as I felt my heart jumping out of my chest. My palms were sweating, and I felt a knot form in my stomach. My anxiety was going through the roof. Take some deep breaths Daniel, breath in and out, exhale.

Tell me Sevashkish, why did you come to me? How do I fall into all of this? Why me? How exactly did you find me? As I waited for his answers I took another long look at Sevashkish and I noticed that he was crouching his wings by my door. I felt bad. Had he been crouched like this that whole time I wondered? Sevashkish do you want to speak somewhere differently, somewhere you can stretch your wings out?

[I am okay Daniel, but thank you for asking.] His eyes got bigger, and I knew now for sure that the widened eyes meant that he was smiling. [Daniel, I came to you because your planet is crying for help.] [Earth cries out for help, but like I told you we Lukens cannot do anything to get directly involved without some sort of consequence.] [The only reason I can speak to you is because I am speaking to you from the 7th dimension, and you are one of the rare ones who can communicate with no consequences.]

Sevashkish, how did you hear the Earth cry for help? [Planets are in a dimension so advanced that they can communicate with beings from any dimension with no issues, Daniel.] They can? [Yes.] Sevashkish how is Earth crying for help? Why can't we humans hear the Earth? I know you said that Earth is alive, but is Earth a true sentient being like you told me?

[Humans do not hear Earth cry because, after years of harvesting, the Phylmecs have cut that strand that connected humans to Earth.] [Daniel you still have this strand.] [Daniel, Earth, and all the planets are alive, and very much sentient as I mentioned to you before.] [Some planets are in a dimension that we can only suspect to be one of the last ones, and that is why they can seed their own life.]

I am totally confused, Sevashkish, but please go on. [Just know this Daniel, once a planet starts to seed its own life, it can no longer directly defend itself from danger.] [That is something they sacrifice when they enter that new dimension.] [They sacrifice their direct defenses in order to seed life within themselves.] Are you saying that planets are what create life? [I am not saying that directly, but when a planet enters a new dimension, whatever allowed them to enter that dimension also gave them the energy to create life.] What allowed them, Sevashkish? [That, not even we Lukens know.] [Just know that Earth, your home planet, is alive and gives life and pure energy to its children.]

[Daniel, I know I already said this, but Earth, your planet, is one of the most diverse planets in the entire known universe.] [It has more creatures living in one place than anywhere else in all the known galaxies.] [Earth has such a strong energy, and that is what attracted the Phylmecs to it.] [It is also what attracted us Lukens to it.] From everything that I had just been told this entire night, hearing that Earth was so unique in the universe made me feel a sense of pride, but also a sense of shame. If Earth was the most diverse planet in the universe, we as humans really have done a poor job protecting it. I am by no means a "tree hugger," but at that moment I regretted not doing more to help keep the Earth clean and sustainable for generations to come.

[Daniel, I do not have much time left to speak to you because I have to be heading back to my planet, but I will be back.] [I want you to trust me, and know that I will do all that I can to help you and humanity fight the Phylmecs.] [We Lukens are with Earth.] Thank you Sevashkish, but I honestly have no clue how to do this. [Daniel, look and listen to this.] I stared as he pulled out a small device that looked like a remote control. He pressed a button on it. Suddenly 3 other beings who looked a lot like Sevashkish appeared as very realistic holograms. Are they Lukens? They looked at me with puzzlement in their huge owl eyes.

I waved at them, and they were stunned to see that I could see them. They spoke to me, and said "Sevashkish was right when he found you, you will help stop the Phylmecs threat and you will save Earth." "It is incredible that a human can see us!" "Maybe Earth has a fighting chance." [You see Daniel, you have the power to communicate with other dimensions.] [This means that you will be able to communicate directly with your planet.] [Earth will be able to lend you its powers, but first you must establish communication with your planet.]

Wait, Earth will lend me its power? How in the world do I communicate with my planet? How does a planet even talk? I started to get that nasty anxious feeling in my body. It was becoming too surreal again. I mean just last night I thought the Earth was just a rock in space that contained life. I had no clue that it was a living sentient being, that I now had to save. Sevashkish, how do I communicate directly with Earth? Where can I find Earth, does it have a body?

[Earth is all around you.] [You are inside Earth.] [In fact, the Earth sees and hears what we are talking about.] Then why doesn't the Earth just reach out and speak to me? [There is only one way to establish direct communication with your planet.] Please explain. [There must be four sentient beings together.] You mean I must have three others with me? [Yes.] [You must have four sentient beings hold their hands together while you call out for Earth.] [Earth will establish a communication directly with you Daniel.] Why only with me? [You are the only inter-dimensional human that I am aware of.] [After direct communication, then all the knowledge and shared power of Earth will flow to you and everyone who has established communication with Earth.]

Four sentient beings? How was I going to find others to tell this to? [Daniel you only need to find two other individuals.] [You are one, and I will be the other, so you must find two others to help you.] [This means you must convince 2 others to start the communication call with Earth.] How in the world was I going to convince two other people to help me? I knew that no one would believe me. I also knew now that I couldn't trust the government because if they found out they would just inform the Phylmecs. They would kill me instantly. What to do?

Sevashkish, you know that no one, and I mean absolutely no one will believe me if I tell them what you just told me right? [You must try, and I believe you will succeed.] [Daniel, I must go now because the longer that I stay on your planet, the harder it is to get back to my home.] [I will be here tomorrow at 6 pm, and we will establish communication to speak to Earth.] [I believe that you have the power to convince two others to speak to Earth tomorrow.] [I believe in you!] [I must go now.] Just like that, Sevashkish left my room and flew away into the dark sky.

I was once again alone outside in the dark. I looked all around and he was gone. Was this true? Had I been dream-walking? No, there is no way that this had been a dream. My body was shaking too badly. I also felt different in this strange way. I felt somehow older, and I felt wiser. I felt changed.

In my heart and mind, I knew that my world had changed forever. But not just my world, but every single human being on this planet. Their world would forever be changed too. I looked up to the stars and thought, somewhere out there the Phylmecs are coming, and starting tomorrow my life would be a huge battle. My mind was thinking of a million things at once, but I knew that wasn't healthy. I had to relax.

There's no reason why I should start to worry right now. I gently reminded myself. Something I have learned from being bullied was to live in the exact moment in time. I can't predict the future, so I might as well relax till tomorrow. I went back inside the house and decided the best thing to do was get some rest. I had to keep up my strength to be the best version of myself, and that meant rest. I locked the doors and headed to bed. The next day I woke up at 8 am. I felt refreshed. Now it was time to face my new reality.

Okay, I need to find two people by 6 pm when Sevashkish comes back, and the only two people that I am willing to tell are my two best friends Javier and Valerie. My parents cannot know because they would worry an insane amount. Plus they would lock me up in an asylum instantly. They would think I was completely insane. It had to be Valerie and Javier. One of the reasons why they were my best friends was because they were both genuinely open-minded people. I believe the best people are open-minded.

Bring, bring, bring, I glanced at my phone. It was Valerie calling. What perfect timing I thought. Hey Val, what's up? <Daniel, are you feeling better?> <I have been worried about you since last night.> I am feeling better. I just needed to rest, and not study as much. Who knew college would be so difficult right? <You got that right.> Oh, and Valerie, can you please meet me at my house today at 5 pm after classes? She agreed but sounded a little weary. After I hung up the call with Valerie, I decided that there was no way that I would go to school today. Yesterday I could barely concentrate, today would be a total disaster.

Instead, I called my parents and checked up on them. They were doing great, and that made me feel better. They will be back home in three days. I texted Javier one simple text, "My place 5, bring Mario Kart. He replied, "Wouldn't miss it." Okay cool, that is all settled. Now what? I could not focus on anything. All I could think about was what Sevashkish had told me.

On top of that, all I could see was Sevashkish in my mind. He was an alien for crying out loud. All my life I had thought aliens were hoaxes, yet they were real. If only people had raided Area 51 as they had planned. I said to myself while laughing. I had to joke about the absurdity of all of this or else the anxiety was going to eat me alive.

I couldn't let that happen, so I decided to get productive. I would learn as much as I could about aliens and ancient Earth and its cultures. Besides that would help me better explain to Valerie and Javier what I was talking about.

I googled ancient civilizations that had gone as fast as they came. I looked up Atlantis and other mysterious civilizations. I looked up what it means to be sentient. I looked up how planets formed. I looked up different dimensions. It was so interesting and yet so confusing. I even went as far as to search secret government organizations around the world.

I do dare say that I looked up the Illuminati. I used a VPN throughout all my searches, not that it would do anything for someone tracking me, but it did give me a false sense of safety. I even found groups on Reddit who claim that they have been abducted by aliens. I read what they said, but didn't comment on them. I do not know if these people truly got abducted or are genuinely crazy, but it was an interesting read.

How would Valerie and Javier react after I told them what I was about to tell them? Would they trust me? Would they think I was joking, or would they just laugh? No clue, but I knew that I had to tell them in a way that they knew I was being genuine and truthful. I had to show them evidence somehow. I printed everything that I could on different dimensions and planets. On sentient beings and the soul. I printed everything I found useful.

By 4 pm I decided that the best way to tell them would be together, and to just tell them everything in detail in a chronological manner. I would sit them down on my couch and just speak the truth. It is always better to be direct and honest, I thought.

Chapter 6
INTO THE TUNNEL

5 o'clock came around and Javier arrived with Valerie. Here we go, now or never Daniel. They looked excited to see me. Valerie gave me a tight hug and Javier whispered in my ear, <Everything ok man?> Good grief I thought, Valerie must have told him about my situation at the gym. I felt my cheeks get red. Yeah, everything good I told him. Okay, guys please take a seat. I have to show you something. <Daniel, why are you talking to us like you are about to sell something?> Javier, just take a seat. Okay, I am going to show you guys something, and you have to promise to not make any comments until my video and presentation are done, okay?

<Yes, yes of course.> They both said. Okay cool, just give me a second. I went over to open my curtains. I wanted to let the natural sunshine flow into the living room. Might as well make the atmosphere look less dark and tense. The looks on Javier's and

Valerie's faces already looked scared, so I was hoping natural light would make them feel more at ease.

Okay here we go, I mumbled to myself as I rubbed my hands together, and I began. I began to tell them everything that had happened from yesterday morning to this exact moment in time. It took me 15 minutes to tell them my entire story, but in those 15 minutes, I saw looks of confusion, sadness, empathy, and finally disbelief from my friends.

Before they could speak I handed them printed papers of ancient civilizations that "randomly" went extinct. I told them in detail about my encounter with Sevashkish and a bit about how he looked. Then I let my friends express their opinions. So what do you guys think? <Daniel, I know midterms are just around the corner, but if you are this stressed you probably just need a break.> <School will always be there, but your health should come first.>

Javier, I am stressed, but I am not that stressed to the point that I am imagining things. I know this sounds crazy, and guess what? Maybe I am crazy, but if what I am telling you is the truth, then we only have 8 weeks left before the extermination.

Valerie ran to me and hugged me. <Daniel, I am here for you, and I won't judge you.> < If you think what you are saying is true then I believe you.> Javier shot Valerie a look of "Give me a break." Valerie looked back at him with a look of, "I know something is wrong with him, but he needs us." <One of my cousins once had a breakdown from stress, but after going to therapy he got

better, Daniel.> Valerie I truly appreciate you caring so much, but I promise you what I am saying is the truth. Please, just take a seat again and stay till 6 o'clock, I asked them. They agreed.

Sevashkish will be here any minute, but only I will be able to see him, I told them. When the words slipped my mouth I knew I sounded crazy that it even made me laugh. <Yes of course only you will be able to see him.> Javier said while cringing his forehead. Valerie jabbed him with her elbow. It is okay, Valerie I said, you and Javier will see what I mean soon enough. I know I sound like I just ran away from an insane asylum, and honestly, I wish that were the case. I was about to give Javier a playful punch when I heard the voice.

[I am back Daniel, are you ready?] [I see your friends are here.] [I am glad you were able to convince them to help us save Earth.] Not exactly, I muttered to Sevashkish. Sevashkish, I know my friends, and they will help, but they need physical proof that what you are saying is true. Javier looked at me with his mouth wide open. <Daniel, who are you talking to?> <There is literally no one there!>

<Valerie look at him, we need to get someone to help him.> <I am going to call his parents.> <I don't think he is even hearing us right now.> Oh boy was Javier wrong. I was hearing everything they said, but I had just thought about the only possible plan that would work. The plan that would get me to speak to Earth. I would have to trick my friends since telling them the truth did not help.

My plan was simple. I would get Valerie and Javier to hold my hand, and then I would call Sevashkish to hold their hands. I do not like tricking anyone, but this was the only way that we would be able to contact Earth, and then they would get the proof that they needed.

Guys, can you please come next to me? I am not feeling well at all. I feel lightheaded. They both shot up and ran to me. I am so sorry for putting you both through all of this. I guess I have been so stressed, and it is partially because of my exams. I feel like a failure. My life hasn't been going like I wanted it to go. College is definitely harder than I imagined. The look on Valerie's face made me feel bad for lying, but I had no choice. I reached over and grabbed both of their hands tightly. Sevashkish! It is time! Please hold their hands! I yelled. They both looked at me with surprise, but it was too late, Sevashkish came and grabbed their hands. Suddenly the four of us were falling in complete darkness.

We were spinning in circles. It felt like that scene in Alice in Wonderland when she fell into the rabbit hole. I could see the look of fear and total amazement that Javier and Valerie had. They were shocked to see that we were falling. Don't let go of our hands I told them. <Why does it feel like someone else is holding my hand?> Valerie yelled. Sevashkish is holding both your hand and Javier's. I am sorry for tricking you two, but you guys did not believe me, and it was crucial that we made direct communication with Earth! Also, Javier, see there was no reason to think that I had gone crazy.

<I mean, I am totally sorry, but what is going on?> <Are we going somewhere?>

<I have no clue Javier, but I know we will be okay and safe. <I guess you were telling the truth, but this is WILD, oh and I am sorry for not trusting you.> Don't be, I told him. Valerie looked at me and squeezed my hand twice. That was the way she always apologized to me. She looked beyond scared but did not say a word. <I guess this means that all of us are crazy.> Javier said while laughing. <That or whatever chemicals are in your house have also affected our brains.>

As we were falling I told them Sevashkish was actually with us, and to not be scared if they were to see him. I guess having a presentation in a calm setting before something out of this world happens really does help a person out. We were falling into a pit of darkness and Javier and Valerie were not nearly as freaked out by what was happening as I had been yesterday when I met Sevaskish. I wish someone had told me in a calm setting what was going on too. All I got was a real-life alien staring right at my face in the middle of the night.

The falling felt like a lifetime. We were just going down. I felt weightless, but at least we were falling feet forward. <How did the ground just open up in your living room, and why can't we see Sevashkish?> Valerie asked. Honestly, I do not know how that happened. I didn't even know that was going to happen. But one thing I can tell you guys is that we are going to be safe here. <How can you be so sure Daniel?>

Well Valerie, if we are entering a place to talk to planet Earth it will be safe. It has to. <I really hope so.> As for Sevashkish, it is because he is from the 7th dimension, remember? <Oh yes, I am sorry this is very confusing Daniel.> Don't apologize, Valerie, this is confusing and scary for all of us.

<Valerie don't forget Daniel is the special one here.> Javier looked at me with his sly smile. <He is the chosen one here, let's not forget.> I know Javier meant his words as a joke, but they made me feel a little uneasy. Hey, I am not special in any way okay? Besides you guys are with me, so if I am special then so are you. <Daniel I am joking.> <Besides I am glad that we are all together in this.> So am I Javier.

After about five minutes of falling into empty dark space, we were finally starting to slow down in our fall. I felt that we were about to be back on solid ground, and that is when Javier started to yell his lungs out right along with Valerie. What is going on? I turned my head in the direction where they were yelling. I didn't see anything, but Sevashkish.

Why are you yelling Javier? <Don't you see that big winged-thing!> <Look at those eyes!> Wow, were they seeing Sevashkish? Are you seeing Sevashkish? They were afraid, but at the same time too afraid to let go of his hand and gaze. <Yes I think so!> <How is this possible?> Javier yelled! Well Javier I am not sure, but here is Sevashkish, and do not be afraid of him. He is here to help us. I was super happy that I wasn't the only one who could see Sevashkish anymore. I felt relieved.

We finally landed softly on what felt like the softest marshmallows in the world. I felt a little wobbly for a second or two then my legs stabilized. Kind of like when you get off a roller coaster. We let go of each other's hands, but Valerie was still holding Sevashkish's hand, <Are you Sevashkish?> [Yes, nice to meet you Valerie, and nice to meet you, Javier.]

<How do you know our names?> [I have a sense for these things.] He looked at them with that strange alien smile of his. Sevashkish, how are they able to see you if you are from the 7th dimension? [Earth has created a ripple that blocks our dimensions from colliding allowing us to coexist naturally.]

Okay, that makes sense I guess. <So Mister Luken, you are from the 7th dimension, can you please tell us where we are now?> [We are within Earth's center, and this is actually my first time here.] [Every time that I have ever spoken to Earth it has been through the body of one of its animals.] [Earth is very protective of who or what it is.] That ran a chill down my spine. I always assumed Sevashkish talked directly with Earth in a physical way, but that wasn't the case. I started to get a tad nervous when Javier broke my concentration. <Sevashkish, man I have to say you have some amazing-looking wings.> <How long are those big boys?> I glanced over toward Sevashkish, and I do not know how I knew, but I knew Sevashkish had gotten shy over the comment.

Javier and Valerie were just in awe of Sevashkish, so I took this time to do a bit of exploring. I started to look around the dark soft area where we landed. I took a couple of steps from the area where we landed, and the entire room lit up. The room that we were in was a strong golden color and the ceiling was a bright strong white. The walls were covered in what looked like solid gold. The floor where we landed was replaced by golden tiles, as clear as the ocean waves. All around the room, everything was clear and bright. There was a smell of lavender haze. It felt peaceful and welcoming.

I felt immense happiness pass through my body. I felt connected to this place. Valerie looked at me with a smile that showed both amazement and fear. [We are somewhere within Earth's soul.] [A being of such a high dimension that we cannot fathom.] At that very moment, I could not contain my happiness and anger. Earth was a being of life, that loved life, and Phylmecs were too egocentric and cowardly of their own fate that they had essentially sucked the life out of Earth for thousands of years. They would pay for that.

<Sevashkish, what do we do next?> Valerie asked. <It is beautiful here, but kind of scary at the same time.> [We must wait for Earth to make direct communication with Daniel, or one of us Valerie.] [Though I believe the communication will come to Daniel first, as I believe he has the power to speak directly to a being as strong as Earth]

<Well that definitely makes all of us feel special.> <I mean not to make you feel bad Daniel.> Javier, don't start again. This is not the time, I am already freaked out as it is. <I'm sorry Daniel, you know that I joke when I am scared.> <It does make sense though that you would be the one that Earth chooses to speak with.> Why do you say that, Javier?

<I always thought you were weird, but special you know that, right?> Yes, you told me that several times. <Well I just want to remind you that I was correct.> <If you can put up with my sarcasm then you definitely can put up with Earth and any alien.> He came over and playfully punched my arm. <Daniel, maybe you should try to communicate with Earth.> I will do that Valerie, once I figure out how to do that. [Look deep down in your soul and you'll find the answer.] Hmmm, that helps, Sevashkish I silently thought. How do I get my soul to speak to planet Earth? I closed my eyes. I began to search for what Earth meant to me in my mind and body.

Earth this is Daniel, I am here to do my best to assist you in anything that you may need from me. I kept my eyes closed for about a minute and nothing happened. I opened them and Sevashkish, Valerie, and Javier were all staring at me. Guys, a little privacy, please! I yelled. After looking for Earth in my mind for well over five minutes, I headed back with my friends. Sorry, I couldn't communicate with Earth. <You said Earth gave us our souls, right Sevashkish?> [Yes Valerie, that is correct.] <Daniel, maybe you

need to speak to Earth as if you were speaking to yourself, to your soul.> <Let Earth know that we are here and that we genuinely want to help.> <Let Earth know that we care not only about humans but all the life on it.> <Valerie, can you please explain to me how in the world he is supposed to do that?> <Javier!> <It is not hard.> <When you really like someone, when you are hurt, when you feel happy, or when you are relaxed.> <That little voice in your head that you talk to, that voice that is you.> <That is our soul!>

I smiled at Valerie's last statement, "That is your soul." I had not thought about that, but she was right. That little voice in our heads is our soul. <Valerie, I do not want to sound offensive but how do you know that?> How do you know that the voice in our head is our soul?> Javier asked. <I can feel it, and besides it is something that is personal to each person.> [You are correct Valerie, that voice is your soul.] [All sentient beings have it, it is what makes them sentient.] I turned around to look at Sevashkish and he had a hint of a smile and nodded yes to me. I will give it a try, I told everyone. I will speak to Earth as if it were part of myself, my own soul.

Chapter 7
EARTH SPEAKS

I closed my eyes and tried to relax. Okay, I need to try to speak to the Earth as if I were speaking to myself. I searched my mind and imagined everything that I loved about life. I imagined the beautiful beaches that I have been to. I imagined the tasty food that I had eaten. I imagined all the great times that I have had with my family and friends. Every Christmas and birthday party that I had. I even started to imagine the bad times that have made me stronger after overcoming them. I hope this gets Earth's attention. I felt kind of stupid just standing in the room while my friends and an actual alien watched me. What is life? The craziness of it all made me laugh.

Maybe I am crazy and I will wake up soon in a white room with doctors asking me a million questions. Kind of like in the ending of the movie Inception. Dream or no dream I will still try to communicate with Earth, as crazy as it might sound. Okay, Daniel, stay focused. I pictured myself riding my bike for the first time. Faster and faster the images came to my mind like the first time I saw the beauty of Yosemite. I tried to imagine all the continents and all the oceans that I have seen on maps in my life from the view of a plane. I saw the time that I got lost at a Walmart when I was a kid. I even pictured the time a dog chased me when I was just 8 years old. I started to feel all the sensations I could too.

I felt the grass under my feet, and the waves around my body when I went to Santa Monica Beach. I am here Earth, and I am here to do my best to help you. Suddenly, images, videos, smells, and audio rushed to my mind. I saw a white bright light collide with an asteroid. I saw lava covered all around this ball of light and rocks.

I saw water overtake the lava. I saw islands and continents emerge from the water. I saw animals being born. I saw humans that did not look like normal humans, but humans nonetheless. I saw the Earth being born in a mixture of golden bright lights. I saw the crust of Earth's body molding together to form the planet. The golden bright light covered all of the planet as it formed. I saw and heard water rushing to fill its seas. It sounded like the sound Niagara Falls makes when pouring down. Strong and powerful.

Earth was speaking to me, but it wasn't normal speech. It was more of a feeling that was mixed with mental images, and videos. Earth told me that it needed help to survive. Earth told me that humans had the power to one day become galactic dimensional beings. Earth showed me its cries for help, to a higher power that even Earth had just started to understand what this higher power was. Earth called this being Thou.

Earth showed me the desperation of not knowing whether Thou still existed or was gone, or not allowed to help it because of the rules of inter-dimensional conflicts. I had goosebumps all over my body hearing Earth "talk."

So much information was being shown to me. Earth played back videos of the Phylmecs and how it was unable to stop them from attacking it because it was now a planet, and that meant it had sacrificed its own defenses to seed life within itself. I saw Earth look at the life it created with great enjoyment, but sorrow because it could not protect itself, so how would it protect its own creatures? I saw how Earth came to the realization that it could defend itself, but it would need help from its children. All of its creatures, from the smallest single cell to the most complex beasts.

Lastly, Earth showed me its cries through the millennia to its sentient children, humans, and even to the ones it calls the sea children. Over thousands of years, earth has cried to humans for help, some have heard but none have understood. No one understood. Thankfully Earth made a friend, Sevashkish. Sevashkish who was millions of light years away from Earth, but had a connection with the beauty of life that Earth had to offer. He came to help. He helped spread Earth's cry for help to its children without directly interfering. Year after year failing until now.

Finally, I saw it. I saw how we were all part of Earth. I saw how Earth gives its life force to help humans and every single living thing on it get a soul. I saw how our beautiful planet evolved from its last dimension into this new dimension that allowed it to bring life within itself. My mind was going to places that I could not even begin to describe. I saw some things that I could not even express with my own human emotions, even if I lived thousands of years. It felt beautiful.

I now understood that every time humans evolved, Earth evolved too. Growing stronger, and to a higher dimension. Sadly, with all the great things Earth showed me, I also saw how the Earth was weakening and dying. The Phylmecs have stunted human evolutions and that has caused Earth to grow weak with life energy. With overpopulation and no evolutionary growth, Earth could not survive another Phylmec harvest. This was the last round for all of humanity to stay alive and for every single organism for that matter.

As quickly as they came the images and video stopped. I was once again in my mind. It was dark like normal, but then I saw something that connected to me on a deep level. It was a bright golden circle heading towards someone who was about to be born. I instinctively knew it was a soul traveling to a newborn baby. In my mind and heart, I knew that the soul was mine. I looked around and saw thousands of souls traveling to newborn humans, and even to the tiniest of creatures. This must be how Earth gives its energy to its children I thought. Then something caught my eye, and that was that only a handful of souls looked like mine.

Most of the souls were bright white lights traveling to their physical bodies, but mine and a few others were crystal golden bright. As golden as the brightest gold ring. At that moment I understood. My soul and a few select others carried a piece of Earth's soul within themselves. This realization made me have a feeling of bravery mixed with a feeling of leadership and responsibility. I am not sure if I am one of Earth's saviors or fighters, but at that moment I knew I would do everything I could to save Earth and its children.

All of a sudden my mind went completely blank again. I opened my eyes and it was as black as a moonless night. Hey Valerie, Javier, and Sevashish are you there? There was no answer from any of them. I was starting to panic, and then I saw a silhouette that was bright, so bright that I felt like I was looking directly at the sun on a bright summer day.

My eyes were burning, but I knew that I could not look away. I could not make out a face, but just the silhouette of a body on this being. A body that was maybe only 4 feet tall and thin. It was bipedal and oddly shaped like a human. This being was coming closer to me. I wanted to run away, but something told me that I should stay. The being came towards me and touched my chest. My chest felt like it was on fire. I felt my skin would tear in shreds.

I felt like I was being burned alive, but at the same time, I felt a sensation of great pleasure running through my body. It was a combination of feelings. The bright being turned its head up to face right at me. It was looking directly at my eyes, and I tilted my head down to see it directly in the eyes. I felt like time itself stopped.

It didn't say my name in any words or sounds, but it said my name in a way that ran through my entire body and soul. **Daniel.** Oh my gosh. I knew who this was. What I was seeing was "Earth" before it moved on to the dimension that turned it into a planet. I was seeing Earth as an individual and not just a planet.

I could not look away from its eyes. They were so bright that for a second I thought that there was no true color, but then some color started to appear behind the diamond-shaped eyes. Earth was a being with eyes so dark green that it made my head feel dizzy. Earth looked at me and spoke not with words but with pictures in my mind again. The name Terramondetierra repeated in my head over 20 times, and I knew that this was Earth's real name.

Terramondetierra is the name Earth still goes by. Terramondetierra no longer had a physical body, but its spirit was projecting one of the bodies it once had. Terramondetierra was still touching my chest, and I asked why it was touching and burning my chest. Terramondetierra did not respond, but somehow I knew it was transferring part of its powers to me. The powers of the animals, the weather, the plants, and the terrain were being transferred to my body and soul.

I finally understood how I was the perfect candidate, since I had part of Terramondetierra's soul I would be able to handle the powers and fight in the current dimension without causing harm to the overall universe. This would also allow Terrmondeteirra to defend itself through its children. The powers felt so heavy in my body, and they hurt every single cell in my body. The pressure felt immense. I felt like I was being squeezed together. With all the pain that I felt, at that moment I also understood why we needed four sentient beings other than myself to be here. The powers of Terramondetierra would be shared amongst us. Just one person holding them is not safe.

<Daniel, can you hear me?> <Daniel, wake up, wake up.> He is starting to scare me, he isn't waking up.> [Do not worry Valerie, he will wake up.] [His mind and body are going through an intense situation speaking to a being so high in dimension such as Earth.] <Sevashkish, how do you know this?> <I mean how can we even trust you that you are telling us the truth?> <Javier how can you not trust him?> <Look into your own soul and you will feel the bright energy that Sevashkish is giving.> <Valerie, I feel his energy, but I am scared.>

<Sevashkish, I am sorry for making you feel like I didn't trust you, I know you are a good being, but I am just scared!> [There is no offense, Javier.] [Also, I wanted to let both of you know that

you both are equally as important as Daniel.] <What do you mean Sevashkish?> <You did not come to Valerie or me, you came to Daniel.> [It is not that I chose Daniel, he heard my pleas for help and he was able to bring me to him.]

<That is what I mean, what good are Valerie and me in this mission that seems to be impossible?> <It seems like we will do more harm than good.> <We may be a distraction for Daniel as well, he will be worrying about us.> <He is my best friend and he always puts others before himself.> <I do not want my friend to come to harm because of me.> [You are stronger than you think Javier, and you and Valerie are here for a reason.] [Do not forget that.] <Thank you, Sevashkish, and again I am sorry for having doubted you.>

Chapter 8
POWERS

<Sevashkish, Javier, look he is waking up!> <Oh my gosh why is he compulsing like that?> <Javier please help me hold him, so he won't hurt himself.> <Ouch, he feels hot!> <Sevashkish, Daniel's body is burning up!> <What do we do?> [We must wait, Valerie, we must wait for Daniel to control whatever is going on with him and Earth]. <I am sorry Sevashkish I just cannot sit around and watch Daniel have compulsions like this.> <He can get seriously hurt, and then who will save Earth and everyone?>

I felt a hard slap go across my face and slowly I opened my eyes. Valerie was frantically slapping my face. I felt a pressure on my chest and turned my head down and saw that Javier was performing CPR on me. I rolled my eyes to the side and noticed that Sevashkish was about to drive something that looked a lot like an Epi pen down my chest.

Guys, stop! I am awake! I managed to say in a sleep-driven voice. Please stop what you are doing. <Dude don't you ever scare us like that again!> <We thought we had lost you!> I was shocked to see tears falling from Javeir's face. He is not someone who cries, ever. [I am glad that you made it through Daniel.] [Even though I must admit that I was scared that you may not come back.]

<How are you feeling Daniel, do you need me to do something for you?> <Get something for you?> I am okay Valerie, but can you please loosen the grip of your hug you are choking me. <I'm sorry, we were just all scared.> I am feeling a bit nauseous but nothing that I can't handle.

How long was I out for? [You were out for over 30 minutes Daniel.] Oh wow, that is a long time. I didn't expect to get that response. I turned to look at my friends. Javier looked like a truck had run him over. Valerie looked like she had lost someone, and Sevashkish looked like he had been defeated. I felt bad for putting them through that.

You guys are amazing, I told them with a big smile. I stood up cautiously, and instinctively I grabbed everyone's hand and placed it on my chest. They all stared at me oddly, but suddenly their eyes opened wide as they all stared into blank space. They were being "shown" what Terrmondetierra had shown me. They now understood. One by one they each pressed their hands deeper into my chest. It hurt a bit, but it was the only way to give them what I had in me. Sevashkish was given the power of the Earth's weather.

He would control everything from the rain to the winds and even the mist in the air.

I am not sure how I knew this but Terramondtierra had also given Sevashkish the power to temporarily stay in the 3rd dimension, but this meant that he couldn't go back to the 7th. What shocked me was that Sevashkish willingly gave up the ability to go back home in order to save Earth. He would only go home if the war was over, and we were victorious. Earth did not have enough power to override what it had done. Next, Javier was given the power of the terrains. He would be able to move mountains and Earth from the very core of the planet if he wanted. Valerie was given the power of the plants. She could make any plant on this planet grow or die in the blink of an eye. Lastly, I was given the power of creatures. I had the power to control any organism on planet Earth. From the smallest microbe to the largest whale.

After everyone had gotten their powers Terramondetierra's silhouette reappeared in my mind. Everyone saw it instantly since they were still touching my chest. In Terramondetierra's strange way, it "spoke." It told us that we had these powers, and we must use them wisely. It gave us its blessing to save the planet and every single creature in it. <We cannot go back home, can we?> [I am afraid going home will not be a good idea, Valerie.] [The Phylmecs have technology that can scout Earth's energy in as little as five minutes, and now we all have part of Terramondetierra's energy, so we can't risk using our powers when all of you are near your loved ones.]

This made my stomach turn. I wouldn't be able to say bye to my parents. No, that would be impossible. It would be too dangerous if we accidentally used our powers. We would be targeted by every Phylmec already on this planet, and that meant the top leaders of the Earth. We would be killed at first glance, or worse yet, we would be harvested. [We all must leave immediately now!] [The Phylmecs will be here in five minutes.]

<What do you mean?> Javier asked. [As I said, they have technology that can detect Earth's energy as fast as five minutes, and the informants have surely detected this surge in energy.] [It is no longer safe to be here.] <Are you sure, Sevashkish?> [I am 100% certain, Javier.]

Wait, we cannot go yet! I am getting another message from Terramondetierra. [We must go, Daniel, there is no time.] No Sevashkish, we need to see this. I closed my eyes and the images and vivid scenes started to pour in as I felt Sevashkish pulling me away. I saw a large object shaped like a golden heart. It was the size of a basketball. It was frozen somewhere, under blocks of ice. What was this? It felt pure and then I knew, and I felt that Sevashkish knew too since he was holding on to me. This heart-shaped object was what we needed to defeat the Phylmecs.

This was Terrmondetierra's physical golden heart which is where most of Earth's life energy is stored. The heart looked heavy and as golden as the sun was bright on a warm sunny day. Terramondetierra showed me its location. It is currently buried in the largest frozen mountain of Antarctica, Mount Vison. Terramondetierra was doing its best to give us as much information as possible, but only Sevashkish and I were able to see all of this, so I began to explain to Valerie and Javier what I was seeing.

Guys, Terramondetierra moved its physical heart from within its own core two hundred thousand years ago when it found out that a strange alien species not from this galaxy, "the Phylmecs," had used and consumed all the energy of two planets, rendering them lifeless.

One of those planets still remains today as a mere moon of what it once was, "Pluto." Earth knew that the Phylmecs would come to it, so it made a deadly decision. It made the decision that to this day it still weeps over.

It made the lush green continent of Antarctica, which at the time was a place filled with biodiversity like in the Amazon, into the cold winter wonderland that it is now. Sadly every single living creature in Antarctica died, millions of life forms all frozen in time under sheets of ice. Terramondetierra knew that only in a place so void of life, so cold, where no real strong ray of sunlight hits, would its own energy be hidden from any Phylmec sensor. This is also the reason why Earth is now on an axis, to always keep that side of Antarctica under complete and utter darkness.

Thankfully, when the Phylmecs arrived on Earth, they automatically assumed that Terramondetierra had broken its heart and spread it throughout itself so the life energy wouldn't be able to be acquired, just like the other living planets had already done in the third dimension to prevent Phylmecs from stealing their energy. The Phylmecs were partially right in their assumption, that Earth had spread its life energy through all its organisms, plants, and terrains, but not all of it. [The Phylmecs had no clue that Earth had more life energy than the other planets.]

[It has so much life energy that it did not break its heart, but hid it!] Yes Sevashkish, but sadly, The Phylmecs did not mind not finding Earth's physical heart for two good reasons. [Yes you are right, Daniel.] Javier looked at me, <What are those reasons?> On planet Earth they got the bodies they so desperately needed, and the souls or life energy of humans that will help them move to the next dimension. <Even though they did not steal all of Earth's energy all at once, they have slowly been torturing it to death.> [That is right, Valerie.]

<I still do not understand why we need this heart, Daniel, what will we do with it?> Wait, Javier, Earth is still transmitting its message.> My head was starting to hurt as Earth was showing me as much as it could. The heart needs to be broken, and once it is broken all the life energy stored will be released together and it will eliminate any non-earth organism from this planet.

<Why didn't Earth release this power on its own when the Phylmecs first arrived?> Before I could try to answer Valerie, Terramondetierra showed me the reason or reasons I should say. At the time the first homo sapiens were just coming to be, and if Earth had used its own heart it would have stunted the growth and development of its dominant sentient beings, and that was not a risk that Terramondetierra wanted to take. The second reason is that it takes over ten minutes to properly break the heart and for the energy to spread throughout the planet.

[It makes sense, and as we know the Phylmecs can be anywhere on Earth within five minutes of an energy surge.] <The last reason is the simplest.> Javier spoke, <Earth cannot defend itself anymore since seeding life, only its creatures can, so that means it itself cannot break its own heart.> You are right, Javier. [Everyone, they are here in one minute.] I heard Sevashkish talking, but I was too busy absorbing everything Terramondetierra had told us. I felt a sense of fear as Earth warned us of one thing.

The destruction of this heart can possibly mean that unless humans evolve to the next dimension the planet will surely die. Thankfully, Terramondetierra is confident that after the Phylmecs are destroyed humanity will continue to evolve like they were supposed to. Terramondetierra feels so strongly that humans will evolve again that it is willing to break its own energy source. In one last show of pictures and videos, Earth said, **TEN MINUTES** for the chemical to be fully released into the entire planet, to drive out any Non-Earth organisms. [Here they come.] I felt myself being yanked by Sevashkish.

While Terramondetierra was "talking" an explosion that sounded like one thousand of the loudest fireworks I've ever heard went off. I felt Sevashkish stumble to the floor. Shortly after I fell hard to the ground. The skin on my elbows and knees burned. I was stunned and my head felt like it would explode. I was drifting in and out of consciousness. I managed to open my eyes and noticed there was smoke all around. I felt blood falling through my nose, and that is when Terramondetierra reappeared in my mind. It quickly showed me that the explosion was caused by "an informant of the Phylmecs." [Everyone we must move from here, we must run, they will shoot again.] [They noticed the high amount of energy coming from Earth and decided to attack.]

Terramondetierra rapidly showed me that we had to hold hands again in order to leave this place. Guys! "We must grab each other's hands together, so we can leave here!" Before I could confirm that we all held each other's hand we started to fall. Within half a second we were falling back into a dark space. Just like when we first arrived, but this time bloody and injured. Shortly after, Terramondetierra's "voice" started to get fainter. It must have been cutting communication to ensure our safety and its safety, but not before sending us one last visual of what happened.

Images and videos of what had happened played back in our minds. It was an actual spaceship. It didn't look like the flying saucers that you see online, no. This ship was shaped like a long deadly cube. On the sides, it has blades pointed up and down. On the tips of the blades, it had what looked like big guns. The images stopped. I felt Terramondetierra wish us luck on our soon-to-be journey for the fight of our very existence, and I know everyone felt Earth wishing us luck because we were all holding hands thankfully.

As we fell Sevashkish told us that he was sure Terramondetierra would take us as close as it could to our destination. I stared at Javier and Valerie. They were equally as scrapped as I was, but we would be fine. Javier yelled, <If it's cool with everyone can we never repeat that again, and can we all call Terramondetierra TT for short?> To my surprise all of us but Sevashkish laughed out loud. <TT it is Valerie agreed.> Sevashkish, do you think that, wait where am I? I was lying on the ground, and my head felt heavy. I touched my head and there was blood on my hand. It was pitch black and I could see nothing but darkness. I pulled my phone out and saw that it was 1:23 am.

What happened? The last thing I remember is asking Sevashkish a question, while we were falling. I seriously hope my head was not that hurt. It did not hurt too much, but the blood concerned me a little. Hopefully, it was just superficial. What should I do? I need to find my friends. I started to dial Javier's number and then it instantly clicked in my head that I could not say anything through any technological means to my friends. Not that the Phylmecs knew who we were, but you can never be too cautious. The calls and texts would be traced. Everything would be bugged and we would be killed without hesitation. I decided to get up slowly to try and look for the others.

I walked maybe 40 feet when I saw someone lying on the floor. I ran to them. It was Valerie. Her bright red hair was tangled on some rocks, but she looked to be okay. She was unconscious. Her breathing was a bit heavy, but she was stable. I gently pushed her a bit to the side and she woke up, "Valerie stay put I will go look for Sevashkish and Javier," she nodded in agreement. I walked for about two minutes when I saw Javier lying with his hand bent backward.

I hurried to him and noticed that his middle finger was either broken or he had seriously sprained it. I put my head to his chest and his breathing was normal. I will let him rest till I find Sevashkish, I told myself. Before I could turn around I saw Sevashkish flying as quietly as an owl with his massive wings. Even though it was pitch black, his giant purple wings glowed lightly in the darkness. He looked to be bruised and cut everywhere, and his wings were torn on the sides, but yet he flew as silent as a real owl.

Chapter 9
IT STARTS NOW

Sevashkish are you okay? He landed right next to me. [I am okay, but a little bruised.] Do you need me to help clean your wounds? [No, it is okay Daniel, the cuts are only superficial.] Okay, but I am here if you need me. Sevashkish, what happened, and where are we? The last thing I remember was that I was in the middle of asking you a question. [Terramondetierra was attacked while sending us away I presume.] [Terramondetierra had to leave us in a spot where we could not be tracked by the Phylmecs, and I think we are somewhere in India if I am not mistaken.]

While Sevashkish was talking to me he stumbled a bit to the floor. One of his wings collapsed under his weight. You need to lie down right now, you are hurt! How did you get hurt so badly compared to the rest of us? [I did my best to shield you all from the explosion.] Wait, you shielded us? [Yes, that is correct.]

I couldn't believe it, Sevashkish had risked his life to save the three of us. He had risked himself for beings that were not even his species or in his same dimension. Sevashkish I do not know what to say, but thank you so much. You are a true friend, and you can count on me to do the same for you. I went over next to him and did my best to place him in a comfortable position. I smiled at him and did my best to comfort him.

He was a being from the 7th dimension now inhabiting the 3rd dimension, and unless we won he would never see home or his family. He was brave, and I hated myself for feeling like an absolute coward at that moment. I was feeling terrified. Everything was falling apart before it even started. We almost got killed before even getting instructions on how to save our planet.

Things weren't going well at all. Javier, Valerie, and I were knocked unconscious from just a simple fall. How could three kids and an alien save the world? If only I could ask someone for help, like my parents. My parents I thought, I may never see them ever again in my life. I felt utter sadness flow through me. There was a lump in my throat.

Why is this happening? My eyes started to swell with tears. I was about to let the tears flow when I heard footsteps behind me, and then I felt two hands across my back. I turned around and saw Javier and Valerie looking at me. They gave me a huge hug, and I don't know how, but I held it in and did not cry. I knew if I did they would lose it. I smiled at them and thanked them for joining me on this trip to *literally* save Earth and mankind.

I am sorry for dragging you guys into all of this. <Come on Daniel, how were we going to let you have all the fun?> Javier punched my shoulder gently. <Yeah, plus you wouldn't know what to do without us.> Valerie said with a smile. I hugged them tightly. We have an issue, guys. We have to find a place to move Sevashkish to because he got injured by shielding us. It is not safe to keep him out in the open like this, he isn't exactly human.

It took us about ten minutes of wandering around silently until we realized that we were in some sort of forested area. We ended up finding an entrance to a little cave that was abandoned. It took a good 5 minutes, but we managed to carefully move Sevashkish into the cave. Thankfully Javier's fingers were not broken like I had assumed, but they were still pretty swollen. <Let me tell you this boy weighs a lot.> <I mean a lot, he's probably heavier than me and that tells you something.> <Javier, you are not fat you are just thick.> Valerie said.

Oh yeah, he is thick alright. I slightly shoved Javier so he would know that I was joking. I wouldn't want you any other way, Javier. I laughed but I was being truthful. I was glad Javier was here. He is extremely strong, so without him, we wouldn't have been able to carry Sevashkish anywhere. Sevashkish must weigh a good 400 pounds. I think we all felt happy to be safely in a cave where no one could see us without us seeing them. We found a soft patch of grass growing in the back of the cave where we all sat down. I do think it even took us five minutes before we all fell asleep. The next thing I remember is waking up to Sevashkish looking at us with a smile on his face.

<Um why are you staring at us while we sleep Sevashkish?> [I am just happy Javier, and thank you all for saving me.] <I am glad we got to help you a bit Sevashkish.> <Daniel told us what you did for us.> [It was nothing, Valerie, really, but you are very welcome.] Your wings are looking healed up! [Yes we Lukens heal fast.] [In fact, if we were in the 7th dimension we would be healed within a minute.]

<Sevashkish, Daniel told us that you suspect that we are in India.> [I am afraid I was mistaken, Valerie, based on my internal compass we are actually in eastern China.] <Okay, let me just be clear did you just say we were in eastern China, as in Ni Hao China?> [Yes, Javier we are in Eastern China about 3 kilometers north of the nearest village.]

Wow, we were in China. I couldn't even believe it. Are you sure we are in China? [I am 100% sure that we are in China.]. It was a bittersweet moment for me right in that second. See I always wanted to go to China as a kid, and my goal was to go one day before turning 21, but here I am now. I was beyond happy, but then sad at the reasoning as to why I was in China. I wouldn't be able to visit the Great Wall, nor would I be able to eat delicious

Chinese food. But that was my reality right now. I had to stay focused.

I checked my phone to look at the time and it was only 5:35 in the morning. I am not sure how much we had slept, but I felt well rested plus the sun was starting to come up. <Okay, I am up and feeling pretty good, so what should we do now?> I stared at Valerie as she asked us the question, and to my fear, I saw something big and black charging toward her. It was going to reach her in 5 seconds. There was no way she could move away in time. I quickly pushed her away and got in front of the black bear. Yes, in front of the black bear. With my right hand facing it I whispered, "STOP and Kneel."

To my utter amazement, the bear stopped and kneeled. The bear went from a dangerous wild animal to a cuddly teddy bear in an instant. I could feel my friends looking at me with great intensity. "Go on along your way and leave us alone" I finished telling the bear. The bear did exactly that. <How in the world did you do that Daniel?> <How did you get the bear to listen to you?> Uhhh I honestly don't know Javier. I just knew I had to save Valerie, and I instinctively knew it would work. [We must leave this place at once.]

<Why would we leave this place if Daniel got rid of the bear for us?> [Valerie, remember the Phylmecs can pinpoint any surge in Earth's energy within seconds and be in the exact location within five minutes.] [Daniel just used one of Earth's powers.] [Daniel has

released a great surge of energy by controlling the bear, especially since it was his first time using his powers.]

<Where do you expect us to go if we are on foot and your wings are still healing?> Javier asked. Sevashkish is right, guys. Javier, we got to run, wings or no wings. I feel energy flowing through me, and it feels like I can take on the world. It feels like someone gave me a supercharged energy drink. I am sure the Phylmecs have picked up this surge. No one said anything else after I explained that.

We ran in the opposite direction of the cave for 4 minutes and that is when we saw the spaceship that I had seen only a day before. The deadly-looking cubed ship with the jagged edges. The ship hovered in the cave and we heard an announcement being made. Surprisingly this wasn't in our minds like when Sevashkish talks. This was an audio announcement that we heard through our ears.

"We know you think you have connected with your planet, and we know that you think you are helping your planet, but we want to let you know that you are wrong." "Someone is trying to trick people into believing that the Earth has a soul and is alive, but we want to let you know that Earth is not alive." "It is just a planet floating in space." A hacker has gotten into our base and is trying to cause paranoia." "The hacker doesn't want humans to advance technologically speaking." "He wants humans to remain in the dark ages." "Come outside and we will explain everything to you."

<That can't be true, can it?> Valerie asked. We heard a noise coming from the cave just as the message finished playing. Two

cute little black cubs came out, sniffing the air and turning their heads toward the spaceship. Before they could even reach twenty feet from the entrance of the cave the ship blasted two of its dark black beams towards the cubs. We heard no cries, but we smelled burned fur, and when the dust cleared there was nothing there. The bears had been blasted into mere particles.

We looked at each other in total bewilderment. <Wow, they just killed two innocent creatures like it was nothing.> <They are vile!> <How do they sense the energy that Daniel emitted?> Javier had a look of fear and hatred in his eyes. A look that I had never seen. [The Phylmecs may be a species from the third dimension, but that does not mean that they are medieval in technology.]

[Everyone, I want you all to understand the Phylmecs may suspect that something is helping Earth.] [That being said, by blasting the bears they do not know if it is a human or an animal that is helping.] [That is good for us and our safety, and we should stay undercover as long as possible.]

I was hearing what Sevashkish was saying, but from a distance. I was beyond mad. They had killed two innocent creatures like their lives weren't worth anything. Calm down, Daniel. I told myself. I was no good to anyone if I lost control of my emotions. I was dumbfounded by how evil the Phylmecs were. Imagine if we had believed the lie that the Phylmec informant in the spaceship had told us.

We would have walked out and been blasted without hesitation. Plus our families would have been killed, just by association. These creatures were vile. What made it worse was that they appeared to be humans. It is always harder to hate someone who looks like you versus someone who is completely different from you.

As I finished cooling down I was glad to see that Javier, Sevashkish, and Valerie seemed more calm too. Sevashkish was explaining all that he could. [Moving dimensions does not necessarily mean you get more intelligent.] [When you move dimensions you live much longer for one thing, and your soul gets more freedom to travel outside your body.] [You are also able to heal quicker.] [The list goes on and on, but most importantly one day if you are able to reach a high enough dimension, you will be able to seed your own life like Earth did.] [This is a dream that we Lukens have.]

It had been over an hour since the Phylmec spaceship left. I was still upset and frankly scared. I think we all were. [I suggest that we do not move until it gets dark because the Phylmec informant will be around to make sure that it did not miss anything.] Why do the Phylmecs have informants? I mean, am I really the first one that Earth has directly communicated with?

[You are the first human, yes, but Earth has used animals in the past to try to sabotage Phylmec stations and outposts.] [The Phylmecs once suffered a huge loss while on Earth.] [A giant flood swopped through their outpost and animals from all walks of life came to attack them.]

[They lost over 50k of their own kind, and they learned from their mistakes.] [Earth hasn't just sat down and done nothing, Earth has fought and sent its children to fight too.] [Unfortunately, none did enough damage, only the time that 50k Phylmecs died in the flood.] [The Phylmecs know that any surge of energy is Terramondetierra setting up an attack.] It made me feel happy that Terramondetierra has been fighting in any way possible to save itself and its children. Sevashkish, how long do we have until the Phylmecs get here?

[From what we Lukens know they just left their home planet almost two weeks ago, so that puts it at 2 weeks till they reach Earth.] [Then after this will be a two-week period where they try to convince humanity how they are here to save them, and how they are here to teach them the sciences etc.] Their way of having a secret invasion. [Exactly.]

<Okay, so that gives us about a month to get to Antarctica before they start harvesting, right?> <I wouldn't count on that timeline, Valerie.> <What do you mean Javier?> <Look, what if they arrive earlier, or what if they arrive and start attacking right away?> <You have a point, Javier.> <Yes, so we have to get a move on!> [You are right Javier, we must get a move on, but you can rest assured that they will not attack right away.] <Oh, why is that, Sevashkish?> [The Phylmecs can't risk getting into an all-out war with humans.] [The invasion has to be secret at the beginning, or

else they risk a war that can damage all those crucial bodies that they need.]

I guess we can all agree that we need to get moving right? We rest only at night but other than that we keep moving. <I agree with you Daniel, but I think the only way we can reach Antarctica in time is to use the powers that Terramondetierra gave us.> I glanced over at Valerie. I was quite shocked that she had made the comment, but I agreed with her. You are right Valerie, but we must use our powers wisely, and be gone right away after we use them. Does everyone agree on that?

Valerie, Javier, and Sevashkish all looked at me and agreed. <Look at you becoming a little leader.> Javier giggled. Oh shut up Javier. I said while holding onto a laugh. Javier was right though. I surprised myself with the initiative that I was taking. I felt bad for taking "charge," but everyone seemed receptive. I just hoped we would all be okay.

After we all agreed on our plan we simply waited all day in the forest, as Sevashkish had recommended. We didn't talk much to each other the entire day. I think we all needed our own space to absorb our new reality. We hid in some bushes near the cave where the poor bears had been blasted, and we stayed there till nightfall. Once nightfall hit we were all starving. We had to get food before we could do anything else. We all agreed that it was best that only two of us go and try to find food. It would be Valerie and I who went to search for food.

Sevashkish and Javier stayed back because they still had small injuries to rest, even though Sevashkish would never admit it. <Do you think we will find food?> I am sure we will. There are lights outside by the road which means there is a town there. We carefully walked along the edge of the forest, careful to not be seen by anyone. Surprisingly it only took us 30 minutes to reach the town, and no one saw us along the way. To our luck, we immediately saw a little convenience store. The lights were on, but we did not see anyone inside. This probably wasn't the smartest idea, but without thinking we ran toward the store. When we got there it was completely empty and unlocked.

<Where is everyone?> I am not sure, but I see that the restroom door is closed, maybe the owner is in there? <Who knows, but we have to take the risk and go inside.> You are right Valerie. We may not get a better chance than this. I felt bad. I have never stolen food in my life, but we knew if we waited for someone to show up then that may cause issues as we are not from China. That would raise red flags, and everything else would fall apart.

Okay, let's go for it! Valerie and I grabbed everything that we could fit in our hands. Things like: canned food, chocolate bars, chips, egg rolls, and I grabbed a case of water. After no more than two minutes we quietly ran back into the forest. <I feel really bad about stealing someone's food Daniel, something just seems morally wrong about that.> Valerie when all this is over we will personally buy all the food we took I said with a smile. Just remember exactly what we took. Valerie turned to look at me and smiled slightly.

We ran back to the bushes where we were hiding, and the four of us devoured the food. <I know the world is ending and all, but can we take some time and say how insanely good this food is?> <I mean it feels like I haven't eaten in ages.> Javier, it's only been a day, but I totally agree with you. [This food is mighty delicious if I do say so myself.] We all started laughing. Sevashkish was having Doritos. How crazy had life gotten in just a matter of days? I was in China hiding in the forest with an alien and my two best friends, and to top it off we were the only ones that stood in the way of Earth being destroyed. <These egg rolls are heavenly.> <I seriously need to have a talk with my favorite Chinese restaurant back home.>

<They are not making the same egg rolls as they are in China.> <Um, Javier, those egg rolls were for all of us.> I stared at Javier as his cheeks got bright red. It is okay Javier. You need to heal and keep up your strength. We all laughed out loud together again. Night time soon came and we all decided to stay put for the night. We decided to rest the night in the forest and tomorrow we would get up bright and early and head toward Antarctica.

We all woke up at dawn. We all slept pretty well and felt rested. It was still dark out, so we decided we should get to the ocean before the sun rose. Sevashkish told us the ocean was only about an hour's walk, but his wings had healed enough and he said he could carry us all to the ocean. We had one simple plan, and that plan was to go to the ocean where I would call upon an ocean creature big enough to take us to Antarctica.

We figured by the time the Phylmecs informants got a hold of the energy surge we'd be long gone. <Okay, I know Sevashkish is big and strong, but how is he supposed to carry the three of us such a distance?> <I mean I am 6'4 and weigh a good 300 pounds.> In a blink of an eye Sevashkish came and tossed Javier over his back like he was a rag doll. [Do not worry about me Javier, I am quite strong by human standards]. <Well I'll be damned.> Javier had a big smile on his face. [Daniel and Valerie I will carry you in each hand because this will free up my wings to their full potential.]

[Are you all ready?] I am, me too, and so am I. Sevashkish took off quite fast from the ground. It felt a bit like a roller coaster going down. It made my stomach turn around a little, but when we got to the right altitude it felt fine. Wow, I can't even describe the feeling of flying through the air with absolutely no protection but the arms of someone. It was one of the best experiences that I have ever had. I guess it must be like skydiving in a way, but not exactly because we weren't falling. We were keeping the same pace and altitude. I felt like those people in those fantasy movies you see riding on the backs of dragons.

It was so liberating! The only annoying thing was that the air was making my eyes water, so I had to close them after a minute. Thankfully, the trip to the ocean was only about 25 minutes by air.

I opened my eyes before we landed and noticed that Valerie and Javier had the biggest smiles on their faces, and I am sure I did too.

We landed in the cave by the edge of a cliff. <That was absolutely insane, and I loved it!> [I am glad that you enjoyed it, Javier.] [We have about twenty minutes of dawn left, so we must move fast.] We all left the cave and started to walk down towards the edge of the sea. Walking down a mountain cliff in the early morning is not fun. It was cold and slippery from the morning mist, so we had to be careful while heading down. <Hey what is that over there?> I turned my head in the direction where Valerie was pointing to.

Chapter 10
HI TO A NEW FACE

<Is that someone out there?> Valerie asked. [Yes, I think there is someone out there.] [We should be careful to not be seen.] I rubbed my eyes to see better and there was someone there. There was someone that looked to be very old. He had a hunched back and walked super slow. He seemed to be walking with a cane too. Wait, there is a little kid next to him too! The man stumbled a bit as he walked. He had to be no younger than 90 and the kid next to him was no older than 4. <This is pretty strange.> <Why is there an old man and a little boy walking on the beach at this time?> <They may be lost Javier, maybe we should go ask them if they need help?> <Yea maybe you are right Valerie.>

Guys, let's just wait a minute or two and see what they do. I am getting this weird feeling. [I agree with Daniel, I believe we should wait a couple of minutes before helping them.] We waited and watched as they both walked by the edge of the water and that is when the old man stopped walking. He did his best to kneel at eye level with the boy. He carefully grabbed the boy's head towards his and that is when Sevashkish told us, [I believe this man is a Phylmec informant who is transferring his being to this young human child.] [His body must be giving out, so he cannot wait any longer before the Phylmecs come, he must harvest the child now, or die.]

We all stopped breathing. We were too far away to help, and we couldn't risk using our powers to save him because then we would be killed. Plus Sevashkish had told me that the Phylmecs were weak after the transfer, so that meant another Phylmec would be coming soon to help carry "the boy/Phylmec" away. We watched in horror as the man placed his head on the boy's head. We saw how the boy's body got limp and the old man's body stopped moving.

The old man's dead body dropped into the ocean and was swept by the waves. The young kid moved his head but couldn't walk. I don't know how I felt at that moment, but I stared at each of my friends, and the look on Valerie's face truly scared me. She had a look of hatred that I had never seen on her face before. This is not good I thought, and that is when things got ugly.

The long ropes of seaweed on the sand started to rise, and they quickly started to go towards the old man who was already face down in the water. The seaweeds tied around the man's flank and pulled him out of the water. The weeds threw him across the sand, and he landed with a boom. Sand went flying in all directions. That is when Valerie went running towards the boy. It all happened within seconds. I stared in horror when I realized what Valerie had done. She had used her power to try and save the boy, but she had forgotten that once a Phylmec touches your head you are dead forever.

[We must go now!] Sevashkish yelled as the cube spaceship rose from behind the rocks towards Valerie. Of course, there was a ship hidden somewhere, this was the other Phylmec informant who had come to help the Phylmec who had just harvested a new body. It shot a fiery black beam towards Valerie. She stared at it blankly, not moving. She was going to get hit. I stared like an idiot that I didn't even see when Sevashkish flew by and pushed Valerie out of the way. He did all this before I could even blink. He was fast. I was beyond impressed.

We need to get out of here now! I yelled, and that is when I saw two big rocks fly through the air. They were two massive rocks each probably the size of two small school buses, and they both crushed the Phylmec spaceship flat like a pancake. I turned my back and saw Javier looking at me and nodded. He had the power of terrain and had crushed the spaceship. We ran over to meet with Sevashkish and Valerie. I kept stumbling as I ran across the cold thick sand.

As I was running across the sand I noticed something that looked like a tablet that was still fully intact. I ran towards it, and it was on. The screen was bright and there were numbers and letters all over the screen. I think it was a message, but in a weird language.

It looked like ancient Chinese mixed with Hebrew. The tablet was about the size of a notebook and it was as light as a feather. It did not even have a scratch even though it was all glass.

I quickly grabbed it and gave it to Sevashkish. [You have found a Phylmec tablet.] [This will be highly useful for us.] [Please, give me 3 minutes to hack this software, and once I do this we can safely take it and learn all that we can.] [We can hopefully learn when their next harvest will occur.] [In the meantime, may you please call upon a sea animal to take us from here?]

[We have maybe 4 minutes before they send multiple reinforcements.] I'll do that Sevashkish. I ran to the sea just about knee-deep. The water felt surprisingly warm. Which was quite weird because it was starting to get beyond foggy. I couldn't even see what was in front of me, and I instantly knew Sevashkish was forming a fog pillow over us, so we wouldn't be recognized or found.

Okay, Daniel, time to focus. You need to call upon something big and smart. I am still not sure how I knew what to do, but I simply said whale, and within 30 seconds I felt the presence of a creature believed to have sentientism, or at least close to it.

I could see the whale in my mind. It was massive. Beyond massive. It was gigantic. It was the blue whale. The largest animal to ever live on Earth. Guys our ride out of here is here! Sevashkish and Javier ran towards me with Valerie right behind. [The tablet is hacked and now we can safely use it without being traced or spied on.] <You are the man Sevashkish.>

Javier looked at him with pleasure. Guys, I have called upon a whale, and it is here, but we must go at least neck deep into the water to reach it. It took us about 20 seconds to reach neck deep into the water, and then I felt the rubbery skin of the whale. I gently touched its tail and told him "Thank you, friend," and just like that we were on our way. We were in the vast ocean on top of the back of a blue whale.

About 30 seconds after we took off on the blue whale we heard the ships. We did not see them due to the fog, but we heard them sweeping by. They made a low humming sound, kind of like those toy drones that they sell at the mall. Sevashkish thinks there were at least three different Phylmec ships. Ten minutes passed by and none of us talked until Valerie broke the silence. <I am so sorry everyone.> <I could have gotten all of us killed and ruined humanity for my impulsive action.> <I knew the boy was gone when the Phylmec head touched his, but I could not just sit around and stare, I guess I had some blind hope that he would still be okay.>

<I am so sorry>, she said as tears ran down her face. Javier went over next to her and gave her a big hug. <It was a very stupid move Valerie, but I wouldn't say that I wouldn't have done the same thing.> <We cannot keep making these mistakes, I know we were just thrown into this, but this is real life now.> <We have a mission to complete, and we have to stay together.>

I gave Javier and Valerie a shoulder hug and stared at Sevashkish. Sevashkish had a look of worry as he stared at the tablet. He looked like something was bothering him. Is there something wrong? [The Phylmecs will be here tomorrow.] [They encountered something called a dark loop spring that allows them to get to Earth in two days instead of four weeks.] [It seems that the Phylmecs also believe what we Lukens feared.] What is that? [After this harvesting they will jump directly into the 7th dimension.] [The dimension that we Lukens are in.] Sevashkish looked angrier than I had ever seen him. His big dark eyes got so big that looking into them felt like looking at a dark sky.

This mission just turned personal for him. [The Phylmecs truly value the body of the Luken, so they will do everything they can to have that body.] Javeir broke Sevashkish's dark death stare. <What exactly is a dark loop spring?> [A dark loop spring is a ripple in a black hole that allows a spaceship to travel billions of miles in mere hours.] [It is extremely rare for this to happen, but unfortunately it did.] [The only positive thing is that they will not directly harvest until after two weeks of gaining human trust.]

As Sevashkish was doing his best to explain a technology that we could not even begin to understand I could see the look of frustration sweep through Valerie and Javier, and I felt it sweep over my face as well. We were feeling hopeless, we had more barriers now than we did just a day before. I was starting to get a pit feeling in my stomach when I heard a strange call. It was a call I could only hear in my head. Like when Sevashkish speaks. Where is that sound coming from? Who are you? I thought. Am I turning crazy?

{You and your friends are on me.} I probably jumped three feet in the air. I got goosebumps all over my body. All over my body. The blue whale! It was the blue whale that was communicating with me! I yelled with a smile. {Humans are the dominant sentient species of the earth, but Terramondetierra has also passed this gift to some blue whales, and a handful of other whales and dolphins.} <Are you guys hearing a voice in your head, saying it is the blue whale talking?> Javier asked. [I most certainly am.] <I am too.> Yes, so am I Javier. <Good then I am not crazy.>

{Our first sentient ancestors learned about the Phylmecs thousands of years ago, but they could not do much to help Earth.} {There were not enough sentient whales, or dolphins to help.} {Now I can proudly say we are over 1000 sentient whales and dolphins swimming through this ocean.} {We will do all that we can to help out in any way or form.} Thank you so much, and what is your name? {My name is Tailfin, and I am honored to meet you, Daniel.} {Tailfin the honor is mine, and I would love for you to form a part of our little team of misfit heroes. {It would be my pleasure.}

We might have just found out about the Phylmecs arriving tomorrow, but at least we met a new ally, and I mean how cool is it to find out that humans are not the only sentient beings on Earth? To top things off Tailfin is a blue whale; the biggest and mightiest animal on this planet. In all of Earth's history, I should add. I was feeling better. The empty pit feeling that I had in my stomach was gone. I was happy, and as we slowly sailed all I could think about was Tailfin. Tailfin had self-awareness and lived in an entirely different world, within our own "human" world. That is just amazing.

We sailed for over 7 hours just getting to know each other. It was nice and much needed, but soon enough Tailfin had to go. He had to get something to eat and rest for the night. He found a small island to leave us for the night. {I must go feed, but I will be back tomorrow at dawn.} {Will you guys be okay here, tonight?} <Do not worry about it Tailfin we will manage.> {Perfect, so see you all tomorrow.} <Um, Javier, how exactly are we going to manage on an island with no stores?> <Elementary my dear Valerie.> <We will find something.> <I hope you are right Javier, because I am tired and hungry!>

[It seems that Tailfin has left us on a small remote island near the Philippines.] <Do you think we will be able to find food, Sevashkish?> [I am sure of it Valerie, please do not worry.] As my friends were talking about food a feeling of bewilderment struck me. Guys, imagine this, a couple of days ago we were all in class and everything in our lives was pretty good, not perfect but good. Now we are on an island in the Philippines trying to get something to eat, <and sweating up a storm with all the humidity!> <All I want to eat right now is a big fat burger from In n Out.> <Don't you

mean a big leaf from one of these trees, Javier?> <Oh yes, that is exactly what I meant.>

Man, life had changed so much, but at least Javier and Valerie were still teasing each other like always. That made me smile, but I also felt bad for Sevashkish. While Valerie and Javier were teasing each other I started to think about Sevashkish. I don't even want to know what poor Sevashkish was thinking. This wasn't even his world, but he had a lot to fear as well.

If the Phylmecs succeeded with their last harvesting of humans they would have gained enough life-energy to jump to the 7th dimension and go for the Lukens. They knew very well of the existence of the Lukens "the police of the universe." I shook my head. I had to stop thinking about negative thoughts. I had to think positively that we would be able to stop the Phylmecs.

<I wonder what is going on back at home?> <Do you think everyone is looking for us?> Valerie broke me from my train of thought. Daniel, did you hear me? Yes, of course, Valerie, sorry I was kind of daydreaming. I don't think anyone is looking for me, Valerie. You know my parents are away on their trip, and I set my phone to send timed text messages.

<What about me and Javier?> <We haven't been home in two days.> <There must be a giant search going on for us right now.> <I am sure our parents are worried to death Valerie, but for the police, they will just see us as two teens who left a little early for Spring break.> <You are probably right, but our poor parents.>

<The only thing that gives me consolation is that my parents kept annoying me to head out to spring break one day early this year.> <They got that sick of you, Valerie?> <Shut up Javier they just thought it would be a good time to remodel the house.> Well let's hope that they think we all went early to Spring Break, and are just being teenagers keeping our parents in the dark. We have to look at the bright side. We are all together and safe. Three human teenagers, one alien, and a whale. I smiled and started to laugh. How crazy is that, right? It sounded like the beginning of a joke.

We spent that evening looking for food to eat. There were plenty of non-poisonous fruits and berries on the island. There were also coconuts, so we had plenty to drink as well. It was decently good and after we ate we decided to go to sleep early. It was a smart idea because Tailfin showed up at 4:30 am according to Sevashkish, who for some reason can tell time pretty accurately. We all got up and started our journey back to Antarctica. Tailfin explained to us a bit of what he knew of Antarctica.

He had been there a few times and told us it was cold beyond belief and that we had to get a change of clothes or we wouldn't make it. <How are we supposed to get a change of clothes if there is no mall in the middle of the ocean exactly?> <You have a good point, Valerie.> Javier said. <On top of that don't we need equipment to find the heart once we get there?> Valerie we won't need equipment. TT gave us its power for a reason, and that is to help us. Sevashkish can control the weather, you can control plants, Javier can control terrain and I can control animals' minds. Let's just worry about getting warm clothes and food for now. <Yeah, I guess you are right, Daniel.>

<The only problem is the 5-minute limit that we have when we use our powers before getting killed by the Phylmecs.> <You have a point there Javier.> <I mean how are we going to deploy the heart in ten minutes when we get caught in 5?> I stared at Javier as he asked the question that I hadn't thought about. [Mount Vinson is extremely large so I am sure we will find a way of breaking the heart and escaping safely] <I hope so, Sevashkish.> Keep your head up Javier, I am sure we will find a way. <Yes, we will.> <Anyway, Tailfin, how long do you think that it will take us to reach Antarctica?> {I believe that it will take us another two full days to get there, Javier.}

Okay, so we have two more days to get there, so the next island that we stop at should be the place where we get our clothes and food. Tailfin do you know of any island along the way that may have stores with warm clothes? {Yes we will be stopping in Australia, and we can get all that we need there.} <Are we really going to go to Australia?> {Yes.} <You all know in another life, that would have made my entire year?>. You got that right Javier. I was doing my best to sound brave, but I was feeling nervous about what was to come. I guess Valerie sensed my hesitation because she came beside me and gave me a little hug. <Don't worry Daniel we will win this.> How can you be so sure? <I have faith.>

This day of sailing turned out to be very similar to yesterday. We talked and learned more about each other. It turns out Tailfin is technically a teenager too. <So you're telling me you are only the whale equivalent of an 18-year-old human?> {Yes, that is correct Javier.} <Wow so I guess we are all pretty young.> <How about you Sevashkish?> We all turned our gaze toward Sevashkish as Javier asked him the question. We had all been a bit curious to learn more about Sevashkish, but since he was so reserved we didn't want to ask him anything for fear of offending him. I guess Javier felt comfortable enough to ask him now. [I am the human equivalent of a 19-year-old.] Wow, we are all teenagers here. {Yes we are.} It made me feel better knowing that we were all around the same age.

As the hours went by we played games. It turns out that blue whales have a very similar sense of humor to us humans. Tailfin kept telling us the jokes and riddles he knew of. It was quite fun, except for one fact. The fact that was lingering in the back of my mind and I am sure the minds of my friends was, the arrival of the Phylmecs tomorrow. I did my best to shake off the thought and just enjoy the moment, but it was impossible. My mind kept coming back to it, and I am sure everyone was dealing with the same conflict. There was nothing to do but wait.

Finally, as the sun started to set we reached Australia. Tailfin had chosen the perfect docking place. A nice secluded cliff. We were far enough from civilization to not be bothered, but close enough that the nearest town was within walking distance. The cliff was also huge so it could easily hide us. {I will be back tomorrow at dawn, okay? <Sounds perfect Tailfin.> Javier smiled as Tailfin dove into the ocean and we waved goodbye to him.

When nighttime came Valerie and I went to a store right by the edge of the beach. It was one of those souvenir shops that sell super expensive last-minute beach attire. It was closed, so we broke in from the back. It was not a good feeling to be stealing, and it was a worse feeling to break into a store. Unfortunately, we had no other way. We got all that we needed. We grabbed all that we could. We got sweaters, underwear, shoes and a backpack. <Daniel, I just don't like the feeling of taking something that isn't mine.> Yes, I know what you mean, and when this is all over we will make it up to every place that we have done wrong to.

Well at least we will get to change our clothes, and surprisingly we got clothes not just in my size, but also in Javier's size. We went back to the edge of the cliff by the shore and were surprisingly pleased when we smelled cooked fish. Sevashkish and Javier had caught some fish and even cooked them. It was a nice dinner, and slowly but surely we all fell asleep. I woke up just as Tailfin was arriving. He looked majestic from the view that I had on the cliff.

. {One more day of traveling till we get there.} Just one more day. <Yes and today is the day that the Phylmecs will arrive.> <Thanks Valerie, I was seriously trying to forget that.> Today was the day that the Phylmecs would arrive on Earth and announce their existence to every human on this beautiful planet. I wonder quietly when and at what time it will happen. Little did I know that I would get my answer sooner than later. Suddenly the sky began to darken. We all instinctively looked up. In a matter of seconds, it became pitch black. There was an eerie silence. They are here, I whispered.

Chapter 11
THEY'RE HERE

A spaceship so enormous that it blocked out the entire sun flew over our heads. My jaw dropped. The ship was an opaque color and it was shaped strangely enough a lot like the Eiffel Tower. It had four big thrusters on the end and a long center that went on for at least a quarter of a mile. I could not make out the front, but I could see windows throughout the entire ship. People were staring out of this ship. Old people that looked older than the average grandparent. My heart dropped to my feet. This was real. They were here, and they were here to wipe out all of humanity and our Earth.

I turned around and saw Valerie fall to her knees. I saw Javier stumble backward. The only one who looked normal was Sevashk-ish. To him, this was not new. He had seen this before. [We have to be strong, and we have to stay together to defeat them.] [We will defeat them.] [Their time was up a long time ago, and we must defend this planet and every living thing on it.] [For every being that they destroy there will be consequences.] [All of us are Earth's warriors and we are strong.]

[We must fight for every species that has been wiped out by these viruses throughout hundreds of thousands of years.] Sevashkish's little speech got us grounded and we all nodded simultaneously in agreement. We were not going to go down without a fight. If we fell we would get back up. As long as one of us was breathing, we would fight till the very last breath was taken from our body.

{I believe that we should get out of here quickly.} {We do not want them to notice three humans and an alien on top of a whale, that isn't exactly normal.} <You are right Tailfin, please get us out of here.> Javier and Sevashkish nodded in agreement with Valerie, and with that, we left Australia, and the big Eiffel Tower-shaped ship behind. [I am able to watch local news and world news on this tablet, would you all like me to do that?] <Yes, yes, and yes,> Javier said with a shaking lip. With that, we started to watch the news around the world on the tablet.

"A humanoid alien species is here to teach humanity about space." "They come in peace and wisdom." "Earth welcomes new heroes with open arms." We spent the next couple of hours watching interviews given by the Presidents of the USA, France, China, Russia, Germany, and India. All these countries were thrilled to meet "beings" from another galaxy. Especially since they came in peace. They had nothing negative to say. The president of the

USA said, "We will learn vastly from them." The French president said, "La France est avec vous." <Well we can surely agree that the presidents from these countries are Phylmec informants. You got that right, Javier.> There were also videos being shown of people all around the world who were celebrating the Phylmecs as they landed.

<How are the news stations just reporting about how happy everyone is over these aliens coming?> <I mean where is the reporting on the fear and mania?> <Valerie, news stations are all run and owned by the same people.> <They must all be Phylmec informants.> <Javier, so you're telling me that every single person who works in a new station is a Phylmec informant?> <No, all I am saying is most people do what they are told in fear of not losing their job.>

Valerie rubbed her temples in frustration and Javier just laid down on Tailfin's back. He was flustered, but he was right. Okay, everyone, I know we are shocked that they are here. I know we are surprised about how the media is handling the coverage, but we must stop this. We must accept that they have arrived. We must accept they have been coming for over one hundred and twelve thousand years, and that top leadership officials are also Phylmec informants.

We cannot change that, but what we can do is defend the 99% of humanity who are humans and not Phylmecs. We must focus on defending our world and everything in it! [You are right Daniel, the faster that we realize who the enemy is, the better we can protect ourselves.] <I just hate that they look like your average grandparents.> < Fragile-looking people who are coming ready to share their life stories with anyone who would listen.> Javier said. [You must remember that these people may have human bodies Javier, but they are not humans.] [They are everything but human.]

I stared at Javier as he talked to Sevashkish, and then I stared at the tablet. I saw the president of the USA shaking hands with this short old man who looked like he was about 85. This old man went to the podium where the president usually gave his State of the Union speech, and he began to speak. I will never forget that moment in my life. ALLOW ME TO INTRODUCE MYSELF, MY NAME IS Tindawnstong, AND I AM THE OFFICIAL ELECTED OFFICIAL OF THE PHYLMECS.

He stopped and took a breath, and repeated this same introduction in over 10 languages. Tindawnstong spoke every major earth language, English, Spanish, French, Chinese, Russian, Arabic, and even Hebrew. He told everyone who the "Phlymecs" were, and how they were here to save humanity.

He was such a good actor that I almost fell for it. He spoke about the fear of those to travel out to the stars, and how he would help humanity. This guy was smart. He even spoke about Gods, he said "Just because there is life out in space does not mean that there is no God." THE UNIVERSE IS VAST AND NO ONE HAS THE ANSWERS AS TO WHAT HAPPENS AFTER LIFE IF

ANYTHING OR EVERYTHING. He spoke the perfect words to reach the religious and the nonreligious crowd, and everything in between.

All the major TV stations like CNN, Fox, MSNBC, and PBS were showing images all over the world of the Phylmecs space-ships landing in every major city in the world. The World Leaders of those countries were seen welcoming the Phylmecs to "planet Earth." It was unbelievable how easily they were being introduced. <Won't anyone question why the Phylmecs look exactly like us?> <Like humans?> Javier's question was answered as soon as the last word slipped from his mouth.

A reporter asked, "Why do you look like elderly humans?" THAT IS AN EXCELLENT QUESTION. IT SEEMS LIKE WHOEVER CREATED US, OR WHATEVER NATURAL SOURCES GAVE US LIFE. ALSO MADE US CO-EVOLVED INTO VERY SIMILAR SPECIES, BUT I CAN ASSURE YOU THAT WE ARE PHYLMECS AND NOT HUMANS.

<The answer was simple and to the point.> Javier looked at me with worried eyes. <They know how humans work, and they are not going to waste time complicating and answering questions that would get them questioned.> <Sevashkish, is this the normal way that the Phylmecs work?> [Yes Javier, they do their best to get humans to trust them because it makes their harvest much easier.] [It is always easier to have your victim not know that they are a victim.]

I felt such intense anger at that very moment. These creatures had been coming to Earth for over a hundred and twelve thousand years, and they had gotten away with murdering us, and using our planet's resources. They had interrupted our natural evolution, and the evolution of Earth just for their own selfish needs.

They saw us as objects and nothing more. I knew one thing at that very moment. They would not have the success that they were hoping for. They would have a battle for Earth, a battle that they never could imagine. I may just be a 17-year-old kid, but it only takes one butterfly to start a Tsunami. We would not be taken without a fight. We would die trying, but if we died we would make sure they were badly injured as well. Earth has its defenders and that is us.

I am going to go ahead and put the tablet away, Sevashkish. [Yes you are right Daniel, there's nothing left to do but reach Antarctica.] We might as well not stress for now. I turned to look at Javier and Valerie and they both approved that we should put the tablet away {Hey sorry for interrupting, but we are 18 hours from reaching Antarctica, at the 12-hour mark we will rest and get some sleep and food.} {We must be fully prepared for the journey that lies ahead.} <Tailfin, you do not interrupt, you are part of the team.> <Plus I want you to know that I always thought whales were smarter than humans.> <There is just a feeling that you all transmit, a feeling of peace and intelligence.> {Thank you Valerie for your kind words.}

{My species is just entering its sentientism, and I aspire to be like the great humans that came before, and that are here like you.} I turned and saw Valerie blush. {We will teach about human mistakes too, and try to not commit the same ones as well.} <Hey cut us some slack Tailfin, Javier said with a sly smirk.> <You know the Phylmecs have been interfering with us humans since we reached sentientism.>

{Yes you are right, Javier, but I don't think the Phylmecs taught humans to throw trash away in the ocean.} I don't know why, but all of us started laughing, even Sevashkish. <Well I guess you are right about that, I'm sorry on behalf of all humans.> {Your apology is accepted}.

After the conversation ended, we mostly stayed silent. The next couple of hours were quite boring, but there were moments of some small talk. I think we were all too scared to have much of a conversation, but at least the ride felt nice. The temperature was perfect, and nothing beats sailing in the vast blue ocean.

Twelve hours came and went like the wind. I wished they hadn't gone so fast. {Okay everyone here is the little island that I will leave you on.} {I will be back here by dawn tomorrow morning.} Thank you Tailfin, please get some rest yourself. We gently got off Tailfin and waved bye as he left for the night. This island was quite small, but it had a lot of vegetation, plus it had a small cave. That would keep us warm.

We all went inside the cave. It was nice and cozy. I was kind of happy to be on dry land. <Sevashkish and I will go grab some fish for us to eat.> Thank you Javier and Sevashkish. <Yes, thank you so much you two.> [It is my pleasure.] While Javier and Sevashkish were gone, Valerie and I scouted the cave to make sure it was empty. It was.

Javier and Sevashkish came back relatively quickly and we all ate cooked fish. I felt tired after the meal, and called it quits for the night. As I got ready to sleep I just kept thinking about tomorrow. In a couple of hours, we would be in Antarctica. We would hopefully find Terramondetierra's golden heart, and save the world. The fate of the human world would be in our hands.

I was feeling lightheaded and a tad anxious but I closed my eyes and fell asleep. *Hey, it's not working! The heart does not open. What do we do? Jungle, sea, and a peninsula. The humid air made it hard to breathe. Where am I? Bring the heart to the top of Chichen Itza. Use the power of the sun. Lay it on the altar and it will open. Fighting all around me. People screaming and crying for help. Release your energy.* <Daniel, Daniel wake up!> <Tailfin is here and we have to get going now.> I opened my eyes and saw Javier staring at me. <Come on man you slept enough.> Woah, had I been dreaming all of that? No, it was not a dream. It was a message from Terramondetierra.

It showed me where to take its heart so it would properly open and release its life force energy. I quickly got up and joined the rest of my friends on Tailfin. I explained to them that Terramondetierra had found a way to speak to me without expelling any energy. I told them that going to Antarctica wasn't enough.

We had to find the heart and then keep it safe till we got to Mexico. It was there on the altar that it would open with the help of the sun's life giving energy. <Wow I guess I never thought about how it would open.> <I just thought there was a button or something.> <Yeah, neither did I, Valerie, but I am glad we have an answer now.>

I turned to look at each of my friends as I told them about my dream. Sevashkish looked determined and ready, Valerie looked worried but courageous and Javier looked blank but motivated. With Tailfin's face in the water, it's hard to tell his expression but he told me he was ready for the challenge. {Plus, I prefer the warmer waters in the Mexican Gulf, so it would be a pleasure to go there.} {We are four hours from reaching Mount Vinson, our destination.} It was starting to get quite cold, so we put on all the warm clothes that we had gathered in Australia, and for the most part, it did its job in helping us not get too cold.

An hour before reaching our destination the weather drastically changed. It was beyond cold, it was freezing. I was starting to shiver. It was so cold that I could see my breath. Thirty minutes before getting there, Sevashkish had to open his wings up so we could all cuddle together to stay warm. I could only imagine how funny we looked. As cold as I was, I was relieved that we were finally getting to Antarctica after a few days of traveling.

{We are here.} Tailfin stopped by the edge of a giant ice bridge that led straight to a giant mountain. This mountain was enormously huge. It was covered with ice and halfway up you could not see anything but fog. Wow, the mountain was so big and all the ice on it made it look magical. I was in awe, and lost in its beauty until Valerie interrupted my day-dreaming. <Daniel, did TT tell you how to find its golden heart?>

No, Valerie, I was not given any information on how to find it, but somehow I know we have to start walking in that direction over there. I pointed to a road that led to the right. <It must have transmitted the directions in your subconscious at some point.> You are probably right, Javier. [I believe we have one hour with this clothes attire before we start going through hyperthermic shock.] [To be safe and give us time to get back to Tailfin we only have 30 minutes to find Terramondetierra's heart.] That got us all moving. {Please just call me when you are all ready.} {I will be in this exact spot waiting for you.}

We quickly got off from Tailfin and started our journey. After walking for five minutes I knew we had to go all the way straight, and then turn right and then walk for two minutes and turn left again. After walking in the same direction for 10 minutes I knew we had reached our destination. Terramondetierra definitely put this information in my subconscious in my dream last night. We reached the rocky edge of the mountain, Mount Vision I assumed. We were on the side of the mountain that never got any sun. It was more than ice cold to the touch. It was so cold that it burned to the touch. This side of the mountain had rugged sharp edges that looked like small jaggers. This is the place.

Earth's heart is safely snuggled inside this part of the mountain. It is jammed about one kilometer into the mountain. <How will reach the heart?> <Even if Javier can open up the mountain he may cause the heart to sink into the ocean.> [Do not worry Valerie.] [Javier has the power of Terrain, he can open the mountain without opening the ice sheet below it.] Plus, for safety reasons, I will send an animal in there to get the heart for us. Just to make sure it doesn't slip into the cold sea floor. <The other issue we have is that the Phylmecs will be here within five minutes, of us using our powers.>

You are right, Valerie. That is why we have to make this quick and efficient. <Is that such a good plan?> <To simply go in and go out as fast as we can?> <Valerie, we do not have time for a better plan, but we have to act now.> <I know, I am sorry everyone, I am just nervous.> <It is okay, we are all scared, but we will succeed!>

Don't worry everyone, as long as we get inside the mountain we can hide and decide what our next course of action is! Sevashkish, please form the densest fog that you have ever formed. [I will.] Within seconds everything around us looked snow white. Javier, please open a hole that is big enough for all of us to be able to get in and out of the mountain. Also, make a hole in the mountain that is wide enough for us to freely move in the mountain just in case you have to close up the entrance hole. <You got it.>

Valerie, make sure you wake up in plants in the area just in case we need them. <I will do everything that I can.> "Tailfin", I thought in my mind if we are not here in 40 minutes leave and save yourself. Finally, to that bird that was near us (who I later found out was called an Arctic Tern), "come here and help me find Earth's golden heart," and just like that, our rushed plan was set in motion.

Chapter 12
THE BATTLE FOR THE HEART

The Arctic Tern came flying low over my head. Its black feathers stood out in the white snowy atmosphere. When it was near me I noticed that I felt its emotions. I was connected to the bird. "Go get Earth's heart." It headed straight for the hole that was slowly cracking open in the mountain. The Tern quickly went inside once it was able to fit. Dust started to fly all around as the hole in the mountain got bigger, but at the same time, thanks to Valerie, there was grass growing around the edges of the inner rock. That helped control the spread of the dust.

A thick grass that wrapped itself like a cast over our bodies was also forming. Thanks to Valerie. It made me feel much warmer as it covered my body and the area where we were standing. It wasn't by any means a warm blanket, but it kept me from feeling like I was going to die in five minutes from hypothermia. After a few more seconds, the hole in the mountain was big enough for us to enter. We quickly stepped inside, and within 30 seconds the Arctic Tern came back flying with something in its beak. It was carrying something the size and shape of a small basketball. It was struggling to carry it, but it brought it to me, and I signaled for it to leave the mountain. Right when the bird left Javier made the mountain close behind us.

In my hand, I was now carrying a very important "ball," so smooth and bright. Bright enough that it was hard to stare at it directly, so bright that it illuminated the dark cavern that we were in. In my hand, I was carrying the most important thing on this planet. I was carrying the heart of Terramondetierra, where Earth stored a good chunk of its life-giving energy.

This heart had the power to officially remove the Phylmecs from within Earth. <I just finished carving a hole in the side of the mountain.> <We can hide in it, and hopefully wait out the Phylmecs.> <Do you think they will leave soon if they don't spot us?> [I am not sure, Valerie, but we will soon find out.] [Two minutes have passed since we first used our powers.]

As my friends were talking amongst each other I quietly prayed that the Phylmecs would leave as soon as they didn't see us. I was scared that Tailfin would come looking for us after we didn't show up in time. I did not want him to get hurt. To make matters worse, the wait for the Phylmecs to arrive was agonizing. Every second that passed felt like an eternity. How long would we be able to survive stuck in here? I thought to myself.

[It has been 6 minutes since we first used our powers, but still no Phylmecs.] <Maybe they didn't see us and left?> Javier said. Boom, boom, crash the sides of the mountain shook as an explosion hit them. We were all dropped to the floor.

Then the second explosion, and the third, and then a fourth explosion. They happened so fast. My ears were ringing like crazy. It felt like a blow horn had gone off in my head. Thankfully, I wasn't hurt, and neither were the others. The mountain stayed intact, and the hole that Javier had made was deep enough for us to not absorb much of the impact. <Oh my gosh they will destroy the entire mountain to find us, won't they?> Valerie asked in a panic tone. [They cannot risk their fighter-informant-craft being picked up on human radar so early on because it will risk their easy conquest, so I believe that they will not destroy the mountains.]

<Hey guys, a "still-living" Phylmec has not seen us, right?> Javier asked. <I mean do they know that humans are helping Earth?> [I believe like I said last time, the Phylmecs do not know that humans are helping Earth yet.] [In our last encounters with them either we weren't seen, or they were terminated.] [That being said I am sure they highly suspect that it is a sentient Earth crea-ture.] <Okay, so what does that mean for us?> Valerie asked.

[I believe it means that they will send ground Phylmecs to search for tracks on the snow to see what is really helping Terramondetierra.] <Exactly.> Javier said. <So what do we do?> Valerie looked concerned. [We should wait till we no longer hear any more craft flying around.] [We also have a better chance of escaping ground Phylmecs than we do those flying over us.]

Five long minutes passed since we heard the last explosion, and the last ship flying around. <How long do you suggest we stay here Sevashkish?> [We must stay here as long as possible Valerie.] [Like I said before, the longer we stay here the higher the probability that the Phylmecs will be gone.] <Yeah, until they see our tracks in the snow.> <Maybe the wind covered up our tracks already, Javier.> <Yeah, well let's hope so.>

[Based on my understanding of human anatomy and my own anatomy we can stay here for 3 hours, and then freeze to death.] In other words, we can only really stay here two hours because it will take us 30 minutes to get back to Tailfin, and any unforeseen events that may occur once outside if the Phylmecs are still there. [Yes, that is correct, Daniel.] <Hopefully Tailfin is safe.> Yeah I hope so too Valerie, but I hope he does not try to swim under the ice to save us. He needs to continue the fight if something happens to us.

Thirty minutes passed since the last explosion and I slowly drifted to sleep. I am not sure how I even did that, but I guess I was more tired than I realized. [Daniel, you must wake up, it is time to move.] I shot straight up and saw Sevashkish waking up Valerie and Javier. <I was having the best dream that I was sleeping in my bed,

and then I woke up to Sevashkish staring at me.> <Almost scared me half to death, no offense Sevashkish.> [None taken Javier.]

[We must all move now.] I moved my hand and noticed that it was starting to go numb. Guys we need to leave now because my body is feeling numb. <Mine too, yea, and mine as well.> We have to get back to Tailfin as soon as possible. [I am not feeling numb yet, so I believe we should fly to Tailfin as it will be quicker.] [I do not think you all can last much longer outside like this.] [Javier's nose is turning purple and it can die if we don't get warm soon.] <Let's go, you don't have to tell me twice.> Javier said, while gently rubbing his nose.

Okay, we need to get out of here now, but we need a plan just in case the Phylmecs are still out there. What do you all suggest that we do? [I suggest that I start a winter storm that blanks the entire sky.] [This will prevent any spaceship from flying, and give us a better playing field.] That is a good idea, but is it feasible? I mean how far away are we from Tailfin? If we use our powers now they can pinpoint our location within five minutes. [Uninterrupted, we are ten minutes from Tailfin, but I believe that we must take the risk.] [It is now or never.] [Our bodies cannot handle the cold anymore.] I agree with you, Sevashkish. I hope your storm will be able to keep us covered long enough because if it doesn't we must be ready for a fight. Is everyone in agreement with that? <This will be a terrifying 10 minutes> [Yes it will be Valerie, but we have to do it.]

<I know Sevashkish and I am ready.> <I will go ahead and add more "cast" layering of plants all over our bodies to shield us from potential hits.> That sounds like a good plan Valerie. I said with a smile. How about you Javier? <I will do my best to throw any rocks that I can to any pursuing Phylmecs. That sounds perfect. As for me, I will call upon any animal that I can to help. I feel a lot of leopard seals around this area. I will call them to get any Phylmecs on the ground, but I will need your help Javier to break up any ice that the Phylmecs are standing on.

That way the leopard seals can drag them into the ocean. I will also call on the birds to help us, but guys, before we leave this mountain I have a question. Who will carry Earth's heart? They all looked at me and gave me a nod. <You will Daniel, we trust you and that heart is a part of you too.> Javier came over and gave me a half hug. I looked at him with worried eyes, but he whispered in my ear. "<You got this, Daniel.>"

I turned and stared at Valerie and Sevashkish. They both smiled. Well if everyone believes in me, I will believe in myself. Okay, well let's get going everyone! I faked a little fist bump in the air to motivate the others. Truth be told I was beyond scared. We were about to leave the protection of the mountain to unknown territory, and I was in charge of the most important object to ever exist on earth. How crazy has my life gotten?

[We all have to act together at the same time.] Okay on the count of three we all start using our powers, okay? 1, 2, 3, the mountain started to open, while my body began to be covered by the extra vegetation that Valerie was able to call upon from deep within the mountain soil. As the hole of the mountain got bigger I saw a blizzard start. Before I could react Sevashkish grabbed me, and the others and we left the mountain. Off we went flying, and Sevashkish warmed the air around us. I held on tight to Earth's heart. While we were in the air, I called upon every leopard seal in the area to come towards the sound of my call and to meet us at the shore.

I called upon all the birds that I could and told them to fly to the ocean. I felt my heart start to beat loudly from the rush of trying to leave Antarctica. Unfortunately, four minutes after we made our way to the ocean we saw the first Phylmec Spaceship coming our way. Sevashkish thickened the air even more. Visibility was so low that I wasn't able to see my hands. Thankfully, Sevashkish was able to form a clear spot for his eyes, but those eyes are big and purple. They are not necessarily unnoticeable. A few seconds after seeing the first ship I heard a crash. It must have been the first spaceship crashing because of the low visibility and high winds.

<Things are getting crazy fast!> <They sure are, Javier.> <Woah, what was that?> Before I could ask Javier what he meant I felt and saw shots fly by me. We were being fired at from the ground up. Javier, please try to break the ice apart beneath our feet. <You got it!> The next thing I saw in my mind was a leopard seal grabbing what looked like a man and dragging him under the ice. I felt flash-

es of heat as they fired. I was getting dizzy as Sevashkish zigzagged in every direction possible. It was chaos. I did my best to hold onto Sevashkish and the heart.

As I repositioned myself, I got hit. It felt like being hit by a hammer. My leg got a tingling sensation, and before I could react I heard Valerie yell as got hit as well. The pain was intense but those shots wouldn't kill us. Thankfully Valerie's thick "cast" layer of plants had protected us from any serious harm. Nothing would be broken from our hits, but we would be bruised.

<Daniel your leg is on fire!> I looked at my leg as Javier pointed at it. The vegetation had caught on fire! Sevashkish we need rain, please! My leg is on fire. The rain started to fall instantaneously, and the flames were put out. [I see the shore where we left Tailfin, we are only two minutes away.] [Daniel, call him please.] I closed my eyes and called for Tailfin. "We're almost there, Tailfin." To my utter happiness, he answered. He is underwater waiting for us, everyone!

We have some good and bad news. <Tell us, Daniel.> The Phylmecs do not suspect Tailfin of anything, nor did they see him, but there are over 20 Phylmecs standing around the shore. They all have weapons, big weapons. To make matters worse about 30 more Phylmecs are coming to the shore to join the 20 that are already there. [We are 30 seconds away from reaching Tailfin!] Okay, everyone, it is now or never. We must fight!

"Birds attack," I thought in my mind. "Do what you have to do, but attack these invaders of Earth." In the blink of an eye, penguins started to jump out of the water. They brought down the men surrounding the area where Tailfin was submerged. I saw birds diving towards the eyes of the other men. Javier started to rip the ice floats where many were standing, and Sevashkish called on ice wind to free as many as he could. Within a minute there was only about 15 left.

Sadly, our element of surprise was over as they looked up to the sky and saw us. They saw us for what we really were. Three humans and a Luken. Our cover was blown, and that is when they opened fire. I was hit hard all over my body. It was the worst pain I had ever experienced in my life.

I felt an intense burning all over myself. Imagine being splattered by hot oil, and multiply that by twenty. Maybe then you'll get a sense of what I felt. Parts of my cast of vegetation started to fall off. I had lost all the air in my body, but still, I was alive. I still held tightly onto the heart. How was it possible that I wasn't dead?

Then I understood. It was Valerie. She had called on all the vegetation from the ocean to rise in the air and form a barrier between us and the ground Phylmecs. The barrier had taken most of the beating. [We must land, my wings are giving out on me.] We crashed lightly on the snow by the shore. Thankfully the snow cooled off the hot flames that were starting to catch on fire. I SEE EARTH HAS FINALLY FOUND SOMEONE TO

DO ITS BIDDING FOR IT, BUT YOUR TIME IS UP, said an old woman who could have easily been my grandmother. IT IS USELESS TO TRY TO PREVENT US FROM OUR GREAT HARVEST. YOU HUMANS HAVE DONE YOUR JOB AND NOW YOUR TIME IS UP.

<Who do you think you are telling us that our time is up?> <It was your species who stopped evolving, so your time was up a long time ago.> YOU, I WILL HARVEST YOU PERSONALLY. The old lady came walking and pointed her weapon slowly to Javier. He simply looked at her frozen and afraid. She was about to place her head on his when Sevashkish slashed her head with the sword on his wing. She staggered back and cried in pain as her face had been cut open.

SHOOT THEM ALL! SHOOT THEM WHILE THEY ARE ON THE GROUND! I closed my eyes and did my best to call every animal to attack the Phylmecs because even if we died these animals would at least finish them off. The fewer Phylmecs in the world the better for the universe. The gunfire started, but I wasn't hit. What happened? I opened my eyes and saw a thick layer of frozen ice in front of us. Sevashkish had formed a frozen ice barrier. An ice barrier that was about to break. It would not take another round of fire. I prayed that the animals that I called for would hurry.

Then suddenly, the place where we were standing was ripped apart and taken out to sea. I saw what looked like a little Tsunami of water come down on every single Phylmec that was standing there waiting to have us killed. {I brought some of my friends to cause a mini Tsunami wave to wash those vile creatures.} Thank you so much Tailfin. You saved our lives! I emotionally yelled at him. {You are welcome, now get on me so we can get out of here.}

We got on him and left in a hurry. I looked at everyone and there was a sense of happiness and confusion. We had gone into battle and barely survived, but we survived. It was Euphoric until I noticed several leopard seals dragging the Phylmecs underwater. I closed my eyes in sadness.

It was awful to see that, but they were the invaders and not us, and besides it was a small victory for us. We had to be happy. We got away alive, and the cherry on top was that the Phylmecs did not know about the existence of Earth's heart. They may now know who is helping Earth, but they do not know of our plans. In my book that's victory!

As we sailed away from the scene of the battle I observed each of my friends. The euphoria of battle was quite distinctive in everyone's face. Javier had a look of hope in his eyes, while Valerie had a look of sadness. Sevashkish had a look of great pride and optimism. As for me? I had a look of determination and anger. This would not happen again. They could not come this close to killing us again. As much as I hate violence I have to defend my planet and its creatures, with everything that I have. I felt the power of Earth's creatures flowing through my body. At that very moment, I decided I would have to do everything I could to ensure that we won. The good and the ugly.

Earth, our beautiful planet, deserved nothing but the best. The Phylmecs would be defeated. This was going to stop. I looked around at everyone and made direct eye contact. Guys, we have to be strong, and we are stronger together. This isn't a game. We almost got killed back there, and that would have been the end of the resistance for the human race, the planet, and everything that lives here, big or small. We have to fight. We have to use the powers that Terramondetierra blessed us with. Use every bit of strength that we have. I turned and they each nodded in agreement. That nod would bond us for life.

We sailed on Tailfin for over 2 hours, and we did not say much at all. The only time there was some interaction was when poor Javier would have to throw up due to his seasickness. <I am sorry everyone I just feel a little dizzy.> Do not apologize for feeling bad Javier, <yea Javier it is okay, please don't feel bad.> <You two know how to make a guy feel better.> I gave him a small punch on the shoulder, but Javier wasn't who I was worried about. I felt worried for Tailfin. I am not sure how I knew, but I knew that Tailfin was tired beyond belief. I am sure he hadn't eaten properly.

Tailfin thank you for saving us back there. You are amazing and do not forget that if you are tired, take a break. We will understand. {I am so happy that I was able to help Daniel, and do not worry about me.} {I will let you know when I am tired.} I gently gave

Tailfin a pat on his back. {So I think we should stay on this small island right past the harsh Antarctic weather.} {It is a little cold, but nothing that a little fire can't warm up.}

[That sounds like a plan to me because I believe we all need a well-rested night.] <Don't forget a good meal.> <Oh Javier I just love how even though you are seasick and throwing up, you are still thinking about food.> <Don't you get in the way of my food Valerie.> We all started laughing. We were feeling better that we were nearing the next island. {We are about 3 days away from the Gulf of Mexico (with rest included), everyone.} {The place where Terramondetierra's heart will open.} <Okay, so we have been traveling for about 4 days now.> <If we reach Mexico in 3 days that would mean that Phylmec would have been here a week at that point.>

<That leaves them with one more week of confusing the masses that they are here for something great before they start their harvest.> <Thus if we reach Mexico in that time frame that would put us at a week before the official harvesting began.> Thank you Javier for explaining all of that. I smiled. It is good to have someone good with numbers when the rest of us cannot even think straight. We had over a week to arrive in Mexico, but we would do our best to get there in 3 days instead of a week. It felt good having a little "wiggle room."

We finally reached the island and it was fairly small. It was maybe only half a mile across, but there was vegetation all around which meant we would be able to make a small fire. {I will be back tomorrow at 8 am, please all of you get some rest and some food.} <You need to rest as well Tailfin, and go eat!> {Thank you, Valerie, I will.} Tailfin left, and just like that, we were on our own again. <Guys I know this will sound lame, but after we eat, we should tell ghost stories by the campfire, maybe it will help us distract our minds?> I think that is an excellent idea, Javier. <Me too.> We quickly started a fire and then our night began.

Valerie told us a few scary stories. They were extremely scary. She loves to write, and she thinks she may want to become a writer. I am sure when this is all over she will write a book about it, and it will go on to be a major success. I was happy for her. Javier told us a story about a mad scientist, and it wasn't scary at all, but at least he got to talk about his love for numbers. [You are very good with numbers Javier, your mind is great.] Sevashkish was quite surprised and said he had a gifted mind. Javier was grinning from ear to ear. He loved compliments. I am sure Javier will become a mathematician of some sort. Maybe a comedic one? He loves all the attention he gets.

Sevashkish told us about Luken folklore, and we didn't quite understand it, so we asked him a bit more about his family. He is an only child. On their planet, parents only have one child, because after they finish raising them their life cycle ends. We apologized to Sevashkish, but he was quite pleased and told us not to feel bad for him because in Luken society it is believed that once a person passes they evolve to the 8th dimension. They are also quite spiritual in that aspect. <Daniel, show Sevashkish what you are really good at.> What do you mean Javier? <You know what I mean!> <Tell him you speak 6 fluent languages, and that you are researching the original language.>

Sevashkish turned his eyes to me, [Do you speak Humanta?] What is that? [That was the first official human language of course.] [Sevashkish started to speak, and to my surprise, I understood about 30% of his sentence, and I responded back. He walked over and shook my hand. He was quite happy. [You are an old soul Daniel, and now I see quite well why Earth's soul chose you.] Thanks, Sevashkish. I do not believe you but thank you for making me feel better. As the night ended we goofed around a little more, and each told our best corny joke that we could think of. We needed this night. We needed to feel like normal teens again.

Chapter 13
A FRIEND OR FOE?

After our campfire, we all went to bed. Well if you can call lying on cold wet sand a bed. It was still better than having nowhere to put my head on. At least the sand was smooth, plus I buried myself a bit into the sand, so it kept me from freezing too much. I curled my body together to stay warm, and I quickly fell asleep and slept the entire night like a baby. The next morning we got up bright and early, and we all felt super rested and excited to go to Mexico. <Time to save the world.> <Yeah, mister Superman time to save the world.> Valerie said. While she gently hugged Javier.

I looked at Javier and I swear his beard had grown two inches overnight. He had a full beard by this point. We were only 17, but Javier was one of those guys who had facial hair since middle school. I had no facial hair whatsoever, and I was glad at that point, because Javier kept complaining about how itchy it was, and I believed him as he kept scratching it.

Javier was just about to start to complain again when Tailfin showed up right on time to save us from a Javier rant about how lucky I was to not have a beard. Tailfin informed us that we would swim for the next 8 hours, then we would rest for the day. <Tailfin how fast are we going?> {Do you mean the speed in miles per hour, Valerie?} <Yes, how are we getting to our destinations so fast? I thought dolphins and whales were not as fast as boats?>

{I thought none of you were going to ever ask me, haha!} {Valerie, we are using a secret ocean "highway" that allows us to go over 150 miles an hour, but you all do not feel it because of how massive my body is.} {It is very tiring for me, but also so much fun, and it keeps me in shape.}

<Thank you so much for doing this Tailfin.> <Yes, thank you,> Javier agreed and gently put his hand on Tailfin's back. [I am impressed with how efficient your water highways are.] {Well only the sentient ocean life knows about them.} {It can be dangerous for a non-sentient ocean creature to use it.} [It makes sense.]. {I will try to swim slower today, so no one will hopefully get seasick.] <Thank you, Tailfin, my boy!> Yesterday we had all gotten quite seasick. If you have ever been on a boat and you start to get seasick, imagine being on a boat with no back support, and where you are constantly getting wet. That is how it felt to be on Tailfin.

About an hour after we took off I asked Sevashkish to take out the Phylmec tablet. [Let us see what the Phylmecs have been up to since the last time we checked the news.] Sevashkish turned it to BBC News, and what we saw next we did not expect. I was shocked. Javier's mouth was open, Valerie had her hands to her face and Sevashkish had a look of anger on him. There was a video of us hurting "old people in Antarctica." The reporter said, "Innocent scientists were ruthlessly attacked by an aggressive alien who has taken control of 3 human youth in an attempt to stop Phylmecs from sharing technological advances with humans." "They are presumed dangerous." "If seen they should be reported to the local authority." {What is going on?} Tailfin the Phylmecs have broadcasted videos of us worldwide "hurting the Phylmecs." They are painting us as the bad people who are under the Lukens' control.

They have warned the world whoever sees us to presume that we are dangerous and that we are trying to prevent humanity from evolving. {Oh no, that is definitely not good.} <They are beyond evil.> Valerie said. <They cannot get away with this> <People will look for our parents!> <They will think our parents have something to do with this.> <Sevashkish, please what can we do to protect our parents?> <I do not want them to be harvested!> <My stupid phone hasn't worked since we first contacted Earth, how will I contact my parents?> Valerie was practically yelling. I turned to face Valerie and saw how overwhelmed she looked. Her face was so red that it almost matched her hair. <We must go back and save our parents because they will be the first ones taken.>

Sevashkish went over to Valerie and wrapped his strong arms around her and said, [Valerie, you all need to try to reach your parents mentally.] [Naturally, when a species is nearing the 4th dimension they get to dabble a bit with mental thought sharing.] [It may not work, and you surely won't get any answer, but maybe it will reach your parents' soul.] [Share your thoughts only with those that you want to warn.] [I suggest you all hold hands to form a stronger connection.]

Valerie came and grabbed my hand and Javier's. We closed our eyes, and I thought about my parents. I thought long and hard about how they looked and everything they had ever done for me. "I have a message for you two, please leave the city and go hide somewhere." "Do not contact anyone for at least two weeks because it will be very dangerous." "Please trust me and just go, and I will find you." "You two were right all along, we have souls." "Use your soul to contact me, but please do not go on any social media and get rid of any phones." After five minutes we let go of each other's hands and stayed silent. Valerie looked flustered. She was talking at a million words per minute.

<The absolute worst thing that can happen to anyone is to lose their soul.> <Without our souls we cease to exist.> <I have always valued life at any level, from the smallest ant to the biggest whale, but these creatures are true monsters.> <They have been

killing billions of people over the millennia.> <They have to be destroyed!> <They just have to!> I had never seen Valerie so upset. It made me sad. She is such a kind soul, and the Phylmecs are making her change who she is. Valerie cried for over an hour silently after that speech, but she apologized after.

She had bottled everything up, and with her parents, everything just got more personal to her. [I hope that all your parents are alive and well, but just know this, your parents give a part of their soul when they have you all.] [You will always carry a part of your parents within yourself.] I guess Sevashkish's speech was supposed to make us feel better, but in my case, it didn't. It made me mad, but also more motivated to stop the Phylmecs. I decided to try to change the conversation and learn more about the enemy. Sevashkish has any species ever won the invasion against the Phylmecs? [There have been no species of beings to have ever won against the Phylmecs, Daniel.] <Well I guess it is time for us to stop them, right Sevashkish?>

[Yes Javier, it is time that we stop them.] [If they go into the 7th dimension they will not only go after the Lukens, but they will use the resources of the many alien races that we protect.] [There are many species in the 7th dimension who are very spiritual and do not even have an army.] Sevashkish, we need to learn more about the Phylmecs. Do they have many leaders or just one? How does their government work? [They have an establishment of leaders called the 10.] [The 10 are a group of ten Phylmecs who each lead a harvest every time that there is one.] [They are chosen in elections and consist of five females and five males.] Hmm, the 10 I thought in my mind.

Are they on earth? Do they take on human forms or any other form?] One member of the 10 is on Earth and the rest are on their home planet.] Tindawnstong? [Yes, he is the current leader of this harvest.] How many Phylmecs do the Lukens estimate are out there? [There are an estimated 3.5-5 billion Phylmecs out there.] [The Phylmecs' population used to be much higher.] [There were around 11 billion Phylmecs before their evolutionary downfall.] [There was terrible war and chaos amongst themselves when they first discovered that they were a dying species] [They started killing each other trying to survive.] [Fearing their downfall since they could no longer evolve or reproduce.] How did they stop the fighting? [It was the founder of the technology that allowed them to harvest the self of other beings that brought stability to their world.]

[He brought their world together once more and showed them how "powerful, strong and intelligent" they were.] [He promised them that they would evolve by their own conquest and technology.] [The remaining 3.5-5 billion Phylmecs live their lives in sort of a utopian functioning society, ruled over by the 10.] <Who is the creator of this horrid technology that the Phylmecs invented, Sevashkish?> Javier asked. [We are not quite sure, but we know it was a highly intelligent Phylmec scientist who invented it.] [The intelligence of a species is not equal to the dimension that they're in.] [The creator of the harvesting technology was seen as a hero, and he started the 10.] Is he still living?

[That we do not know.] Sevashkish, do you believe that all Phylmecs are evil, or just the leaders in charge? [Daniel, I believe that a vast majority of Phylmecs are vile beings if not all of them.] [They can choose to not participate in the harvest, but yet they do.] [They have been living the same life for hundreds of thousands of years taking the souls and bodies of other beings with no mercy.] [They are cowards who are scared to die.]

This conversation must've taken several hours because before I knew it we had arrived on the next island, which meant only two more days until we reached Mexico. I was excited to finally be sitting on dry land. {I'll be here tomorrow at dawn.} That sounds perfect Tailfin, see you tomorrow, and get plenty of rest! <This island looks dead, I guess I have some fishing to do.> Javier was not wrong. The island did not have many choices for food, so Javier and Sevashkish hardly caught any fish. I was still hungry after dinner. That night I struggled a bit to sleep because my mind was racing. I was thinking of how many innocent races had been exterminated, and how the Phylmecs were okay with doing this. Eventually, I closed my eyes and drifted to sleep.

The next day I woke up before everyone, and when I got up to go use the restroom I noticed a man looking at me. Was I dreaming? I rubbed my eyes again, and I was definitely awake. He was right in front of me. This man was maybe between the ages of 25-30 years old. He had no shirt on. He had underwear on, hiding all the important parts, but that was it. He had bushy long hair, and he was very dark. He had big expressive dark eyes and a squared nose. I looked at him and I decided to wave at him. He waved back at me with a smile. That made me not tense up as much.

He slowly came up to me. He was small in stature, no more than 5'4. He started to come closer to me, but I put my hand up to form a stop sign. I knew that this was a universal sign that meant stop. I did not want him to get too close to me. Thankfully, he listened and stopped. This must be a native person living on this island, I thought. He looked kind. He extended his arm out and bowed his head down. I went over and shook his hand, and at this point, the others had awakened and they were staring at us. <Daniel, are you okay?> Yes, Javier, I think this man is just curious to see other people randomly show up on his island.

Chapter 14
THE UNDERGROUND CITY

Sevashkish came up to introduce himself, and the man did not flinch. He simply smiled and stuck his hand out so Sevashkish could shake it. Sevashkish smiled in return. The man started to speak. It was not a language that I was familiar with at all, but thankfully Sevashkish understood it. "We are the fugitive humans from the last harvest of 15 thousand years ago." "We have hid on this small island for all this time (our ancestors came here)." "We were waiting for the time when these viruses came back to Earth." "We have a member of our tribe who lives in the outside society." "She told us that the Phylmecs were back, and she told us about a group of four beings who are probably here to help stop them."

"Never in my life would I have suspected these beings to show up on our little island." "I must take you to meet the others." We all looked at each other with skepticism. Tailfin was supposed to show up in about 30 minutes. Sevashkish, may you tell this man to give us 20 minutes to talk it through with each other? Sevashkish nodded and spoke a few words that I did not understand, but I noticed that the man smiled and nodded his head and then left us alone. <I don't know about you guys, but this man seems genuine and kind.>

<Valeire, you think everyone is genuine and kind, but we all checked this island yesterday before sleeping here and there was no one here.> <How did he come out of nowhere?> <Maybe he is a Phylmec informant who wants to harvest our bodies to get Earth's powers?> <No, Javier I know you may think I am gullible, but my heart tells me that this man is someone that we can trust.>

<I feel his positive energy radiating out of him.> Javier and Valerie turned to look at me and Sevashkish. They were waiting for our opinions. [I am quite confused about how this man got here, as Javier said we checked the island and there were no humans.] [The question is, how did this man get here?] I felt their eyes staring at me, they wanted my opinion. We were all asleep when this man was looking at us. If he was a Phylmec he could have easily hurt us as we slept, but he didn't. He could have stolen TT's heart, but I have it here in my backpack. I pointed at it, so everyone could see that I had it safe and sound. I say we go, but before we warn Tailfin about it.

That way if we are captured then Tailfin can still fight to save this planet. Sevashkish went to tell the man to come back in forty-five minutes. This would help us keep Tailfin hidden from this person if it were a trap. Half an hour passed, and Tailfin came and we told him all about it. He understood and said he would be back in an hour to come and take us off this island. {If you all are not here in an hour, I will flood this entire island!} We all smiled at him and waved bye. The man came back to us fifteen minutes after Tailfin left, and he signaled for us to follow him.

He did not say any words as we followed him, but he always had a giant smile on his face. It made me feel safe. The more I looked at this man, the more convinced I was that he was a Mayan. He had very dark skin. Almost as dark as Javier's, and he had very impressive dark almond-shaped eyes. He is for sure indigenous that much I know.

After about ten minutes the man started to speak again, so Sevashkish began to translate. "Our ancestors say when the Phylmecs came 15,000 years ago they announced that they were Gods and creators of the Earth." "They came to help humans come together in harmony and prosperity." "For two weeks they brought happiness and joy across the world, and people loved every minute of it."

"Two nights before the 14th day after their arrival, one local boy from the tribe had a vision." "In that vision, he saw the Phylmecs destroying humans and taking their life force from them." "He also saw a vision of a small island that would keep a small amount of humans safe if they made it there on time." "This boy told the elders and most did not believe him, but he was insistent, and he was able to convince twenty-five people to come with him and to seek out this island." "Off they went and they found this island about two days from the coast of the Yucatan Peninsula, and this island, like in the boy's vision, had a secret passage that led to a hidden underground paradise."

[We will see this underground paradise once he finishes his story.] I nodded okay at Sevashkish. "After finding this hidden island the people decided to go back to their home and tell their family about it, and when they got back there, there was nothing but dead bodies all around." "Dead bodies for miles and miles." "Most of the dead bodies were not of their tribe members, but of the old Phylmecs." "Trees were cut down to the root." "There were scavengers consuming the remains of Phylmecs and the younger and older tribal members who were not of age to be harvested." "At that very moment, the boy had one last vision." "The Phylmecs would come back to Earth one last time in 15,000 years."

"They would come one last time and destroy the entire planet of Earth." [He says this is all they understood from the vision.] [They have been hiding on this small island for the last 15,000 years.] Javier came over to me and whispered, <If they knew about the Phylmecs why did they not try to warn others?>

I guess Valerie overheard and said, <Can you imagine who would believe some native people living on a secluded island that aliens that looked like humans would come kill every human in 15,000 years?> <Yeah, you do have a point, Valerie.> <Even I would not believe that.> <These poor people have probably been living in constant fear and paranoia thinking of how they could stop these powerful alien creatures.> Yes, both of you bring up a point. They are just trying to survive and save their family.

We walked for about five more minutes when we stopped in front of a big tree. It was a huge tree. It was almost as round as a Sequoia tree, but not nearly as tall. The man pushed the middle of the tree and a door appeared. An actual door! He opened the door and walked in. He held it open and stared at us. [I believe he wants us to follow him there.] Are you sure that is a good idea, Sevashkish? [I believe what this man is saying is true, and I believe one of the elders of his tribe will have more information than he did.]

One by one we went into the tree. I was the last one to step inside. Once inside there was a little sidewalk path, and the man sat down, and then he started to slide down the path. He slid down to the bottom. I smiled. It was a real slide. <Man I am way too tall for this, but here goes anything.> Javier complained. After everyone slid down, I went. The platform was as smooth as marble. It took fifteen seconds for me to reach the grass at the bottom. I now understood why they had a slide made. Climbing down all the stairs would take ages.

We walked for thirty more seconds in almost complete darkness, when the man opened another door. The entire room was lit. It was as bright as day down here. <It feels like we are outside.> <You are right Valerie, you can even see the sky through the roof, but man they need to make the doorways taller!> <I keep hitting my head.> As Javier complained about everything being too small, I was starstruck. There was an entire little village underneath the ground here.

There were about 150-200 people that I could see. The people stood outside their homes. Their homes looked like small huts. Kind of like the ones the natives would use back in the day. There was one key difference. Each small hut had its own satellite. A big satellite was on top of the hut. I stared all around, and it was marvelous.

From what I could gather there was a sense of keeping the old traditions, but incorporating the new. There was a feeling of peace. The man took us to the biggest building in this underground village. This building was shaped like the pyramid in Chichen Itza, but a big difference was the TV screens in various parts of the pyramid.

A woman came out of the front door. She was about 60 years old. She stood strong and confident. She was maybe 5 feet tall. She had long black hair and no smile. She came towards me and pointed at me. She then spoke in perfectly good English, "My name is Kach'ma'o-k, and I am the tribal elder of the original Mayan tribe that once settled and ruled over most of Mexico and Central America." "I am glad all of you are here, and wish you nothing but the best possible things." "I do not have all the answers to questions you may have, but I can tell you some of what I do know." "You are the one who has been chosen to defend us."

Before I could speak she spoke again, "I have gotten visions from the elders that a boy would come to free us from the vile creatures who steal the bodies of others." "My visions have told me to give you anything you need on your quest to save all of humanity." "We have three things that can help you succeed." "We can offer you a shelter to stay here, a secret passage that will get you from the Yucatan Peninsula and back to this island in 45 minutes instead of a day. Sadly, the entrance of this passage is at the Yucatan, and it only works one way, so you cannot take the passage from here.

Lastly, a special crystal that helps prevent those creatures from stealing your body." "There is only one crystal, so your friends will not be able to use it, only the person wearing it, and it has to be you." I was only understanding about every other word that this woman was telling me. My head was spinning with so much information that I felt like I would fall. I guess I looked the way I felt because Javier came next to me and put my hand on his shoulder. <Do you have an area where we can rest?> <We value

your offer to shelter us here, but we feel like we need to rest a bit and talk it through,> Javier told the lady with a half smile.

She nodded, "but I must inform you that even though we have a secret passage you may only use it once." <Why is that?> "Well young lady it is because using this passage will cause an enormous amount of energy to be transmitted, so you can only use it once you get to Yucatan." "It will bring you back safely to our secret private island." <How will we know where this passage is?> "I will tell your alien friend where it is located exactly, but just know it leads directly to here." <Thank you so much.> Valerie said. I nodded to show that I understood, and two other people came over and took us into the pyramid.

It was breathtaking. It looked a lot like the inside of the Louvre Museum in Paris. The ceiling was covered in golden tiles. The walls were sparkling like crystals. There was a smell of honey throughout. "We leave you to decide what to do, feel free to sit, please."

<I feel like this place is too luxurious for me.> <Oh just sit down Javier.> We all sat down for a bit and said nothing. Valerie was the one to break the silence. <This is great news.> <After we open TT's heart we do not have to worry about getting captured because we can escape, and hide here until we are sure the Phylmecs are truly being destroyed!>

<You know something, Valerie?> <What is it, Javier?> <I would usually say this is a trap and let's not trust them, but these people have hope in their eyes.> <I see hope in their eyes, and you cannot

fake hope.> <They really think we are here to help, so I say let's do exactly that!> Since when did you get all poetic Javier, I teased him. He instantly flipped me off in retaliation.

Guys, I need to go talk to Tailfin and tell him everything that is going on. Do you guys think it is a good idea that we tell these folks about Tailfin? [I believe that it has to be his decision if he wants other humans to know that there are sentient whales out there.] You are right. I will go out, and tell them I have forgotten something by the beach area. About 30 minutes later I was right by the beach and I saw Tailfin waiting for us.

{Daniel, I was beginning to worry, where is everyone else?} Tailfin, there is a lot that has happened since you brought us to the island. It took me a good hour, but I told Tailfin everything that had happened with the native people. {This is a very interesting situation, Daniel.} {I've never heard of a secret water passage that takes you so fast to a destination, and I live in the ocean.} {May I ask for you to not let them know that there are sentient whales out there?} {I just need to see it myself first before anything.} Do not worry about anything Tailfin, you are my friend and I respect you like I respect the others. You are equally important to me.

{Daniel, do you think I can explore the underground passage-way without using it?} I am sure you can, let me ask the native person who came with me if that is okay. I quickly went over to the man who had come with me, and I explained my situation. The man completely agreed to show "the whale under my control" where part of the passage was. He thought Tailfin was just an animal under my control. Tailfin I quietly whispered to him before the man got to the edge of the shore, please meet us here tomorrow at dawn, so we can head back to Mexico.

{Don't worry Daniel I will be here.} I sat on the sand as the man went on Tailfin's back to show him the area of the passage. They couldn't dive down together, but Tailfin was able to see where it was at. {Wow Daniel I see where it is at!} It is covered by a swirl of sea plants and fish.} {It is so perfectly camouflaged no wonder no one ever sees it, and wow we cannot even hear the force of the water waves, but I can feel it when I am on top of it now.} The man came back to shore and Tailfin left. Okay, good I thought. At least we know that they were not lying about having a secret water passage.

We decided to trust what the ancient Mayan people were telling us, but we would not share any information with them. We told them that we would have to be on our way right before sunrise. Kach'ma'o-k understood and explained to us (well Sevashkish) in great detail where to find the hidden passage back to their hidden place. Of course, Javier, Valerie, and I looked as confused as kids lost in a giant mall but Sevashkish and Tailfin understood perfectly where to find it. That made me happy. It was one less thing that I would have to worry about.

By the time we all finished talking and meeting some of the local people, it was past 4 pm, so Kach'ma'o-k invited us to stay the night in the pyramid, and boy were we happy. She showed us to our room. It was beautiful. It did not have the beds we were used to, but they were comfortable hay-styled beds nonetheless. That would be plenty to enjoy a nice night of sleep. After showing us our room, Kach'ma'o-k gave us a little tour of her underground island. There was a sense of simplicity, but also a mixture of advancement. Some parts of the city had ancient-looking sculptures, but in other places, there were modern-looking buildings.

There were gardens all running through the center of the town, and the people worked them. There were shrines where kids were being taught. There was a beautiful waterfall that allowed the people to secretly be able to see into the exterior part of the island. "We believe in keeping the old traditions, but also incorporating the best of modern advancements." <You have an amazing place here.> Javier looked straight into Kach'ma'o-k 's eyes and said, "<We will do our best to protect all of you.>"

"Thank you, young man, and I have faith in each of you. She eventually brought us back to the room, and we had a tiny meal of some sort of fish and rice. It wasn't too much, but it made us happy that they shared food with us. We were intruders into their society, but yet the people shared with us. Eventually, it was time to go to bed, and we said goodbye to Kach'ma'o-k since we would not be seeing her again; the guide would take us back to Tailfin in the morning. I fell asleep as soon as my head touched the blanket.

I was just beyond tired. Right before sunrise, the guide came in to wake us up. He took us to the shore and Tailfin was waiting for us.

Chapter 15
VALERIE SPIRALS OUT OF CONTROL

I felt comfort in knowing that there were some humans who were innocent and who were aware of the history of the Phylmecs. It felt like we had less of a burden to bear. We were not the only ones who knew the truth. As we sailed through the ocean I had the sudden realization that it was almost a week since the Phylmecs first arrived on earth, and two days since we last saw the news on the tablet.

We were just too mentally tired to look up any more information, but I knew we had to see what was going on again. Sevashkish, may you please turn on the tablet so we can see what is going on? Sevashkish proceeded to turn on the tablet, and I moved to the right of him, and Javier and Valerie moved to his left.

WE ARE SENDING OFFICIAL PERSONNEL TO EVERY CITY, EVERY TOWN NO MATTER THE SIZE TO HELP WORK WITH THE LOCAL GOVERNMENT THERE TO BETTER ASSIST IN THE ADVANCEMENT OF EARTH TECHNOLOGICAL EFFORTS. ON TOP OF THAT WE ARE SENDING SPECIAL PERSONNEL FOR THOSE WHO WANT TO KNOW MORE ABOUT WHAT SOME OF US BELIEVE IN TERMS OF RELIGION. WE ARE HERE TO SHARE OUR CULTURE AND THE UNIVERSAL BOND THAT WE SHARE. I, TINDAWNSTONG MAY BE THE OFFICIAL LEADER OF THE PHYLMECS, BUT THEY LEAD ME, AND JUST LIKE HUMANS WE RESPECT AND VALUE LIBERTY. WE WANT HUMANS TO KNOW THE TRUTH OF NOT ONLY THE WORLD BUT WHAT THE UNIVERSE HAS TO OFFER.

Tindawnstong spoke with incredible grace and passion. <I hate to admit this, but he is charismatic, and to top it off, he looks like he could come from any background.> What do you mean, Javier? <I mean he is racially ambiguous looking.> [He chose the perfect human body that could relate to the masses.] <This man, I mean creature is dangerously smart.> Yeah, Javier, I mean he even gives me this sense of hope and safety. <We really need to hurry.> <They are already heading to every major city and every town around the world.> <This is bad.> Yeah, Valerie, I fear that they may start to harvest some people already, little by little before their second week of arrival.

<I sure hope not!> Valerie said. We need to really hurry. Tailfin, what is the estimated time of arrival to Yucatan? {We will stop on an island off the coast in a few hours, and rest there for the night.} {Tomorrow we will have about 4 hours of sailing and we will get there.} Thank you, Tailfin things are getting bad around the world. Based on what we just saw they are sending their troops all over the world, into the daily lives of most people. It is crunch time. {I will warn my people that they are starting to send out their troops all over the world, so they are made aware as well.}

NO! I turned my head towards the scream. Valerie, what is wrong? <My sister!> <She has been taken.> <She has been harvested by a Phylmec!> <Wait, how do you know that?> Javier asked. <I saw it happen in my mind!> <I saw, and felt her cries, her pleas, her fear!> <I even saw the look of the disgusting Phylmec who did it!> <The laughter on his face, the face of victory of having harvested a family member of one of Earth's defenders.> <Valerie it could just be the stress of this all, and she could be okay.> <No!> <I never warned her, because she was studying in another country.> <I didn't think they would find her.>

<I am so stupid!> <Why did I not warn her?> I felt so bad for Valerie. I knew she was right about her sister. Her sister was gone. What the Phylmecs do is beyond murder. They not only take your body, but they steal your essence, your being, your actual soul, so

when they harvest you, you are really gone. I went over to hug her, but right when I was about to reach her I fell off Tailfin. I went headfirst into the ocean.

My skin touched the cold water, and the cold of the ocean struck me like a slap to the face. I went down under the water and moved my arms to get back up from under the surface. I was struggling to breathe as salty water entered my mouth. I was panicking, but slowly calmed myself down. I kicked up to the surface, and I managed to pop my head up. I started to slowly float and saw that Tailfin had been flipped over. The weight of his body was causing big waves. What was happening?

I swam toward Tailfin and instantly noticed the giant Elodea plants and seaweeds that were extending all around us. They were encasing us in a little prison. [Valerie, this is one of the worst things that can happen to a person, and we will talk about this, but for now, you NEED TO STOP.] I heard Sevashkish in my head. [You have to control yourself for this moment, your sadness has caused you to lose control of your power, and the Phylmecs are on their way.]

[They wanted this reaction.] {He is right, Valerie, you need to gain control.} Tailfin gave me his flipper to hold onto. Where was Sevashkish? I turned my head to the sky, and he was flying overhead with Javier on his back. Where was Valerie? Then I saw her, she was on a surfboard of ocean plants and was on her knees sobbing. Plants were coming out of the water all around us, so much so that

I found I could stand on the bed of plants without sinking back into the water.

<Daniel, I think she is in a state of despair.> <We have to do something drastic or we will all get killed.> I can't move Javier. Tailfin and I are locked in a bed of seaweed, you need to reach her, while we untangle ourselves. <Okay, but it won't be pretty.> "Fish come to me, and rip these beds of plants away from us." Within 10 seconds fish started coming and tearing the prison of oceanic plants that imprisoned Tailfin and me; within 30 seconds we were free.

I had some bites all over my body from the fish, but it was nothing serious. I quickly got on Tailfin's back and we headed towards Valerie who was being subdued by Javier. He had his arms around a screaming and crying Valerie. He brought her towards Sevashkish, who simply touched her with one hand, and she was frozen solid.

Sevashkish had frozen Valerie in a solid block of ice. It was quite shocking to see, but it was the only way to prevent her from hurting us, and herself. <She will be okay, right?> [Do not worry, she is in homeostasis, and once we get out of here, I will carefully bring her out of it with no issues at all.] Okay, we have to get out of here quick, and just as those words slipped my mouth I noticed two Phylmecs crafts coming our way. The nearest cubed craft was getting ready to shoot. Its missile-like blades glowed a dark purple hue as it was ready to fire. Sevashkish! I yelled with all my might. Form an ice crystal barrier between us, please.

Suddenly the molecules in the air froze and formed a barrier between us and the spaceships. "Birds from all around come to me and help clog the engines of these spaceships," I thought. I knew this first spaceship would hit us, but maybe one of us would survive by the time the birds got here. I saw several birds head towards the second spaceship. They would stop the craft from hurting us. Never underestimate the power of birds, they are the direct ancestor of the dinosaurs and are highly intelligent.

Blast, blast, and blast was all I heard as the first ship fired its beam at us. The beam of light was so bright that all I could see was a dark purple hue. The blast hit the frozen barrier of ice but it did not break, so it kept blasting and blasting. It was hard to stay on Tailfin as the waves pushed us around. Little by little the barrier began breaking. Javier could not help us because we were in the middle of the ocean, so there was no natural Earth terrain there to use in time. Another cracking noise and I knew the next shot would get us. {I have an idea, Sevashkish come get Daniel!}

Sevashkish came and grabbed me, and that is when Tailfin leaped into the air and struck the spaceship. He struck it so hard that it fell deep straight into the water with a loud splash. You did it, Tailfin! You stopped the ship, and you saved all of us, my friend. At the same time, I saw the second spaceship crashing down into the ocean. The water steamed as the flames heated the water. I felt bad for the birds because I knew some had sacrificed themselves to take the ship down, but this was a war and unfortunately, we had to make sacrifices for the greater good. When this is all over and if we win, I will personally help protect animals worldwide.

Yeah, I'll do that, wait why is the ocean water getting so red? Sevashkish look at the water! [Oh no.] Oh no, what? I looked closer at the red-stained water and that is when I saw that Tailfin had been hit. The water around him was oozing in warm red liquid. He was bleeding fast. He had a giant wound about one foot deep in his flank. Tailfin! Are you okay? {Daniel, I am badly injured, and I am afraid this cut may be fatal.} {I do not know how much longer I can stay awake, I am feeling very disoriented.} You will not die Tailfin, please stay with me. Talk to me. Hear my voice. Sevashkish, take me by Tailfin's side, please! Tailfin my dear friend stay with me, please.

<We will not let you die Tailfin, please fight to stay awake.> <Do not close your eyes!> <I repeat do not close your eyes.> In a flash movement I saw Sevashkish go towards the ship that Tailfin had hit. His wings skid on the water. He yanked the door open and went inside the ship. I couldn't see what he was looking for, but he was throwing things out of the ship like there was no tomorrow.

[I found it!] He flew out of the ship and came over to us. He was holding something in his hand that looked like a big patch that smokers use to quit smoking. He ran over to Tailfin and put the patch on his injury. <What are you doing Sevashkish?> [The

Phylmecs always carry a cell regenerator with them.] [This will save Tailfin's life, and help him recuperate quickly, but it takes about two hours for it to start to really regenerate new outer skin.] [We need to move Tailfin ourselves during this time, and we have to do it now before the next Phylmec informants arrive.]

<How are we going to move him if he weighs as much as 200 semi-trucks?> Leave that to me, Javier. In my mind, I thought, "Come help us, any ocean creatures that are mighty and big." "Come help us save our world and friend." Waves started to get out of control within 30 seconds, and Sevashkish pulled me out of the water.

I saw three large orcas come to my call. They were not the same size as Tailfin, but they were mighty impressive to see. Their perfectly streamlined bodies glisten in the water. We all got on one, and the other two went under Tailfin to support his weight. Sevashkish made the area where we had battled dense with a cold chilling fog. We left and headed towards the direction of the island that we were supposed to be going to. This was a close call. It was too close. We almost lost Tailfin and Valerie is not doing well. We needed a break.

<When we get to the island we should all hug Valerie.> <She has gone through a lot, and she needs emotional support to be able to help save humanity.> [We can not afford to have her lose control of her powers again.] [This is the second time she has done this and can jeopardize the entire world.] <Yes, we will tell her that she

will have to just stay put somewhere if this is too much for her to handle.> Yeah, you are right Javier. I noticed that Sevashkish was beginning to look a little uneasy and as I was about to ask if anything was wrong, but then he started to speak to me privately. [Daniel this is not a game, and this is the second time Valerie has put our mission in jeopardy.]

[I believe that you should take away her power of "plants" away.] [You have the power to remove any power that Terramondetierra gave us.] I wasn't shocked by what Sevashkish was telling me, but I knew we needed Valerie to control the power of the plants. I would not be able to handle that power. I nodded at Sevashkish and said, "We are all stronger together, and we will speak to Valerie if she wants to continue with this fight or not." If she doesn't we will have to figure out a way to find someone willing to take up that responsibility.

Sevashkish nodded, not looking too convinced by that idea, but too rattled to argue. It took us about 6 hours to get to the Island, more time than we expected, but we got there safely. By the time we reached the island, Tailfin's wound was completely closed. I was happy to see that. The orcas would stay till Tailfin was able to safely move around. I was beyond glad Tailfin was recovering and would be all right. That was one less issue that I had to worry about, and now my next was Valerie.

Sevashkish and Javier, do you think that it is time to unfreeze Valerie? <Yes, I think we should now as the sun is already setting.>

<We want her to be able to see that she is around friends and not enemies.> Sevashkish, may you please unfreeze her? Sevashkish nodded and slowly began to use the blades on his wings to carefully crack the ice prison that Valerie was in. She looked peaceful and rested. Javier and I went to her and grabbed both of her hands. She was ice cold. Javier gave her the sweater that he had on. Valerie, it's me, Daniel, and Javier is with me too. We want you to know that you are safe and we will never let anyone hurt you.

I noticed that her eyes started to flicker and she slowly picked up her head. She looked at me, then to Javier and finally to Sevashkish. She instantly began to cry. <I am so sorry for losing control of myself.> <I didn't mean to lose control of my powers.> <Was anyone hurt?> [Yes, Valerie Tailfin was wounded badly, but he will survive.] [Your misuse of your powers caused two spacecrafts to track us down.] [You are a warrior for your planet now and must learn how to better control your emotions.] I wanted to tell Sevashkish that his words were too harsh and a bit cruel, but I knew that everything he was saying was right. I looked at Javier, and I knew by the look on his face that he was doing everything to not tell off Sevashkish because he also knew that he was right.

<Valerie, what you did was irresponsible, but you are also grieving and you have the right to.> <We are here for you, and we are your family.> <I can't even try to understand what you feel right now, but I can tell you this.> <The Phylmecs are here, and they will try to destroy everyone on this planet.> <You have the

power to stop that, but we need to know that you will not lose yourself again.> <Are we able to trust you, and do you even want that responsibility?> It was touching seeing Javier talk that way to Valerie; sometimes I even forget that he has a big heart since he is always joking and being sarcastic about everything.

Valerie, Sevashkish has told us that we can take your power away if that is what you want. You will not have the burden of protecting Terramondetierra and risking your life anymore. Just let us know now, please. The battle back there was really rough. Valerie got up and looked at each of us. Her red hair was bright and sparkling by the sunset. Her green eyes looked like gems piercing each of us, and then she spoke. <I have made stupid mistakes based on my emotions, but I promise you all that, that is all over now.>

<I am a warrior and I am here to defend my world, and everything in it.> <I will not let the Phylmecs continue to hurt the innocent and murder everyone and everything in their path.> <When this is all over, I will grieve for the loss of my sister, but for now I cannot think of that.> <If you all excuse me, I will go apologize to Tailfin now.>

It made me smile. Valerie was someone that I worried about. She is shy and not secure about herself, but at that moment I saw a different look in her eyes. She was becoming the person she always wanted to be, but never had quite enough bravery to do so. I let her and Tailfin speak in private and I went to talk to Javier and Sevashkish. <Hey, Sevashkish do you think we can take a look at

what is going on around us?> <I have this feeling that we should turn on the tablet and take a look.> [Of course.]

Sevashkish turned the tablet on, "Every island in the world will have Phylmec stations starting tomorrow morning." "These islands will have internet towers that will give everyone free faster than a blink of the eye internet, in every corner of the world." People in less developed countries were seen cheering and thanking the Phylmecs. "Friendly reminder, please remember to pay close attention to these faces as they are highly dangerous and wish to destroy human advancement." Several pictures from my social media were put on the news. Pictures of my parents, of Javier's and Valerie's parents, and social media were displayed. Then her sister went on camera.

"My sister always had psychological issues." "Her friends Javier and Daniel forced her to join some alien cult thing that we thought was a phase." "We thought she was doing it to fit in." "We didn't think too much of it, until about a month ago when she started to say strange things like, "Humans are the inferior species and only deserved to live as slaves to the Luken race." Pictures of Sevashkish hurting Phylmecs were shown.

Of course, to any ordinary human, it looked like a scary alien fighting old people. He even looked scary to me on camera. The news reporters cut away to people in my town. "We will catch these traitors and make them pay!" Out of the corner of my eye, I saw Valerie approaching. Guys, turn it off please, Valerie is coming back our way. I do not want her to see her sister saying these things about her. Well, I should not say sister. Valerie looked more at ease. I am positive she and Tailfin had a good talk. That made me happy, and now it is back to work. Guys, so this is what we know. We have to leave this island no later than sunrise tomorrow. The Phylmecs will come to every island worldwide to add satellite towers. <What are the towers for?> I am not sure actually. Sevashkish do you have a clue? [These are not satellite towers like the ones that you all have on Earth.] [These towers will help absorb the rays of the sun in a very effective manner, and they will help distribute these waves all around the planet.] [In every region of Earth.]

[As you all know the Phylmecs will be vulnerable during the two days after harvesting a person.] [The waves of the sun will help the human body respond faster to having its soul ripped out of it, and having an entirely new soul within it.] [That is the real purpose of these towers.] <We can't let them put those towers up Sevashkish!> I stared at Javier as he shouted. <I mean I know our main mission is to get to Yucatan, Mexico, and open Terramondetierra's heart, but we can also cause the Phylmecs some damage along the way, right?>

I smiled at Javier. You know what? You are right Javier. Sevashkish, do you know if destroying these satellites would have any impact on the Phylmecs? [Yes, if a Phylmec has harvested a human then they need the power of the sun's rays to gain strength in order to fully control the body, and if they do not have proper sun exposure they too can die.] [As you recall there is a two-day time frame where a Phylmec cannot walk or really speak well when they infest a new human body.] [This is why the Phylmec's harvest in a two-week time period.]

[It gives them time to not all be vulnerable in case of an attack.] <Well, well, well looks like we have to strike them first don't we?> <Javier, but they will surely have extra towers, won't they?> Valerie asked him with concern on her face. We all stared at Sevashkish. [Even if they have extra towers let us hope that we at least cause some harm to them.] <It is impossible for us to destroy maybe more than just this tower on this island.> <We cannot be on every island at once.> Valerie said. {It is not impossible!} {I will send a message to my people and let them know to destroy every tower on every island once almost completely placed.} {They will not get their way this time, and we will defend our beautiful planet.}

Tailfin I'm so happy that you are feeling better, and I am so glad you are part of the team. I smiled. How will you all do it? {We will flood the islands temporarily if we have to!} Valerie went over to the shore and caressed Tailfin. I am so sorry again for the pain I caused you, my friend. {All is forgotten, Valerie.}

For the first time since we had first met Tailfin, I was getting a sense of hope again. We finally had an ace up our sleeves. A way to hurt these alien creatures! Maybe, just maybe they were not all powerful. <We should all eat something and rest up for tomorrow.> <We have to be out of here by 5 am I believe> You are right Javier, because the Phylmecs will be here as soon as the sun comes up. [I think we should be out by 4:30 am, just to be on the safe side.] <I am on Sevashkish's side on this one boys.> <You all may want that extra hour of sleep, but we have a world to save!>

I looked at Valerie and gently threw a rock towards her. She caught it in midair and smiled as she tossed it back at me. Javier looked at me and said, "I guess now that she is coming out of her shell, we will have an Amazon on our side." I couldn't help, but laugh. <What are you guys saying back there?> <Do not make me come and beat both of you up.> This got Sevashkish to truly "laugh out loud" in our minds. It was the first time we ever "heard" him laugh this loudly, and it made all of us laugh.

Later that evening we had eggs for dinner. I feel bad for doing this, but we found a nest full of eggs on a tree and we took them. There were about 12 eggs and we ate all of them. That momma bird was not happy, but something told me she knew it was necessary to keep us energized. I really felt stronger after having them. I guess my body needed the protein. After eating we all felt tired. We went to "bed" before 9 pm. At least today my sand-bed on this island was warm. We were nearing the Gulf of Mexico so the weather was warmer too. The sand felt like a light blanket around my body.

I had no issues falling asleep, and thankfully I slept like a baby. The next morning we all kind of woke up around the same time at 4:15 am. I quickly got up and dusted the sand from my body, and then I went over to the water to check on Tailfin. He was swimming happily around the island. The orcas were still there as I had commanded them to be which made me happy. We had two extra bodies to help us if Tailfin needed it. Well, let's get this show on the road, I thought silently.

Chapter 16
CAUGHT IN A BOAT

We were on our way right at 4:30 am. We decided to not go on Tailfin for another couple of hours, even though he said he felt fine. We rode on the orcas, but I missed riding on Tailfin. He was much bigger than them, so riding on him felt more like riding on a train. On the orcas, it felt kind of like when you are on an airplane and there is light turbulence, so we had to hug their tail fins tightly. Which was not fun considering we were getting wet.

Hey, Sevashkish, how far are we from the Yucatan now? [We are only about 6 hours away at this current pace, Daniel.] Wow, we are not that far away. {Unfortunately, we won't be able to get to Mexico today.} <Why not Tailfin?> <Sevashkish said we are only 6 hours away.> {The currents are very rough today and it will be very dangerous as well since there is a storm that is supposed to hit.} {We will swim for 4 hours today, and then rest the entire night in Belize.} <Well at least I can say that I am going to Belize.> Javier said with a smile. {That would only leave us about 3 to 4 hours away from our destination tomorrow when we head out.} How does that sound to everyone?

I turned my head to look at my friends. They didn't seem too happy with the news. The look of sadness in Valerie's eyes was apparent. Whenever she is sad she gets small bags under her eyes. Javier had a look of fear in his eyes. He squints his eyes a bit when he feels uneasy. As for Sevashkish, he did not look happy, but he did look determined and motivated. I, myself, felt mad. I felt mad and scared. I felt mad about what the Phylmecs were doing, and I felt scared for my life and my parents.

I didn't want to die. I started to feel a bit anxious, so I took a deep breath and released. I tried to distract myself and imagine all the good things that would happen once this harvest was over, like peace on the planet. I was deep in my thoughts when I heard Tailfin speak again. {I am getting communication that they are installing sun towers all over the world.} {We believe that we will strike when they are half-installed.}

{This will ensure that any exposed wiring is damaged and destroyed.} <How exactly will you and your family and friends do that Tailfin?> Valerie asked. {We will cause miniature Tsunamis with groups of us working together on different islands.} {This will cause a rise and heavy fall of water that should destroy everything that it touches.} I saw Valerie's face squint a bit because I think she just realized that unfortunately anything that was in the way of the miniature Tsunamis would be destroyed. She didn't say anything after that.

<How do you guys think the world will change after we defeat the Phylmecs?> Javier looked at each of us as he broke the awkward silence. That question kind of caught me off guard. I guess I had not even thought about it. I don't know, I told him in a soft tone. I really do not know. <I think it will bring people closer together as a human species, and we will all be kinder to all animal life,> Valerie said with a smile. <Yeah, but knowing people, that will still be a challenge.>

<You are right Javier, but that is the beautiful part of it, we can create programs to explain how we are all connected with actual evidence to support our claims.> <Yeah, you are right I guess it takes someone as special as Valerie to accomplish that.> <I wouldn't be able to deal with changing the point of view of people who think they are always right.> Valerie smiled and gently hugged Javier. <That is exactly what I will do after all this is over guys,> she said with a huge smile.

<I think I have found my calling; well that and writing short stories,> she added with a smile. <I will write a book of all this for us when it is over.> <I will also write about how every creature on this planet is connected and serves a purpose in nature.> <I will help educate people on how to better protect the animals of this planet.> I looked at Valerie with a smile. I truly hoped she would

accomplish everything she was saying she wanted to do. It will just depend on whether or not humanity survived, I thought silently. <What will you do Sevashkish after this is over?> Javier asked.

[I will find a way to allow inter-dimensional species to speak to each other without consequences.] [That is my goal.] [I don't know how, but I know there is a way.] [Just like how Terramondetierra gave me the power to be in the 3rd dimension, I am sure I will find a way.] He looked so confident and happy while saying that. That made me happy. Sevashkish was truly a kind soul.

<How about you boys?> <Any clue what you guys will do?> Javier looked at me while Valerie asked us the question. <Well I'll add more context to what I said back when we had the campfire, but I am I not 100% sold on the idea.> <I am thinking of something with math and science intertwined with entertainment.> <I always found humor in life, and I believe when this is all over people will need to learn to laugh again.> <That being said people will need to be taught the sciences/math for our species to evolve.> <Maybe I will create educational centers around the world that help people learn while still having fun.> You mean like a school?

<No more of a center where anyone can go, not just to learn or laugh, but to also heal their souls.> <Now that we know that souls are truly real, it is more important than ever to protect and help them grow.>

<I still have to think about exactly what I want to do after this is over, but those are my initial thoughts.> <I guess I'll change my

major to biological/business management/philanthropy now.>
<What about you Daniel?> I was about to answer the question,
but suddenly the orca that Javier and I were on cried in pain,
"OWAAHH." {Our friend has been struck with a whale spear!}

The orca that I was on started to be dragged backward. We have
to jump off Javier and now! We jumped straight onto the next
whale, and as we were in the air it was struck too. "OWAAHH,
the other orca cried in pain. Sevashkish caught Javier and me just
in time before we landed in the water, with Valerie on his back. We
were gliding over the sea. Tailfin dive down and get out of here! I
yelled at him. He looked hesitant but did as I told him.

{I will be back, and with reinforcements!} Should we flee, or
should we try and save the orcas? I turned around to ask everyone.
<We stay with the orcas> Javier said with a smile. <Like Valerie told
us, we have to start protecting the creatures of this planet as much
as we can, especially when those creatures are in the process of getting a soul and becoming sentient beings!> <Plus, I do not think
it is the Phylmecs.> Okay, but it can get messy and dangerous. It
may be the Phylmecs, and they may try to harvest us, so we have to
be very careful.

<Yeah, but if it were the Phylmecs they could easily seize us up
either way.> <We are in the middle of the ocean and they have
a perfect target range on us if they are really that close.> I hope
you are right Javier, and that it is just regular whalemen whaling.
[I think all of you are forgetting that I am not exactly human.]

[I believe it is best that we leave now.] For the life of me, I had forgotten that Sevashkish was not exactly from this planet. A big powerful winged creature would surely get some stares, wouldn't it? I asked everyone.

<Yes it would, I had forgotten that> Javier said. He held onto Sevashkish's powerful arm as we started to rise higher into the air. As we got more altitude we noticed the ship. It had at least 30 men on it, and they were aiming their spear right at us. Sevashkish is fast, but carrying three people slowed him down. Before he had the chance to escape from view a whale spear pierced right through his left wing, and it pulled us down hard in the ocean. Sevashkish instinctively opened his hands and dropped us straight into the ocean, all but Valerie who was on his back. I do not even remember hitting the water, but I remember waking up to Valerie pleading for our lives.

<Please do not kill us, and please do not take us to those alien creatures!> <Do not take us to any government officials, I beg you.> <I am telling you the truth.> I tried to open my eyes fully, but my head was bouncing from the pain that I could not focus. I turned my head slightly and saw that Sevashkish had been tied up on the bridge of the ship. His arms and legs were tied, and his wings were tied too. His left wing was a bloody miss. That got me up. Where was Javier I wondered?

I turned my head a little to the right and saw Javier lying behind me. I couldn't believe my eyes. His left arm was completely blue and swollen. It had to be broken. There was no other answer, and he was still knocked out. I could not tell if he was breathing from this distance. Is he dead? I yelled to the men in frustration and anger. =No he is not dead, he is just unconscious.= =For being a superior alien species you all sure are dumb, or at least are bad actors.= <We are not an alien species!> <We are humans trying to save the world, and that includes you!>

I slowly got up and five men came running to me to hold me down. All of you listen, please. What my friend is telling you is true. The entire world is in danger, and we need to go save the world. =Haha, you expect us to believe that?= I do not expect anything from someone who does not want to see the truth, but I can tell you one thing. Before I could finish my sentence all the fish they had caught started to jump out of their containers and onto the men. The containers burst open, and the fish fell. Hundreds of pounds of fish fell right on them, just as I had instructed them to.

The men tried to struggle free, but it was no use. I looked at the men holding me, and the men on the ground. I gave them all a stern look and a warning. Now here is what is going to happen. We all have five minutes before your so-called heroes come into their spaceships and harvest us all. You can keep us captive, or you can help us. What do you say? The man who I presumed was the captain looked stunned. He let go of my hand. He had a look of fear across his face. I could tell that I was getting through to him. =What can we do to help?=

Firstly, get my friend down from there and bring me a bucket of fresh water. Valerie, please go help clean Sevashkish's wings with the freshwater and do everything that you can to wake him up fast. We will need a deep fog to protect us. I ran to the edge of the boat and I thought of big animals. I thought about whales. I even thought about sharks.

"I need a few of you to come here." "If you can hear me, come to me now, and take these people to the nearest shoreline safely." "My birds, I need your help." "I want all of you to come to the sound of my voice and attack anything that is flying in the air that isn't one of you." I turned to look at the men. We must be prepared because they can arrive at any minute. "Fish, all the fish in the sea I need you to be ready to form a bed for me, Valerie, Javier, and Sevashkish to escape."

At least two minutes have passed, I quietly thought. We were running out of time. The sweat was dripping from my forehead. Valerie, did you clean Sevashkish's wings? <Yes, but he is still out cold Daniel.> Oh no, we are really in trouble this time. Suddenly I remembered the tablet, and I yelled who took my tablet?

There was complete silence, no one answered anything, so I said, "If I do not get that tablet in the next 30 seconds we will leave all of you to fend for yourself." Out of nowhere, a younger taller man yanked the backpack off a fighting shorter older man and came to give it to me. =The tablet is in there, and sorry for what the crew did to all of you.=

Thank you! Four minutes passed, and in one minute they would be here. Valerie, I need you to call on every plant that this sea has, and form a barrier over this boat, and also over every whale and fish that will come. I need you to raise the kelp forest as high as you can to the air and form a barrier. <I will do everything I can, Daniel.> Tailfin if you can hear me I thought, please be close by. Things are getting rough. If Tailfin was around he would help rescue us.

I heard the explosions before I saw them. The sea plants were thankfully almost completely enclosed around us when the shooting began. Valerie faster! I turned my head to look up and the dome of planets was finally closed. The animals I had called were here. Everyone over the boat and landed on these animals, now! They will take you to safety. Please spread the word out as to what is happening! Tell them that the Phylmecs are the true invaders of our planet. Do not let anyone touch your forehead for any reason! Go now move!

I saw several guys jumping over the boat and a few looking confused at me. They say you do not know how you will act when danger faces you in the face. Some will fight, some will run, some will hide and sadly some will freeze. I did not stay around to help those that froze.

I saw a dolphin right by the area where Sevashkish was, and it took all my strength, but I pushed his body over and he landed on the dolphin. He was on his way. I ran over to Javier and there was a shark, a great white waiting by the area of where he was located.

I mustered all the strength I had in my aching body, but I pushed Javier down onto the shark. Javier was on his way.

Next, I ran toward Valerie and noticed that her body was covered in thick layers of kelp. She was forming a body suit around her, and I saw and felt the same was happening to me. The suit fell heavy and protective around my body. Valerie! I yelled, come towards me. We will jump down and be taken away by this bed of fish. Right as I said the word "fish," the spaceships appeared. There were 4 of them. They were slicing and dicing through the plant forest like it was nothing. Chaos everywhere.

Fires were spreading rapidly through the dome, and my ears were ringing from the sound of the explosions. Within seconds the dome of plants was breached. HAHA, YOU ARE TRYING TO ESCAPE FROM US ON THESE LITTLE EARTH CREATURES? YOU SURELY WILL NOT GET FAR.

Blast! A whale and the 3 men on it were turned into atoms. They disappeared into nothingness. It was terrible. Birds, attack now! I yelled. Right down from the sky, thousands of birds came diving right at the spaceships. From the smallest to the largest seagull. It looked like a scene from a nature documentary where thousands of birds are simultaneously migrating to warmer places. It was madness as the sky was darkened by all the birds. It is time to go Valerie. Jump!

We both jumped straight onto the bed of fish. They took us about 800 meters when we started to rise in the air. {Did someone call?} Tailfin! You are here! I yelled in happiness. {Yes my friend, I am here.} {Javier and Sevashkish are safe too, two of my good friends have them and they are heading east to Cuba.} <Why to Cuba?> {I will explain later, but now we must get out of here!} Valerie and I held onto Tailfin's fin tighter than we had ever before. He was swimming as fast as he could possibly swim.

I turned my head back, and what I saw was a scene of pure madness. The group of birds that I had called upon had taken down two Phylmec ships, but hundreds if not thousands of birds were being burned alive. They were falling like shooting stars into the ocean with millions of feathers flying in every direction. I felt remorse and guilt. Chills ran throughout me. Had I caused this? No, it was the only way to stop the Phylmecs, but still, this was partially my fault for calling them.

I would make this right once this war was over. I gently promised myself as I felt the guilt loom over me. The third ship went down, and then there was only a single Phylmec ship a safe distance away doing all the firing. It was vaporizing anything and everything that it could see. I turned in the other direction, and to my utter horror, I saw two groups of men on two different whales being blasted. Over twenty individuals were killed instantly. The poor whales were cut in half by the blast. Their big bodies were too big to be blasted into atoms since the ship was far away. The poor men on those whales suffered a slow painful death.

The ocean around the area started to turn red. Body parts were floating around the area. I heard screams of despair. Carnage. Pure and simple carnage. <Are all the fishermen dead?> I hope not Valerie. I hoped and prayed to God that at least someone had gotten away safely, at least one person please I thought. It just takes one person to go off and tell others what they witnessed and saw. One person to help the people see the reality of what is happening on Earth. <Daniel, the last ship was just taken down.> Valerie broke me from my thoughts. Okay, good. That is one last thing to have to worry about.

We swam in silence for over a long time. A long time of absorbing what had happened. The image of dead body parts floating in the sea would never leave my mind. I was happy when Tailfin broke the terrible silence. {The towers are being destroyed now.} <I hope this was the correct choice.> It has to be Valerie, it has to be the correct choice. It is the only way to slow them down at least a bit if our plan does not work. Guys, we have to find a way to broadcast what we know on the internet or social media. {When we meet up with the others we can discuss how we can do that.} <Yeah, we should wait and get everyone's input because we may broadcast our location without wanting to.> You guys are right. Let's wait for them.

I am just getting anxious to let others know. On that boat, at least two people took our word. It was only two out of the thirty whalemen, but two nonetheless. <You are right about that

Daniel.> <How far away are we Tailfin from the others?> {We should be reaching Cuba in about one hour.} I think I am going to check the tablet to see what is going on. <Are you sure it's a good idea?>

Yes, I believe we need to know what exactly is going on after the tower attacks and the massacre that we just experienced back there. I pulled the tablet from the backpack that it was in, and it looked just like a regular ipad. Nothing too special about it. It had no buttons anywhere, and it looked surprisingly human. The only real difference was its weight. It was as light as a feather. <Do you know how to turn it on?>

Honestly, I have no clue. There are no buttons on this thing. {Maybe you have to speak to it directly?} "Turn on tablet and show me the news." The tablet did not turn on, and I felt kind of silly. <Maybe you have to speak to it through your mind?> Only one way to find out. I closed my eyes to focus and thought, "Turn on tablet and show me the news worldwide." To my amazement, the tablet turned on and showed the local news in Cuba. Valerie does not speak Spanish, so subtitles on I thought, and the subtitles turned on.

ALIEN FUGITIVES CAUSE MASSIVE BLASTS AND TAKE DOWN 100s OF THE TOWERS BEING PLACED OVER EARTH." "INTERNET SERVICES HAVE BEEN SHUT OFF BY THEM WORLDWIDE" "A LOCAL WHALING SHIP WAS DESTROYED AND ITS MEN WERE ALL

KILLED BY THESE CREATURES. A video of Valerie being covered in sea plants was being played. A video of us jumping out of the boat was being shown.

IF YOU SEE THESE PEOPLE THE UNITED NATIONS HAS ENCOURAGED TO SHOOT ON THE SPOT. THEY ARE DANGEROUS AND ARE KILLING HUMANS. THEY MAY LOOK HUMAN BUT THEY HAVE BEEN TAKEN OVER BY THE POWERFUL ALIEN SPECIES KNOWN AS THE LUKENS. A PICTURE OF SEVASHKISH WAS SHOWN ON THE SCREEN. I turned to look at Valerie and she had a look of disgust on her face. A look of hatred spread over her face, and I am sure I had the same look on my face. I was about to turn off the tablet when I saw a man come running in front of the news reporter who had given the report.

He spoke in broken-out-of-breath English, but I understood what he said. I had to translate a few words to Tailfin and Valerie, but for the most part, they understood what he said as well. What none of us needed confirmation of, was who this man was. We all knew. This man was the individual who forced the other guy to give me the tablet. He was one of the whalemen. <That is the young guy who gave you the tablet Daniel,> yes that's him alright. He started speaking, =The Phylmecs are the real devils who came from the sky!=

=The Lukens and the humans are the ones trying to save the entire human race and planet Earth from being destroyed by the

Phylmecs.= =They are pure evil, and they are demons on earth!= =We need to burn their ships and destroy them all before it's too late.= The man was about to say more when the camera cut off suddenly. <Wow that was intense, but he believed us.> <I saw his eyes when I was telling him the story, and I knew that he believed what I was telling him.>

Yeah, I figured he did when he gave me the bag with the tablet inside. Now more than ever we have to find a way to broadcast the truth out to the world. <We need to let Sevashkish know of our plan, and of course ask Javier what he thinks.> When we all meet up in Cuba we will all make a decision and talk this through. Finally, an hour later we saw Cuba over the horizon. {We cannot go to land until it is dark.} Why is that, Tailfin? {During the day there is a lot of security.} {It is best to go at night when there is less security around the area.} Okay, understood.

We swam around Cuba till it got dark enough. It was boring, but it was beautiful to see the landscape of Cuba. {Okay guys, about 400 meters left of the giant rock that you see over there by the edge of the shore there is a hidden cave.} {The entrance is covered by thick shrubs.}{You must carefully lift the shrubs, but be careful not to break them, or else the cave will be noticeable.} {The hidden cave is big enough for about 10 people where you can comfortably spend the night.} {There are some delicious berries in there I hear, and also a stream of fresh water that flows through the cave.} {I know it isn't the biggest meal, but it will keep all of your bellies full until tomorrow.}

Thank you so much Tailfin, what time should we head out tomorrow? {Well here is the thing about that.} {I have gotten word that 60% of the towers were destroyed worldwide, but now the Phylmecs have people stationed on every seaport in the world.} {This means we have to find another entrance into Yucatan, Mexico.} {Also, we have about 4-5 days before the harvest begins.} How far of a swim are we from the Yucatan right now? {Using the swimming highway that we have been using, it is exactly a 5-hour swim from here.} Thank God. It isn't too far, so four days from tomorrow or five days from today? {It is four days starting tomorrow, yes.}

Okay, we will find a way to enter the Yucatan that doesn't involve getting noticed by the Phylmecs informants. The important thing is to get as close as we can. When we speak to the others I will call you, but please be around this area around 5 am-6 am tomorrow. If you do not hear from us assume the worst and carry on the mission without us. I am going to give you Terramonde-tierra's heart okay? <Where do you have the heart, Daniel?> Well turn around, Valerie. <Oh no, Daniel!> She yelled while laughing.

I took the golden heart out of my pants. It was safely stored in a small sac that I had made from an old shirt. I promise it never left this shirt, Tailfin. {Yeah, yeah, don't worry I believe you.} {I want both of you to know that I believe in all of us, and I will guard the heart with my life.} {It will not go anywhere until I see you all tomorrow night.} With those last words Valerie and I left Tailfin.

It was about a ten-minute crawl to get to the cave from the shore, and it was not fun. We crawled near the sand all the time, so we wouldn't be spotted by anyone. By the time we reached the entrance to the cave we were covered in dirt and cuts from the scraping sand. <Who would have thought that the beach here had so many sharp pebbles?> Not me, but hey it's better to have some scrapes than to be seen by any guards.

<If you say so.> I carefully lifted the shrubs like Tailfin had instructed and we went inside the cave. I immediately saw a small fire that was burning, and then I saw them. <Sevashkish, Javier you guys are here!> I guess Valerie beat me to the punch line. Javier had his left arm against his body supported by a plant cast that Valerie had made for him right before I threw him over the boat. His arm was broken, unfortunately. Sevashkish's wings were pressed against his body. They still had stains of blood. Yellow stains all over his wings. Javier ran to us and gave us a giant one-handed hug.

<You guys are alive!> <I am so happy.> <I thought we had lost you.> <When I woke up I was alone in this cave and very confused.> <I did not know what to do, and that is when he appeared here.> <Sevashkish?> <No, not Sevashkish he came later, but him over there.> I turned to where Javier was pointing but I could not see anything. I don't see anything, Javier. <Look towards the floor.> I lowered my gaze and saw the shape of what looked to be a

child but with a muscular build. <Is that a kid?> Valerie asked with confusion on her face. <That is exactly what I thought at first, but no.> <This is a gnome.>

I stood there like an idiot just thinking about the gnome that my mom used to have in our front yard when I was growing up. I shook my head in confusion. Wow, this is amazing! I yelled. Nice to meet you, my name is Daniel. I guess my sudden enthusiasm took the gnome by surprise because when he spoke he stuttered a little. I could not quite make out what he said, but I heard Hutkis. He came over to me and Valerie and bowed his head. We bowed our heads as well. <He does not speak any languages that I am familiar with Daniel, maybe you can possibly understand what he is saying?> Of course I will ask him, but first I want to know how you and Sevashkish got here. Also, how are you doing Sevashkish?

[Thank you, Daniel, for your concern.] [When I arrived at the cave I was fully conscious, and noticed Hutkis working on Javier's arm.] [He was adding structure to the plant cast that Valerie had made him.] [I did not know exactly what he was because I had never seen a human like him.] [I felt his presence was a good one, so I let him do his work while I sat back and rested.] <Who brought you here Sevashkish?> [I am assuming when Daniel called on the wildlife to rescue us, Tailfin asked one of his friends to find me.] [I woke up on the back of one of his friends who told me that we were heading to a secret cave in Cuba.]

[I asked him if you both had gotten out safely, but he did not know, so I became very worried, and I am quite glad that you are both alright and safe.] <Awww you are so cute Sevashkish, we were worried about you too.> Valerie went over and hugged Sevashkish. [When we got here there were no Phylmec informants on the island of Cuba yet, so I simply walked to the cave, and thankfully my wings are about 20% repaired from the attack that I had this morning.] I am so happy to hear that.

<Yeah, I wish I could heal as fast as you, because my arm still feels like it went through a blender, haha.> [I wish to tell you all something.] [As I was resting I could see and hear an interview going on by a news station glorifying the Phylmecs when one of the men from the ship came and interrupted it.] [They cut the interview, grabbed him, and kneeled him down.] [Just as they were about to touch his forehead, he hit them with the side of his head, and the Phylmec, who of course was an older human, died.] [This gave the young man enough time to run out of there since the reporters were in shock, so he ran.] [They sent 3 big looking humans after him, so I took a risk and spoke to him.]

Sevashkish put his head down while he was saying this. Javier went to him and said, <Do not put your head down or be ashamed Sevashkish, you did what you felt was right, and guess what I think you were right.> What do you mean Javier? <Claude can you step out here?> Lo and behold the young man who had given me the tablet and the backpack came out from behind the shadows. He looked tired but confident. The closer I looked at him the more I noticed that he was young, and probably around my age give or take a year or two. He was dressed like an older person, so he could easily be confused for being older if you didn't look at his face closely. He wore oversized clothes and dark gray colors. I didn't know what to say. This was a lot to take in considering what we had all been through.

Chapter 17
CLAUDE & HUTKIS

So much to take in all at once. I was feeling a bit lightheaded. I hadn't eaten in almost an entire day. If I am feeling this way I can imagine how everyone must be. Hey guys, shall we eat first and then get to know Hutkis and Claude a bit more? Everyone rapidly nodded in agreement. Hutkis looked a bit confused as to what we were saying, but I rubbed my stomach to indicate hunger and he flashed a little excited smile. He went running to the back of the cave. We all stared at each other kind of confused for about a minute, but then he came out with a big wicker basket. It was like one of those picnic baskets that you see in movies.

Hutkis sat the basket in between us and opened it. I was taken aback. The smells were incredible. I am not sure if it is because I hadn't had actual homemade food in over a week, but the food smelled great. I smelled freshly baked bread, honeysuckle, glazed ham, and smells I wasn't familiar with. He handed each of us a sandwich sort of thing and passed a cup to each of us. The cups were only the size of a shot glass, but I was not complaining. He poured something that smelled like sugary tea and used his hands to imitate a spoon going into his mouth.

He wanted us to eat. We did not have to be asked twice. We ate, and it was amazing. I felt like a new person, plus he had enough for us to have seconds. After we ate I was about to try and communicate with Hutkis, but Sevashkish beat me to it. He started to communicate with him. Sevashkish speaks all the major languages on planet Earth, so he has me beat there; even though I do speak several languages myself. Let's see if he speaks gnome. [I will start with the standard human dialect, "The Adam and Eve," which came shortly after Humanata.]

<Ah, I remember you told me about the "Adam and Eve" language Daniel.> <I thought it was cool when you explained to me that in every major language mom and dad basically sound the same.> I smiled at Javier, so you were paying attention, huh? <Oh, of course, you know me, I always pay attention.> Javier said with a wink. It made me happy that Javier had said that. I have always loved cultures and languages, and maybe since I have part of TT's soul in me that could be the reason as to why this is.

Sevashkish used the Adam and Eve language to speak to the gnome, but he had a look of confusion on his face, so he did not speak it. Hutkis ran over to the side of the cave and picked up a stick. He used the stick like a pencil and started to write on the dirt. To all of our shock, he started writing in letters that we mostly recognize. I yelled, it's German! He is writing in German. Sevashkish nodded and started to speak to him. Hutkis responded, and Sevashkish translated for us. [My friends are surprised to see that Gnomes, the species, exists.]

[They thought you were all legends made up in fairytales.] -I am not surprised it has been 15,000 years since we were last with their kind.- -We never truly lived in harmony, but for the most part, we had treaties to respect each other.- -At the time we didn't know much about human evolution, so we thought homo-sapiens were big monsters, and that they were a different sort of creature.- -We now know of course, that Gnomes and Homo-Sapiens are both humans, just a different species.- [Why do you speak German?]

-We Gnome settled in what is now Germany, and this is originally our language.- -We taught the Homo Sapiens our language.- -These humans turned out to be traitors to our people and caused us great harm, but I will not get into that right now.- -All I will say is that we took our revenge.- -The humans feared us a bit since we had more knowledge of the sciences than them.- -They thought we had magical powers and could cast spells on them etc.- -Eventually, we were able to live in our own sections of Germany in mutual respect for the most part, and that is when they came.- -The Phylmecs.- -As you see we Gnomes have always preferred to live in caves, so when they came we were quite shocked at how easily they had manipulated human society.- -We kept our existence a secret without allowing the Phylmecs to learn about us.-

-In the beginning, we also thought they were here to help the human race.- -After two weeks we saw what they did, and we feared for our safety.- -They destroyed everything after the harvest, and left a few people in charge.- -These people came after us with newer, more advanced technology and they tried to kill us.- -There were about 200 of us left, and we fled.- -We fled by boat and ended up in Cuba, which is where we have been hiding and living in peace for the last 15,000 years.-

<Sevashkish can you ask him if he knows anything that can help us against them?> [I will ask him now Valerie.] -They are vulnerable for those two days after the harvest.- -A lot of the German Humans were able to kill many of them while they rested from the Harvest. -Also, this is just a theory, but we believe their spacecraft are biohybrid organisms, so they need water to stay functioning.- -We believe if oil or something poisonous enters the water port of their spacecraft they will cease to function.- Can you ask him why he thinks this Sevashkish?

He nodded yes, and proceeded to tell him. -Right before we fled we saw the humans throw in a thick whale oil in the water portion of the Phylmecs ship while they were filling it up.- -Our ancestors say the ship moaned in pain and fell to its side.- -The ship would not fly, and they had to destroy it at the end before they left.- We all stayed quiet as Sevashkish translated what Hutkis was saying. We all knew how amazing it would be to do that to their ships, but we also knew we would never be able to get close enough to a Phylmec ship. The important thing now was that we had a new ally, Hutkis. Thank you, Danke, Hutkis for all your information. I went over and shook his hand.

<Claude, how about you?> <Where are you from?> <I know you understand English, but are you confident to speak it?> Valerie stared at him with welcoming eyes. She had a way to make sure others felt safe and relaxed. I saw Claude relax his shoulders and take in a deep breath. =I am from Finland.= Javier looked at me with his eyes wide open, <Why were you on a boat in the Caribbean with a majority of sailors speaking Spanish?> Claude looked at Javier like he had not understood the question. Valerie, can you please explain slowly what Javier said, and without such an accusing tone, please?

<Oh I am sorry, I wasn't trying to sound like I was accusing you, Claude, Javier said slowly.> Valerie was about to repeat the question that Javier asked, but Claude smiled and said, =apology accepted.= =My father has an offshore fishing company in the Caribbean, and I decided to take a year off from my studies to work on one of his boats.= =I wanted some time to figure out what I wanted from my life.= =My parents weren't too thrilled about this, so they allowed me to work on the boat, but as a regular sailor.= =I do not get any special treatment whatsoever.= =I guess they wanted me to suffer a bit.= His cheeks got bright red as he said this.

<Hey dude, no problem.> <We know how parents can be; they want the best for us but sometimes forget that we have to figure out our own lives.> Claude smiled and nodded. Sevashkish, why did you decide to bring Claude into the cave? I looked at Claude, no offense Claude, but we are on a dangerous mission. He nodded back at me with a faint smile. [I believe Claude can see the souls of people and sentient beings.] What do you mean? [When I was tied and beaten on the boat, they had ordered Claude to put a dagger through my heart and throat.] [He was about to do it until he saw into my eyes.]

"<The eyes are the window into the soul,>" Valerie said calmly. [Yes he kept the crew from killing me, telling them instead it would be better to turn me in.] [They were very hesitant about this, but he stood his ground until you all got there.] It took me a minute to realize what Sevashkish was saying, but then I understood. Sevashkish, do you believe that Claude can see whether a person, or anyone for that matter has been taken over by a Phylmec?

[I strongly believe that.] I turned to face Claude and looked at him with a serious expression. Claude, growing up did you feel different from others? Have you felt connected to spiritual things, have you seen spirits? I honestly do not know why I asked him those questions, but it was the only thing I could think of asking to get a truthful answer from him.

=I never felt "weird," or "strange," but I did feel unique in the sense that I could see spirits from time to time, especially when visiting old places in Finland.= =I vaguely remember telling my parents about this, but after a while, they kept saying it was just my imagination.= =I eventually quit telling them, and I almost forgot about it until the trip to the United Nations.= =I saw many people there with no shine in their eyes.= We all came closer to Claude when he said this. <What do you mean no shine in their eyes?> Javier asked.

=When I see your eyes Javier there is a gloss over your eyes, like a reflection where I see that you are alive.= =These people did not have that.= =They were simply void of that.= =To me it felt like they were walking zombies.= =I asked my best friend if he had noticed anything strange about that, and he said no, so I asked my teacher, and that is when one of the people with no shine in their eyes overheard me.=

=He said to me, "You seem like a gifted fellow, if this wasn't the official last rodeo, you would have made it to the very end." I felt a cold chill go down my spine. I guess before that very moment I thought that maybe the Phylmecs were not 100% sure that this was truly Earth's last survivable harvest, but they were sure of it. They were mocking us. They would not get away with this.

Claude, I extended my hand out to you, welcome to the team of Earth's warriors. He shook my hand and smiled. =I am beyond honored to accept.= Claude was gleaming with happiness. Sevashkish, may you ask Hutkis if he wants to be part of our team? Sevashkish translated what I had asked, and quickly translated

Hutkis response back to us. -I thank you for your offer to join all of you amazing people, but my duty is to stay here as an official clan leader to my people.- -We have been living in secrecy for thousands of years, and we would prefer to remain that way.- -That being said, I do want all of you to come to spend the night in our little cave village if you will join me.-

-It will be my honor to host all of you.- -That said, I do ask that all of you wear this blindfold, just for security reasons.- -I know that you are amazing people, but no homo sapien-human has ever stepped foot in here, or has known about this place since we left Germany over 15 thousand years ago.- -I only made the secret cave known to Genfin (Tailfin's friend) because I heard of your situation, and I knew that I had to help.- He handed us a bandana blindfold and we put it on without thinking twice. We walked slowly in a straight line one after another for what felt like 10 minutes.

Then Hutkis made us stop, and I kid you know I felt the strongest wind that I have ever felt in my life slap my face. It kind of felt like when you are driving down the freeway and you lower the window and the air hits your face. It made me feel like we went through a sort of vortex, and for all I know we probably did. Hutkis then asked us to walk for about a minute more. He then mumbled some words. Sevashkish translated and said, [We may remove our coverings.] I removed my bandana, and what I saw was AMAZING.

It was like being in Disneyland. There were wonderful colors all around. Trees in every direction and all shapes and colors. All around the edges of the city were the smallest cute houses you could imagine. I could not help but smile with joy. It was another underground city, like with the Mayans, but this city was miniature. I looked at the others and they were equally as mesmerized. Hutkis said something in a loud voice, and soon enough hundreds of gnomes came out of their house to greet us. They stared at us with their big eyes. Some looked afraid, others curious and a few were both happy and angry. I couldn't blame the angry ones. Hutkis started to talk, so Sevashkish began to translate for us.

-These groups of humans and their alien friends are here to save us and the entire planet.- -They wish you no harm, they are here just for the night.- -Do not worry my fellow Gnomes, they do not know how to reach our cave city.- -I will give them a tour of our city and show them the wonders that we have.- -Feel free to come with us, or go back to doing what you were doing before.-

We began the tour. The Gnomes were pretty technologically advanced in my opinion. They had mini cars that they flew in the air. They had a bridge over the water that would move in the direction that a person was moving to. What caught me off guard was that they had a giant hologram projector wall with over 500 pictures on it. Hutkis went over and found himself. He said his name, and a brief virtual hologram appeared describing his life and what he did. I was astonished, but beyond that I was happy. These

Gnomes, like the Mayans, still lived in villages, but they also were highly sophisticated. The best of both worlds.

This was a beautiful place that had to be protected at all costs. I enjoyed walking along the lush green grass. There was no pavement, just beautiful green grass. I soaked up as much of the city as I could. After exploring the city for nearly an hour Hutkis took us to a beautiful park that had four big fluffy beds. -One for each of you.- I was so happy. It had been a long time since I slept in an actual bed before. -This is where you all will be spending the night, and tomorrow I will come wake all of you up and take you back to the shore by 5:30 am.- [I have just confirmed with Hutkis that 5:30 am is a great time for all of us.] Thank you Sevashkish, and Danke Hutkis.

Hutkis left us alone in our comfy beds, and I was relaxed. We had met two different people recently (The Mayans and the Gnomes), and both were great people. I can only imagine how the world will educate us humans on how to be better people. This is amazing, I thought. After the war so much good will happen that people may get motivated to create a better world. "When the war is over," that phrase repeated itself in my head. I got a painful feeling in my gut. I should not get ahead of myself until we defeat the Phylmecs. I had been mesmerized by all the beauty and welcoming people that I had met. I had forgotten how hard it would be to save Earth. One thing was sure, I was now more motivated than ever to defend this big blue marble.

As I got into my bed, I reminded myself that we had at least 3 full days to get to the Yucatan before the harvesting began. Believe it or not, this news made me happy. We still had a little bit of wiggle room. It is surprising how you can find the tiniest glimmers of hope to give you faith. I went to bed that night and do not even remember falling asleep. I woke up the next morning at about 5:25 am. I still felt quite tired, but I dragged myself off the comfy bed. I checked on the others and they were still asleep. Javier was even snoring.

I think we all felt more mentally tired than physically. Yesterday was tough. After Hutkis had left us we all had a serious conversation about whether or not we should do more to let others know about the Phylmecs. We all came to the agreement that it was too risky to broadcast about the Phylmecs to the world for various safety concerns to us. Plus Sevashkish did not think we even had the possibility since the Phylmecs controlled all of Earth's satellites at least for now.

There was no time to think about that now. It was time to get up and prepare for the journey that lay ahead. I woke my friends up, and soon Hutkis was there to lead us back to the ocean to meet Tailfin. It took us about 20 minutes of painful crawling to get to Tailfin, but we reached him. Surprisingly there were no guards that we could see at this time. When we reached Tailfin he looked much better physically. I was glad that he looked much healthier and in better shape. He had been through a lot lately and even lost one of his friends.

Everyone, I have a plan on how we can get to Mexico without being noticed, but let's get sailing out to sea first. {You got it, Daniel.} {Tailfin Express is here to save the day.} That made me smile. I took it as a positive sign that Tailfin had said that. When all of this first started I was watching Futurama, and they have a ship called Planet Express. {Whooh, wait.} What Tailfin? {Why is the man that hurt my orca friends here?} He demanded angrily. <Tailfin, Claude is the one who saved all of us, and he saved you too from being harpooned.> Valerie quickly told Tailfin all she could about Claude. {Thank you Valerie for explaining it to me, and I am more than happy to have you aboard me, Claude. Claude shyly smiled. <Okay Daniel, spill the beans, what is the plan?> Javier asked. {Yes, please tell us the plan because I am getting nervous just waiting to hear it.} {I have word that every coastline in every country, every city, every continent has Phylmecs and regular humans guarding the shores.} {Nothing is getting in or out without permission, and that includes flying as well; since they have guards surveying just the sky for that very thing.}

There is one simple solution, and if we do everything right it will work out, but if we don't then we will just need another plan. Everyone immediately turned their heads towards me. Okay, so this is what we do. We hitchhike a ride on a ship. Either a cruise ship or one of those giant cargo ships. It has to be a big ship though. A ship where they wouldn't notice 4 humans and an amazingly cool alien.

<That is not a bad idea at all, Daniel.> Javier said. <I guess we have to decide which to do, the cruise ship or the cargo ship?> =The cruise ship is the way to go.= Valerie looked at Claude, and asked, <Why is that Claude?> =Even though cargo ships are enormous the sailors know that ship from head to foot.= =They would know if anyone new came on aboard, plus they constantly do hourly checks to make sure all the systems are properly working.= =I've also had the privilege of being on cruise ships, and there are so many workers, that even if you climb to different levels the workers on the new level won't recognize you.=

=They are too busy with their job to focus on details like that.= Javier looked at Claude and smiled, <Well I guess I should say sorry for ever doubting you, Mister Fisher boy.> [I must ask, how will I get to the boat, if I am not human?] We all stared at Claude. Any clue how to get Sevashkish into the boat safely?

=Yes, we go in through one of the safety exits by the lifeboats at the bottom of the boat, but we must do it after sunset, and Sevashkish you must disable the safety codes.= =Is that something that you can do?= Sevashkish looked at us and smiled with his large owl eyes, [Safety codes will not be an issue for me.] We all started laughing. <Oh my bad, I guess we forgot Mr. Sevashkish was a highly advanced alien from the 7th dimension.> [Yes, do not forget Javier again.] <Oh my he is making jokes now.] We all started to

laugh again. It was nice seeing how Sevashkish was learning human humor.

{Okay everyone that should work, but the only issue is that we will have to be swimming in the ocean for 14 hours before sunset, so that means I will have to have a break to feed.} {All of you will have to stay in the ocean for that long period, but I am sure we will make it fun, and I will ask my friends to help me during the time of rest and my feeding time.} We also cannot forget that we have to locate a boat that is headed toward Mexico, and hopefully the Yucatan area. {I am on it.} We spent the next 3 hours just getting to know each other on a deeper level.

Turns out Tailfin was the first one in his family to be truly sentient, but he was not the first of his clan to be truly sentient. {Over the past 300 years or so, about 3 calves out of 100 have been born sentient.} {That is an increase of about 47% from the past 15 thousand years or so.} When a whale isn't sentient just how intelligent are they Tailfin? {Oh they are very intelligent.} {I would put their intelligence level to that of an 8-year-old human.}

Wow, honestly that is incredible and so amazing. <It truly is.> Valerie said. After three hours we all started to get hungry, so Sevashkish flew out to try and get us something to eat. Thankfully after a restful night and a good meal, his wings had healed up. We couldn't ask Tailfin to help, since we were all on him. On a side note, I am not sure if people know this but the ocean is very cold. Especially when you are far into the deep ocean. It is not warm like on beaches. We could not risk getting sick by slipping into the water, so that is why we couldn't find food for ourselves.

Thankfully, Sevashkish came back about an hour later with shrimps and some seaweed for us to eat. We had packed some water bottles from the gnomes. We ate our food. It was not good at all, but it was enough to keep us sustained and in good shape. At the 7-hour mark, Tailfin's friend came and we got on him. He was not a sentient being, but he understood in some strange way that we had to go on him. During this time we asked Sevashkish more about the Phylmecs. <If the Phylmecs do make it to the 7th dimension do you believe that the Lukens would be able to handle their savage invasion?> [Sevaskish looked at Javier and said, I do not doubt that we could handle those vile creatures, but there is one thing that plagues my mind.]

[The Phylmecs are coming with not only their souls but the souls they consumed of other species.] [This could make them very dangerous adversaries.] I have a question, Sevashkish. [Yes, go ahead and ask Daniel.] When I place TT's heart on the altar what exactly will happen? [Well Earth the being will be able to release a chemical that affects anyone that is not Earth-born, or anyone Terramondetierra has not allowed to visit it.]

<Is there going to be destruction everywhere?> Javier looked intensely at Sevashkish while asking. [I honestly do not know what will occur, but I do know that if it works Earth will be saved, and so will its children, but there will be chaos nonetheless.] <Okay

guys, let's change the subject for now, okay?> I looked at Valerie, and gave her a faint smile. I did it to put her at ease, but even she knew it was important to talk about what may happen.

Chapter 18
FINALLY A BREAK

At last, after more than half a day out in the sea, the sun was starting to set. We were all fairly seasick. If you ever want to go in the middle of the ocean, make sure you have a huge boat! That is all I am going to say. <When do you think Tailfin will return?> <I am getting worried.> <It has been a while.> Valerie was right. Tailfin had been gone for about three hours, but I am sure that he was fine. Don't worry, Valerie, remember he needed to find food, and I'm sure he communicated with his family and friends. He will be back soon. <Well, aren't you some magical wizard, Daniel?> Oh, and why is that, Javier? <Mister Tailfin is approaching in 3, 2, 1.>

Well, you can call me the wiz, I jokingly said. <Yeah, no thank you.> Javier said while laughing at me. {Sorry, for taking too long, but I found a ship!} {We are about 35 minutes north of a cruise ship.} {I swam by it, and it is massive!} {I overheard the captain speaking and it should arrive at Cancun at 12:45 pm tomorrow.} {Apparently they arrive at this time to help save cost and not serve lunch.} <Figures, they always cheap out on lunch!> <I think I've lost fifty pounds since this all started!> <Look at me, I'm nothing but bones.> Javier if you are nothing but bones, I guess we are nothing but spirits at this point. We all started laughing, even Claude. Javier is a bigger guy, but he is naturally a big guy. He carries his weight very well.

Not that I would admit this to Javier, but even I was secretly disappointed we wouldn't get lunch, but at least we could have dinner and breakfast on the cruise ship. <I hope they have good desserts on the cruise because I need sweets!> Yeah, me too. <Boys and their sweets.> <Hopefully they have salad.> <Yeah, you can stick to that Valerie, while we eat cake.> While playfully talking nonsense for half an hour we had sailed near enough to the ship that we could see it clearly. From this distance, it looked massive, so I can only imagine how big it must be.

It was darker than light outside now, so we decided that it was best to head for the boat now. It was about 7:45 pm, and most boats had their dinners at this time. There would be fewer people wandering outside. We reached the boat at 8:00 pm, and when I looked up I was honestly surprised how big it was. I had never seen such a massive boat. How does that even stay floating I wondered? [I see the security door and the lock pad.] [I will disable any security, and then we can simply go inside.] <Please be

careful, Sevashkish.> [Do not worry Valerie, I will be fast. =Wait Sevashkish!= =Do not go inside first, I think it is best that I go first because I am the one who knows most about boats.=

[Are you sure that is a good idea, Claude?] =I think that is a good idea because I genuinely know my way around boats.= <I agree with Claude, you are the best person to go in, and I am sure you know the slang if they ask you a question.> We all agreed that Claude was the best option. [Okay I will access the keypad.] [It is a ten-digit code.] We all watched Sevashkish intensely, and to our surprise, he started pressing the numbers 0-9, and to our utter shock, the door opened.

<Are you seriously telling me that this was the code?> <The code that I would even try?> Valerie had a look of embarrassment on her face. <I mean Valerie, who is going to get this close to a boat anyway?> <Cut the people some slack for points in humor.> <Uh huh, humor, Javier?> <Seems like that was the lock the boat came with.> That made all of us get the giggles again.

Sevashkish opened the little hatched door and Claude went in. =There are some stairs that I must climb up to reach the first room.= Up he went, and more than ten minutes passed since we last heard from him. <Do you guys think we should go in looking for him?> <I do not think so Valerie, remember this is a massive boat, and he may be exploring a bit.> <Okay, but if he is not here in ten more minutes one of us has to go in looking for him.> <Why are you so worried?> <It seems like you have a little crush on him

don't you Valerie haha?> I turned to look at Valerie, and her face was bright red, almost as red as her hair. I couldn't help but laugh a little.

<Javier the only crush I'll have is when I crush your other arm.> <Okay, okay I am kidding.> When she looked away he looked at me and blinked. I was happy Valerie had a little crush. It would distract her a bit from losing her sister. I knew she was doing everything in her power to push that situation to the side for now to save Earth, but I was really worried about her emotional and mental state. I mean I was worried about all of us at this point, but even I had to push those feelings to the side.

At the 17-minute mark, we heard something coming down the stairs. We all tensed up, and lastly, Claude returned. =Guys I am sorry that I took so long, this boat is massive!= =It took me some time to find out exactly where to go.= =It is fairly easy to get from here to the first floor of rooms.= =We will need Sevashkish to unlock the last couple of rooms, but I am sure he can bypass security easily.= =I saw that there are four rooms available so that is more than enough, but I suggest we hurry our way up because the kitchen closes in an hour.= Claude please tell me you saw a map of the entire ship and all the schedule and activities it has?

=Yes, there was the entire schedule of the boat next to the engine room.= That is awesome at least we will be in the loop of everything that is going on. Nice work Claude. Okay, Tailfin we will go in now. Please stay close to the boat, but also get some rest soon. Tomorrow is a big day for all of us, and I need you to rest well, my friend. {That sounds like a plan to me, see you tomorrow everyone.}

We all got through the electrical room, and service room quite quickly, and to our surprise, the room on the first floor was unlocked, and we just went right in. Now the tricky part came. Sevashkish had to unlock the 3 of the 4 empty rooms and bypass the security, but according to him, it was easier than pie. We all decided Valerie would get her own room because she was the only girl, and we were sure she didn't want to be next to smelly guys. Claude and Javier took another room, and Sevashkish and I took the last.

When we opened the door to our room I was shocked. It was a big beautiful room. It had two giant beds that were both separated with a little wall to give a bit of privacy. There was a beautiful restroom that had a tub and a shower. There were two sinks also. There was a giant smart TV, and there were two work desks each with a computer chair. The carpet felt so fluffy even with my shoes on. It was amazing. I didn't realize how much I missed my room until that very moment. I could have spent the entire day just looking around, but we had to eat.

I went to the restroom to wash my face, and then I looked at myself in the mirror. When was the last time that I saw my face in a mirror? Almost two weeks I guessed. My hair had gotten long. It was swooping down to the sides, but it looked so much lighter. It was almost a golden brown. I guess from all the sun exposure. My skin was a light tan, but my cheeks were red. I still did not have any facial hair. I guess the sun did not help with that. My teeth were dirty! I was shocked.

It had been a while since I brushed them. I felt bad. I opened one of the drawers and found a toothbrush there. I will be using you tonight. What surprised me the most was my weight and muscle loss. When I started weight lifting I had gained quite a bit of muscle, but it was almost all gone, and I had lost so much weight as well. I am five foot 8, and I probably weigh 125 pounds now. [The others are knocking at the door waiting for you to go up and have dinner.] I'm sorry Sevashkish, let them know I will be out in a minute.

I quickly washed my face and put some extra towels under my shirt to make it look like I had a stomach. I grabbed a face mask and went outside. We had to make sure we disguised our appearance the best we could to not be noticed. We were hoping that no one would be looking for us on a cruise ship during their family vacation. Okay, I am ready. I will bring you back a plate, Sevashkish. [Thank you, please let it be a huge plate.] You got it Sevashkish, I told him with a smile.

<Did you fall asleep back there?> Javier I was two minutes late, cut me some slack. <I am hungry, and you got in between me and food, so no Daniel I will not cut you any slack.> I playfully shoved him to the side. Javier had completely shaved and he wore a cap

that I am assuming he "borrowed" from somewhere, so he looked disguised enough. Okay, so can we just go in and eat, or do we need to have some sort of card? =This is a giant cruise boat, and they are on their meal time, so anyone can come and eat.= =They will not be checking cards etc, they do that only when it is not the boat's meal time.=

<Thank goodness, now can we stop talking, and go eat!> <I missed you being cranky over food Javier>. Valerie gently hugged him. She also had placed towels under her shirt to help disguise her image. <It is crazy the little things that you miss when your life changes completely.> You are right Valeire, but for now, I say we listen to Javier and enjoy our food, so let's get going.

The dining room was massive. Think of a school cafeteria, and multiply that by ten it was huge. There were hundreds of people there laughing and just having a good time. A Fancy chandelier hung over the center of the room, and there were mirrors on each wall. We came in and no one told us anything or looked at us, so I was relieved.

We went over to the buffet table and grabbed a plate. Then we went to the back of the buffet line. Smells, delicious foods all around. I started to fill my plate with salads, pasta, meats, and even sweets. I was so happy. I felt like I was at HomeTown Buffet or Golden Crowel. We found an empty table and sat down. I went over to the beverage area and grabbed myself a Mountain Dew. I do not normally drink soda, but I needed it at that moment. We ate without talking.

We were just so hungry and the food was amazing, or maybe we were just that hungry. After I finished my plate, I went back up to grab a second slice of chocolate cake, and that was heavenly. Right as I was finishing my cake an announcement went off that the dining room would start closing in 30 minutes. I quickly went back up and grabbed a giant plate. I started putting every bit of food I could in it. There were three men in the front door looking out to make sure no one took food from the dining room, so I asked Claude and Valerie to keep them distracted as I snuck the food out.

They both went over and started asking them how they got their jobs, a simple but effective distraction. I snuck around them and left the dining hall. I took the elevator down 6 floors to my room and knocked on the door, Sevashkish it's me. Sevashkish opened the door and let me in. I gave him the plate and his face was glowing from excitement. He ate the food I kid you not in less than a minute. A full giant plate of food including the coke I had gotten him in less than a minute. I was surprised. [This was the best food I have ever had in my life.] [We Lukens do not eat the way humans do.] [In the 7th dimension food is absorbed throughout the body through the air.]

Sevashkish then why do you have a powerful-looking mouth? If you don't mind me asking of course. [This was our original design, and we have preferred to keep it this way as long as we can, throughout the dimensions.] [It helps us remember who we are, and where we came from.] Oh, I understand, well I am glad that you enjoyed the food. [We do not have the same satisfying tastes as humans do.] Well, I may be from the 3rd dimension, but I hope we don't get rid of the taste of food. Humans love to eat and create new things to eat. [I agree with you 100%.]

Sevashkish I am going to shower, okay? Please let me know if the guys come around. [I will do that Daniel.] I was so glad to be taking a shower. When was the last time I took a shower? I do not even remember. I put the water at the perfect temperature. Not too hot, and not too cold. I stepped in the shower and felt the lukewarm water hit my skin. I was in heaven. The water gently removed the dirt from my skin and the sensation of getting clean felt great. Everything was amazing. It amazes me the little things that we take for granted until they are gone. When I was finished I looked down at my dirty clothes and thought, I am not putting those things back on without washing them first. Even if it meant washing them in the bath. They would get clean.

I put on the bathrobe that was hanging on the door, and it felt so smooth. Usually, bathrobes and towels from hotels have this hard scratchy feeling. Oh, not these. This meant it was a luxury cruise I thought. I opened the drawers of the sink and pulled out a toothbrush and some toothpaste, and I brushed my teeth. Gosh, I can't even start to explain how amazing it felt to brush my teeth.

My teeth went from looking dirty to bright white again in a mere two minutes. The little things I muttered to myself again, it is the little things that matter.

I suddenly got an angry feeling. Life isn't just about surviving. Life is about enjoying the little pleasures that we have. The Phylmecs had taken that way from billions of people, and now they wanted to do it to us. That will not happen. That definitely will not happen. I looked at myself in the mirror and noticed my eyes had gone from a dark brown to a solid red. I was about to release a surge of energy from my anger. Calm down Daniel, calm down I told myself. Take in deep breaths and just walk out of the restroom. Just as I stepped back into the room, Sevashkish was opening the door, and Claude came in.

=Hello Daniel, I just came by to let you know that I saw the schedule for docking in Cancun and it is set for 12:45 pm like we had seen earlier.= =Also, Valerie said she was not coming back out, and that she would meet us at 9 am sharp right by your door.= How about Javier? =Well that is another reason I came to talk to you. I think he is sick to his stomach.= =He ate over five big plates of food and refilled his drink over 7 times.= =He is lying on the bed with a stomach ache, and says you know how to make him feel better.=

I rolled my eyes. Javier in a buffet is not safe. I shouldn't have left. I went over to the mini fridge/bar area and got a cup out. Luckily they had a lemon there already cut in half. I'm assuming for those who drink. I poured water into the cup and smashed the two lemon seeds into the drink. Claude, please tell him to drink all of this, and to be ready by 9 tomorrow. Claude smiled at me, and at that moment I realized that he had shaved off his beard. You shaved your beard! It looks good, and you look younger than me now! =Yeah, I am not with the whalemen anymore, so I thought it was time to look my age.= He smiled and went back to his room with Javier.

Sevashkish do you think we will succeed tomorrow? Sevashkish? I turned and he was fast asleep on his bed. I looked at him, and he was truly an amazing thing to look at. Massive purple wings lined with sword-like tips. The body of a person and beast, but yet this being was a being of peace and hope. We may look different, but our mission is the same. Freedom, hope, and peace. I turned off his light and got into my bed. I closed my eyes, and when I opened them it was 7 am.

I woke up and I was not tired at all. If anyone ever tells you that sleeping outdoors or sleeping on the ground is better than sleeping in a soft cushioned bed, then they are lying. I felt so good and a bit happy. Sevashkish was up and had made his bed. [Breakfast is from 8-10 am.] [I would love for more food if you do not mind Daniel.] Of course Sevashkish. I am just going to get up, do my bed, and head to the restroom.

I took my time doing all of this. Today was an important day. Today was the day that we would save the world, or die trying. I tried to distract my mind from these moments by doing everything slowly. [Daniel, it is 8:15 now, Sevashkish knocked on the restroom door.] I had not realized that I had been staring at myself for over 10 minutes. I am almost finished, Sevashkish, I am just finishing up here. I quickly put on the dirty clothes that I forgot to wash and my shoes. I am heading down there now, is there anything in particular that you want?

[I want some eggs if possible.] You got it. I left the room and headed to the dining room. When I got there it was nearly empty. People love to sleep in I guess. <Daniel, we're over here!> I turned my head and saw Valerie casually having breakfast with Claude. I waved and smiled at them. They were sitting right next to each other, and Claude had his hand over Valerie's hand. I was shocked. This was the first person to ever hold Valerie's hand. I felt happy for her. They are totally crushing on each other, and I am glad Javier wasn't here at that moment because he would probably not stop teasing Valerie. You know the saying it takes one thing to change your life forever? Well, that is 100% true, and Valerie is the perfect example of this.

She lost her sister, and yes she hasn't properly dealt with that loss yet, and she lost control for a while, but all of that is making her a different person. It has made her stronger, and more confident. She was wearing her hair up which she never has, and was talking to other people that weren't Javier and me. I went over and grabbed a plate, and I wasn't feeling too hungry so I just served myself some scrambled eggs and orange juice. By the time I got back to the table Valerie and Claude had stopped "holding hands."

Hey guys, where is Javier? =After I gave him the "tea" you made him, he fell asleep within 30 minutes, and when I woke up he was still sleeping.= I'll go wake him up when I finish breakfast. I do not want him to be mad at us for making him miss it, but how are you two? I winked at Valerie. Her cheeks got as red as her hair. Ready for today? <As ready as I'll ever be.> <I am going to use the pain of losing my sister to stop these vile creatures.> <I feel like I can control my powers better now.> By the looks of it you sure can Val. How about you Claude?

=I just hope I can help in some way, in any way honestly.= I am sure you will be. Do not worry. If Sevashkish saw something in you it is because you have something. Speaking of Sevashkish, I am going to serve him a plate of food. See you guys in an hour outside my room. I quickly filled a plate up with food, and thankfully there was no security preventing people from taking food out of the dining hall. I guess they know that breakfast is usually skipped. I ran over to my room and gave Sevashkish his food. I am going to wake up Javier. It is about 8:40, so he needs at least 20 minutes to eat. [I'll be waiting at 9 for you.]

Javier, Javier! I yelled a bit as I knocked on his door. Wake up! We have to get a move on. <Give me another 20 minutes, please.> Javier, breakfast ends in ten minutes (I was lying of course he still had over an hour to eat.) I had my face next to the door and the next thing I knew I was on the floor, and a barefoot Javier ran out of the room. I picked myself up and went back to the room. That was the only way to wake up Javier. He is such a heavy sleeper. Forty minutes later we were all ready in my room. We were all staring at each other knowing we would have to plan out the day that would decide the fate of the world.

Chapter 19
THE LOSS

Is there a way you can direct everything that we are saying to Tailfin Sevashkish? [Yes, he is near the boat, and I spoke to him this morning, so you can also speak to him.] It always weirds me out to "speak" to someone through my mind. Like I understand we each speak to that little voice in our heads (our soul), but when you use your mind to speak to someone it is just bizarre. Okay everyone, so this is what I know about Chichen Itza. I have been to Chichen Itza before, and there are many, many tourists there. That being said, there are not really any guards, so it shouldn't be too difficult to get up to the sun shrine.

<I know what you mean, I've seen videos of creeps running down the pyramids.> Yeah, so I am hoping there aren't too many guards, Valerie. =How do we get around people seeing Sevashkish?= =With us, it is just a matter of disguising ourselves, but he isn't exactly from this world.= Honestly, I am not sure how we will

do that. How do we even get him off the boat and into town? <He can fly, can't he?> Yes, he can Javier, but what if someone shoots him down again? Sevashkish do you have any idea what we should do? We all turned to stare at him.

[I should not fly with all the military and Phylmecs that will be there, but I will do it anyway.] [Claude, do you know how long it will take everyone to get off the boat?] =I believe it will take about an hour.= [Okay, once everyone is off the boat I will fly out to find all of you.] <Are you sure that is a good idea Sevashkish?> <I do not want you to get hurt.> [Valerie, unfortunately, there is no other way.] [But do not worry, I give you my word that I will make it back with all of you without being hurt.] [At the end of the day the mission is to save Terramondetierra and its children, we have to think about that.]

I turned to look at Valerie and her eyes were filling up with tears as she stared at Sevashkish. <Now look here Sevashkish, you are not going to sacrifice yourself for anyone or anything.> <You are a hero, and you will stay an alive hero> Javier had a determined look on his face. I knew he had figured something out. <I saw some ski equipment while I was walking around the cruise ship. I will go take one and bring it here, and remove the ski equipment, and you will go inside it, got it?> <Some of those bags are well over 10 feet long, and you will fit just fine.>

I couldn't help but smile. We had only been together for no more than a week and a half, and we cared deeply for Sevashkish.

I also knew he cared about us deeply. His big eyes lit up in that strange "Luken" smile. [That works well for me.] Okay, so we will make our way to the forest, and figure out what to do once we are there. I know this sounds bad, but I am thinking of taking a car when no one is looking. Everyone turned to look at me. <Daniel, thee Daniel wants to steal a car?> <Daniel who wouldn't let me take a second milk carton when no one was looking in 6th grade?> <I cannot believe it!> <I guess it is the end of the world.> Oh shut up Javier I said, and we all started laughing, even Claude.

We had a plan and I was nervous, but happy that a plan was made. I told Tailfin of our exact plan. He would follow us around the Yucatan Peninsula, and wait for us in the secret escape passage down to the native-Mayan secret island hiding point. He would have a group of his trusted friends with him just in case we had to make a quick escape at any point. It made me happy to know that he would be there. With a loud thud, the boat hit something. I stumbled slightly. What was that? =The boat has just docked.= Perfect, right on time. We have 30 minutes to get out of here boys and girls.

We quickly put our disguises on and we put Sevashkish in the bag. <Do not forget to leave him some breathing holes.> <Valerie, I am not some sort of barbarian, I know.> Javier rolled his eyes at her but then laughed. She pushed him to the side. <Are we all ready?> Valerie asked. <As ready as we'll ever be.> Okay, I said. Let's go for it. We started our journey out of the boat.

From the moment we exited my room I felt my palms sweating, and like my heart was going to leap from my chest. You know that feeling of overwhelming stress and anxiety? That is what I felt, and I am sure what the others also felt. We were on our way to saving the Earth, but first, we had to make sure to leave this public crowded boat without being noticed. Easier said than done since we had a wanted sign for our heads.

I tried to remember my breathing techniques to slow down a total panic disaster. You will do this, I told myself. You can do it. Believe in yourself. I helped Claude pick up one of the wheels from the ski equipment that Javier was maneuvering over the base of the door. We rushed out of the hall and took the stairs to the lobby. We scanned the lobby and there were only two kids there. We passed the lobby and then we were outside. We made it outside the boat. I guess we were right that people would be busy having fun on a ship to notice "criminals" hiding in plain sight. It kind of says something about human nature. As I passed the exit door, warm humid air hit my face as we left the boat, but I did not care. We had made it outside and we were on our way to saving Earth.

<We did it, we left without getting caught.> Javier's eyes were glowing with glee. All of us were laughing without a care in the world, all but Claude. =The people greeting the guests are Phylmecs.= =The locals selling things over to that corner and bowing their heads to the people on the boat are also Phylmecs.= I turned my head to where Claude was pointing. They had

the tourists sit in chairs, while they placed their foreheads on their foreheads. They were being harvested. Then I heard it. COME FOR FREE RELAXING HEAD MASSAGES. WE HAVE HUNDREDS OF TRAINED MASSAGE STUDENTS WAITING TO DO THEIR SERVICE HOURS FOR EVERYONE ON THIS BOAT. COME, COME, COME IN. EVERYONE WILL GET A FREE HEAD MASSAGE GUARANTEED TO STOP ANY FUTURE MIGRAINE.

I looked around, and even the people who were politely saying no to the Phylmecs were still forced to get a "massage." Eventually, they also got a forehead in their face and sadly fell silent. I felt the blood rush to my face. I was angry. I was so mad that I actually couldn't see straight. I always thought that was something people just say to exaggerate, but the anger that I felt at that moment made me almost blind. <Guys we forgot to get our sweaters from the room.> I turned to look at Javier as he yelled loudly while he was making his way back into the ship.

<I need your guys' help because I don't remember exactly where all of you left your sweaters.> Javier was causing a simple distraction. A believable lie to anyone who may have been suspicious. His plan was simple: get us back into the boat and find another form of escape. We gently pushed others aside as we made our way back into the ship. It took us double the time to get in than it did to get out, but we made it back on board. <Let us stay here until most people leave.>

<We should stay here as long as we can, and hopefully they will leave by then.> <We can't let them turn hundreds of people into Phylmecs!> <We cannot let them Javier.> <Look at all the children and families that are here.> <I know!> <You think I want to stay here while hundreds of innocent people get killed?> <Of course not, but we have to think of the billions that will get killed to save the hundreds for this small moment.> They both looked at me to see what my opinion was, but at that very moment I saw the Phylmecs separate two parents from their newborn, and someone who I assumed was the grandma.

They yanked the parents and placed their heads on them. The helping Phylmecs signaled the grandma and the baby to continue walking to the resort just a few feet from the ship. They would not use a baby or someone too old. The vile fact was, that the very young and very old would be left alone to watch their family being made into Phylmecs.

That made my blood boil. I am sorry Javier, but I can't sit around and do nothing while all these people get killed and left behind to die a slow painful death. I have to do something. Javier looked at me like I was an idiot, but nodded. <What do we do then?> Humans are animals, so I will control their minds to run to the resort with their hands extended out. Valerie, I want you to call on every plant in this area, and to tie these Phylmecs so tight that they can't breathe. Javier, I want you to open the ground once the last human is out of the boat dock area and create a massive hole where they can't be followed once they reach the resort.

Drop rocks on any Phylmec that comes their way. I see some horses in the resort. I will call on them to help us escape. This is going to be the biggest use of our powers, but we have to do it. Tailfin I know you are around, so once every human is out of the way I want you to wash out the Phylmecs that are tied into the sea, and this boat as well.

Once the Phylmecs are washed to sea, this will hopefully give us enough of a distraction to get away. Please take care of yourself, my friend. Claude, and Sevashkish once you see the first horses arrive, I want both of you to get on them. They will head towards the forest. Are you guys ready? They each nodded at me. Let's do this then.

I focused my mind and thought "Humans," run with your arms extended and get to the resort. I looked around and nothing happened. I have to try harder. I closed my eyes and thought of the world, and of its destruction. I thought about how we were being invaded. I thought about how we had been invaded for thousands of years, and I thought "Run." People started to run like crazy. Hundreds of people all at once. Some were trampling over others. Cries and screams were heard, but they were getting past the Phylmecs. Horses come to me, I thought.

I ran out of the ship behind everyone, and I ran towards the horses. I saw a giant palm tree fall right on the Phylmecs' "massage" station. I saw the long vines of the forest coming over to tie the Phylmecs up like robbers. I saw the ground being opened up right down the middle, and by the time we reached the horses, I saw rocks fall on the Phylmecs informant running towards the crowd of people. We are doing it! I yelled while climbing on the back of the horse. Claud and Sevashkish each were on their horses.

=Call the people to run back to the forest, or to anywhere that isn't the resort.= =I saw the people that were in the resorts, and none of them had souls Daniel!= I turned my head towards the sky, the first spacecraft was coming down. Birds come to the skies and attack these crafts. While my horse ran I thought, "Humans run everywhere but the resort, get away and spread the word of the invasion." "It is real, just run and don't let anyone touch your head."

Sevashkish! I yelled in pure stress. I need you to cause a huge thunderstorm, and the most intense fog that you can muster around the forest, please. [I am on it!] I felt the heat before I heard the cries. The spaceship that had arrived was burning the people running. It was burning innocent people in broad daylight. Cutting straight through them. Body parts were being sliced as if it were a meat factory. The smell was unbearable. It smelled like a rotten dumpster.

Sevashkish there's no time, do it now, please I yelled, not realizing that I was crying. Sevashkish flew up to the sky as a suit of bark formed over all of us, including the people who were still trying to run away. My birds finally came and sacrificed themselves by going into the small engines of the ship and taking it down. I heard another spacecraft coming, but by this point, Sevashkish had created a fog so deep that we could not even see our hand right in front of us.

At the same time, a thunderstorm was going on behind us as we all made our getaway on the horses. The horses took us straight into the forest running at speeds that had to be over 60 mph until they finally couldn't run anymore and simply fell to the ground exhausted. They ran for over 40 minutes. Impossible for a horse, but even they felt the despair of my pleas. We were over 40 miles from the scene of the destruction.

We all got off the horses and just stood there for five minutes not saying a single word. Sevashkish broke the silence. [What the Phylmecs did back there is only a taste of what they will do once their official harvest starts tomorrow.] [We must not be scared.] [We must fight!] [We are exactly an hour and 30 minutes away from the shrine, and it is only 2 pm.] [We have plenty of time to get there.] You are right, Sevashkish this is not the time to let sorrow and pain consume us. We will have time to grieve, but I do not want people to go through that again without a fair warning. I want you to transmit a message with the tablet everywhere on the web that you can reach.

<Don't you think the Phylmecs have the worldwide web bugged?> <Does the internet even work?> Javier asked. [If there

is internet then it will reach the people, and as for it being bugged, well I am a Luken, and I can bypass any Phylmec security.]

[I am ready to broadcast the message when all of you are ready, let us just hope that the internet is still working.] <Daniel, I suggest Claude and Javier take their shirts off to give you a sort of background with the shirts over you.> <The Phylmecs would recognize the location that we were in instantly if we didn't disguise it.> Go idea Valerie, boys shirts off, please. Sevashkish, please go live. [Going live on 3, 2, 1.]

"Everyone we are being invaded by highly intelligent conscious transferring, body, and soul-stealing viruses called the Phylmecs." "They have been coming to earth for over 100 thousand years harvesting humans and taking their bodies." "The person's soul gets consumed during this harvesting, and the person not only ceases to exist in this life but in all other potential lives." "15,000 Earth years is the equivalent of 100 Phylmec years, or the average age they can keep a human body alive, give or take 30-40 years.

They will commence harvesting tomorrow. They will go after anyone between the ages of 4-40. Everyone else will be killed when they leave the planet. Please believe me when I say all of this and if you don't just know this, just know our planet is alive, and our planet has chosen us as its warriors to defend it. We will try to take our planet back, but we need you to help. Do not let anyone touch your forehead with theirs I repeat. [Daniel, they have tracked our location, and they will be here at any moment!] [We must go now!]

A dense fog rapidly formed around the forest, but this time not so dense that we couldn't see a few feet ahead of us. Sevashkish grabbed each of us, and we flew low out of there. Thirty seconds later we heard the forest being burned down to the ground.

<Do you think they have an idea of why we are here?> Javier asked Sevashkish. [They do not know, but I guarantee they will do all they can to discover why we are here.] [Some Phylmecs may think we are searching for something significant that Earth has hidden.] [While others may think we are trying to destroy their operations.] [For all we know they may think that we have no clue what we are doing, or maybe that we will try to stop the harvesting in some way.]

<Okay, the best thing we can do is get to the shrine now.> You got that right Valerie, so let's get a move on. [I think I should try flying to get us there faster.] I agree, we have to get this over with. I can't sit around and see more innocent people being killed. For the next 40 minutes we flew on Sevashkish, but we flew extremely low to the ground to not be seen from above. Luckily, the Yucatan area is covered by vast vegetation. After 40 minutes we stopped because Sevashkish was getting very tired.

We stopped near the road, and I noticed that there was too much noise happening on the highway even if it was a busy road. I felt a chill go down my spine. I slowly walked closer to the edge of the road making sure to not be seen. The road was a madhouse. They were pulling people over, and many, many too many people to count had old Phylmecs attached to their heads. People were yelling and screaming and trying to get away, and then I felt a shadow cast over me, and I looked up. It was a giant Phylmec ship hovering up ahead. The scene was right out of a movie. I ran back to everyone. The first half of the harvesting has started!

They are doing it now! Sevashkish turn on the tablet, please! THE THREE HUMANS AND THE ALIEN CREATURE HAVE RELEASED SOME SORT OF VIRUS INTO THE AIR THAT IS AFFECTING MILLIONS AND MILLIONS WORLDWIDE, WE PHYLMECS HAVE AN ANTIVIRAL VACCINE THAT WE WILL SPREAD THROUGH THE AIR. IT WILL TAKE A FEW DAYS TO WORK, SO DO NOT WORRY IF ONE OF YOUR LOVED ONES IS INFECTED BY IT. WE GUARANTEE THAT EVERYONE WILL BE CURED FROM THIS. WE HAVE TO FIND THESE MURDERS AND BRING THEM TO JUSTICE!

<I know what I said about leaving the other people behind for the greater good, but we are not leaving these people to be harvested!> I am with you on this man, <as am I> Valerie said. =The people with the brown uniform are the Phylmecs and those who are obviously attached to the forehead, but the soldiers are all humans.= =Try not to attack them because they have their souls.= The first thing we need to do is get that ship away from those people.

Javier, I need you to use all that power you have and move a mountain or something huge, so you can destroy that ship. You can do it. <I will.> Valerie please create a canape of plants that will shield anyone from any fallen debris. <I'm on it now.> Sevashkish I don't know how I know, but I know that spaceships have a force field. Please use all your might to strike that force field from existence, so Javier can do his job. [You got it, one lightning bolt coming right up.] I'll contact every human and tell them to run, to get away, and to seek shelter anywhere they can.

Are we all ready? I turned to look at my friends as they each nodded yes, and then I saw it. I saw right as it was happening from my peripheral vision. Strong-looking men coming from all directions to attack us. Easily over 6'5 and an easy 250 pounds of solid muscle. I hit the ground hard. I was pushed down hard to the ground. I felt my head bounce twice as it hit the floor. I felt the dirt scrap my cheeks, and I felt warm blood dripping from the side of my face. I tried to punch and kick, but the men had my body still. I tried to move my head to see what was going on, but a third person came over and held my head still as they put their head towards mine. [We are being harvested!]

[Do what you can to fight and escape!] I felt a sense of despair rush through me. This cannot be happening right now that we got this close! I felt a surge of power that I never felt in my life before. "Bacteria in the body, viruses in the body eat these people alive I thought!" Within seconds I felt the cold face of another "person" on my forehead. It was terrifying, but since I had the crystal neck-lace that the native Mayan gave me nothing was happening to me. Then I heard the yelling. The "men" who were Phylmecs started to yell in pain. They stood up and I could finally move away, and I saw how their bodies and faces were being eaten alive by the simple bacteria and viruses that they carried in their body.

Back on their planet, they might have killed all Earth-based bacteria and viruses, but they had been on Earth for almost two weeks, so I knew they would have Earth bacteria and viruses. I ran over to my friends. Valerie was sobbing, Sevashkish had killed the four men who had tried to control him. Several of their limbs were all over the floor. Blood was gushing from the severed parts. Javier's plant cast was shattered, but they hadn't managed to take him down since he was pretty tall and very strong himself. Then I turned and saw Claude. He lay on the ground.

His straight blond hair tangled between twigs and rocks. His head was controlled by a very strong-looking Phylmec who at this point was spasming from being killed by his own bacteria. Sevashkish took one swipe at him with his massive wings and his head went flying. It was too late though, we all knew it was too late. There was a Phylmec attached to Claude. [We must get out of here. I hear their spacecraft coming.]

Sevashkish touched Claude, and he and the Phylmec attached to his head were frozen solid. Valerie put a suit of plant armor all around us, and Sevashkish quickly made the forest covered in deep fog. I was just about to call for a bigger animal to come get us, but at that point, I heard the arrival of the Phylmec spacecraft, so we all ran. We ran for 3 minutes straight till we could no longer hear the spacecraft chasing behind us. We didn't see anything at this point, but we continued to walk for another 30 minutes along the busy road, all the time being cautious not to be seen.

<He saved me.> <He took the Phylmec off of me, and they got him.> <He sacrificed himself for me.> Javier went over and hugged Valerie. <I am sorry, Valerie.> <He is gone, but he will always be a hero.> I stared at Valerie and she silently shook her head. <He was my first kiss.> <It was magical.> Valerie stared at us then put her head down. We did not know what to say, so I went over to a patch of soft dirt near a big tree and I started to dig a hole.

<What are you doing Daniel?> I am going to dig a grave for Claude. He deserves a resting place and respect for his bravery. Javier nodded and came over with a large stick and started to help me dig the hole.

Eventually, Sevashkish and Valerie also came over. Within 30 minutes with immense help from Sevashkish, we had a hole that was at least a little over 6ft deep. Sevashkish gently detached the Phylmec from Claude's body and unfrozen Claude. I stared at the others as I stared at Claude. How has life changed so drastically?

I had never even been to a funeral ever in my life, and now I was staring at a deceased person, and about to put him to lay on the ground. [It is almost 4 pm, and we are about 40 minutes away by car.] I stared at Sevashkish, he had spoken to me privately. I am sure about that. He knew I was the person to get the others going, and I would after I gave Claude a farewell speech.

"Claude I may not have known you for a long time, but your death will not be in vain." "We will save Terramondetierra and all of its species, and we will drive these Phylmecs out of our planet once and for all." We all closed our eyes for a moment of silence for Claude, and then I felt his voice in my mind.

=My gift of seeing the souls of others has allowed me to protect my soul and self.= =I am still alive and will go on to my next journey of life.= =I wish you all the best my friends, and thank you for accepting me, even though I was a stranger.= <Did you hear Claude talking to you, or did I just hallucinate all of that?> <You didn't hallucinate anything, Javier!> <I heard him too!> <His body may be dead, but he was able to protect his soul.> <I am so happy he isn't truly gone.>

I ran over to hug Javier and Valerie, and to my surprise, Sevashkish hugged all of us from the back. Maybe Claude's physical body was dead, but his powers had let him protect his actual soul and being. Sevashkish please place his body in the grave, and we will cover it. Five minutes later we left Claude's physical body covered and said our final thoughts to him. Shortly after we were on our way to find a car because the rest of the journey was through open space and we could not risk Sevashkish being seen again.

[The sun will be directly over the shrine in exactly 2 hours, so that leaves us with an hour and 40 minutes to get there.] <How are we going to stop a car right in the middle of a highway?> <Oh leave that to me, oh you leave that just to me.> I looked at Javier and he had a mischievous look. Try not to use your powers Javier, we are too close to the shrine and can be easily tracked. <Oh I won't use my powers.>

Javier took his shirt off and proceeded to tie his shirt over his head in a way moms tie a towel around their heads after a shower. He then took his pants off and tied his jeans over his neck to imitate a cape I assume. Then he ran to the street and started to run in circles yelling, "Where am I?" "Someone help me." I was about to slap him silly when an SUV pulled over to the side of the road. It was an older lady.

She looked like a Mayan to me. She got out of her car, and she couldn't have been more than five feet tall. She had dark skin with long dark white hair that almost reached her feet. She spoke in Spanish, so I translated for Valerie and Javier. "What is the matter with you?" "Are you okay?" "Do you know where you are?" "What is your name?" Before Javier could answer Sevashkish came out from behind the tree and grabbed the lady, and we all ran into her big SUV. I ran into the driver's seat and made sure that everyone was in and we took off.

I looked through the rearview mirror and to my surprise the old lady was not yelling, and she did not seem frightened at all. She then started to speak a language that I can only assume was Mayan. Sevashkish began to translate for us. "So you are the famous aliens that are trying to kill humanity, right?" "You must not be that powerful if you need to steal a car from an old lady."

She smiled at each of us. "I am part of a committee of elders who preserves the ancient customs and traditions of the Mayan people and we know that you aren't bad." "You sir, you are a being from another dimension." "The elder leader felt that you are not from this "dimension." "You do not emit the same energy as us humans, or even as the Phylmecs." "What are you?" "What do you want?"

To us, she spoke in Spanish, "Why are you humans here?" "What is the purpose?" "Please tell me and I will do everything that I can to help you all." So for the next twenty minutes, we told her everything that was truly going on. We told her who we were, and why we were here. She looked at us and got a deep sad look on her face. "You are missing a crucial part of your plan I am afraid, and it hurts me more than you know, but this is what will happen next." We all looked at her in surprise. [What do you mean?] "For your plan to work, for the heart to open you must sacrifice a person."

What do you mean by having to sacrifice a life? "In our old Mayan texts whenever we wanted a good harvest, or the rains to pour down we sacrificed a willing soul to the Gods, or to Earth I now assume." "They granted us with a beautiful harvest and plentiful rain the next year." "If you ask for something you must return what you have asked for." "Life and energy are shared on this planet, and we Mayans have always known this." "It is an act of balance." "Maybe I am wrong, but what if I am right?" "I will say that I believe Earth needs a soul to return to it, for its heart to be fully activated on the shrine." "It is a delicate balance of 3 between Terramondetierra, the sentient being that is being sacrificed, and the sun's brilliant life-giving energy."

<Why must it be on the shrine?> "Well young lady, this shrine is built over a strong magnetic wave of the Earth, and it is built in a way where Terramondetierra can absorb the sun's life-giving energy." I do not know how I feel about this, I told the others. Sevashkish, what do you think? [I think this woman may be correct.] [Earth may need a soul to return to it for the heart to be reactivated.] [It may need this soul as an exchange of energy to be given back between people and itself.] [It could also be just a regular coincidence.]

How about you Javier and Valerie? Valerie looked at me and said, <I do not know what to believe anymore Daniel, but I will trust whatever you say.> <You have the best judgment in my opinion.> <You have always been the most honest person that I've ever known.> <I know that you always have people's best interests in mind.> I glanced at Javier and he smiled. <I agree with everything she said.> <I will add that I believe Sevashkish is correct, I think Earth can only do so much, and sometimes needs its soul or energy back to help let's say the Mayans have a better harvest.> <Plus if

Earth gets the soul back from the person that is being sacrificed then that means that person is not truly dead.>

238

Chapter 20
WE MADE IT TO THE SHRINE

M a'am, I am sorry I never asked, but what is your name? "My name is Joaquina, and may I ask what you all have decided since we are about to arrive in Chichen Itza?" Joaquina we have decided that we will sacrifice a life to save the world, but we do not know where to find this life. I stared at her intensely, and she started to cry. "My son is the one who has the burden of self-sacrifice, and this breaks my heart, but I truly believe that his sacrifice will, as you say, save the world." I stared at her, surprised by her response.

I was taken aback by her revelation, but I let her continue speaking. "I always knew that he was meant for something higher than himself." "You see he was born with a birthmark on his chest that looks like an Earth picture taken from space." "I always knew that his life was connected to Tierramondetierra's life." "Having you all here only proves my point." I felt goosebumps form on my arms.

Javier looked at me and smiled. <You know when she mentioned her son I thought she was maybe a little crazy, but what she is saying makes sense.> <Life is bringing us all together to save Terramondetierra.> Javier gently smiled at a weeping Joaquina. Joaquina wiped her tears and called her son. She spoke in Mayan, so I did not understand. I did not ask Sevashkish to translate either. The conversation was something that had to stay private. That is what I felt at least. Soon after Joaquina ended her call, we arrived at the entrance of one of the 7 Wonders of the World, Chichen Itza.

As we pulled up to the park a man who was maybe around 35 years old came over and knocked on my window. He had a scared look on his face. "Is Joaquina my mother there?" Yes, please come in. The door to the side of the SUV opened and Joaquina's son came in. "My name is Panchueto, and I am pleased to make your acquaintance." He shook all of our hands including Sevashkish's hand.

"I am quite happy to see that my life has a true mission." <Are you sure you want to sacrifice yourself, over something that may not even be true?> "Young lady, I appreciate your concern, but I know deep down in my heart that my life will save the lives of billions of people, plus my soul will live on." He grabbed his mom's hands and they both hugged and cried in each other's arms.

We didn't say anything during this time, but it was Sevashkish who broke the silence. [How will we do this?] [It is 5:00 pm now, and we must be by the shrine at peak sun brightness, which is at 6:00 pm.] [We also need 5-10 minutes to make sure the heart goes into full effect.] His words made my stomach fall onto the floor. This was now or never. The literal fate of the world came down to this last hour. I stared at my friends. They all looked terrified. I believe even Sevashkish looked scared. I was so scared that I could not even swallow my spit.

I turned my gaze toward Joaquina and Panchueto, and they surprisingly looked anything but scared. They looked determined and prideful. They had small smiles on their faces. To them, this was their purpose. It made me smile, and it renewed my motivation. Okay, everyone, any ideas on how we will climb the shrine?

<A distraction would be nice, but not a dangerous distraction.> <We have to make it look like a simple stupid tourist distraction.> Like what Javier? <Have you ever heard of Jerusalem syndrome?> <Oh yes!> Valerie shouted from the back seat. Oh gosh, I muttered under my breath. Yeah, I have heard of it too, and you know what?

That is a perfect idea, but who can we use to cause the distraction? Valerie pointed at Joaquina. <She will.> Javier looked at me and nodded in agreement with Valerie. They were both right. It had to be Joaquina. As bad as it may seem, having an older lady visit an ancient religious sight and have a psychotic breakdown is believable.

I told Joaquina what we needed her to do. She agreed. She would go up to the shrine at 5:40 pm and start to speak in Mayan-Spanish. She would yell hysterically that she was the new God. This would give us time to walk over to the shrine, unnoticed. Once we got there, Sevashkish would simply fly over to the shrine, and then we would put the heart into its place. After that Sevashkish would create a dense fog so no one could see but us. Valerie would arm up our bodies to give us time to get to the underground Cenote.

That is where the secret escape water passage is located. Tailfin would be waiting for us, and we would hopefully escape. That was our plan, and I prayed to God that it worked, or, well let's just not think about the "or" right now. It was 5:20 pm by the time we had our plan planned, so we spent the next 20 minutes in the car just talking about our life back home. We were doing nothing more than keeping our minds distracted from what we were about to do.

We didn't talk about our families. Maybe we were scared that they were no longer there, or maybe we did not want to get too emotional. What we talked about was our friends and school, and what our hometown probably thinks of us. <Guys I am sure everyone is probably like, I knew they were weird.> <They were always studying and super quiet.> Um, Javier I don't think they would be saying that. They would probably be saying, 'Wow, yeah, I knew something was strange with them." "They always hung out with that Javier dude who was always trying to joke over things that were not even funny."

Javier flipped me off, and we all started laughing. It felt good to laugh, especially before a mission that would change the course of human history forever. At around 5:30 pm, we all fell silent in the car. Joaquina and Panchueto were hugging each other silently. They had taken one last photo and video of each other together. It was very heartbreaking to see. He spoke to her in Mayan, so I could not understand what they were saying, but the time came. It was 5:40 pm and we had to get started.

Joaquina kissed her son on the cheek and he said a few words to her, and then she was gone. We saw her reach the shrine at exactly 5:48 pm. Joaquina did not waste one single minute. She started right away with her acting. By 5:51 pm she had a crowd of several hundred people looking at her and taking videos of her. At this point, we left the van. Everyone but Sevashkish. We quietly went around the crowd of people and got to the shrine at 5:57 pm, and at 5:58 pm Sevashkish flew to join us.

My heart felt like it was going to jump out of my chest, but everything was going as planned. All eyes were on Joaquina. At 5:58 pm with 37 seconds right before Sevashkish was about to land, someone turned their head back and yelled. THE ALIENS ARE ON THE MAYAN SHRINE! LOOK! THE ALIENS ARE ON THE MAYAN SHRINE! The mob of people all formed a tight circle around the shrine. WE HAVE TO STOP THEM.

WE MUST KILL THEM BEFORE THEY KILL US. 5:59 pm I took out TT's heart and placed it on the shrine. Instant dense fog blinding everyone but us.

A suit of hard torns formed around my body. As thick as steel. Valerie had gotten good at controlling her powers. Panchueto put his head on TT'S heart. Now it was my turn. I had to dig deep down in my soul to get the heart to unlock. Something in me knew that just having the sacrifice and the sun would not be enough. I used every single ounce of energy that I could muster, and I closed my eyes and formed a mental image in my head of Earth.

Of Earth and its children. Of all its animals and beings big or small. I focused harder, and finally, I opened my mind to the people and the animals. I let them view my story. I felt like Professor Xavier from X-Men. That is what it felt like. I was letting everyone that I could reach, view what had happened to me and my friends the last two weeks.

I was connected to their minds, and they were connected to mine. I was showing them what the Phylmecs were. I no longer needed the tablet. I wasn't sure how many people it would reach, but I knew that I was reaching millions, maybe even billions. I would reach those with an open mind and soul all across the world. I tried to picture different faces and cultures that I had seen throughout my life.

Next, it was time to find Terramondetierra. I had to find Terra-mondetierra and give it its heart back. I heard screams in the far distance, and I tried my best to ignore them. I felt myself shaken as if I were on a roller coaster. I felt intense heat over me. I heard the cracking sound of wood burning as my plant suit was withering away.

Still, I kept my eyes closed and I pictured Terramondetierra. I knew in my heart that I had to form a connection with it, so I could give it back its physical heart that contained all its life-giving energy. That was the only way all of this would end.

Finally, I saw a light so bright that I was once again blinded. I gave Earth its heart back, and it took it, as well as Panchueto's soul. I saw as Earth the physical sentient being took the heart and placed it by its chest. I saw it use as much force as possible to put its heart back into its chest. Panchueto started helping and soon both the heart and Panchueto were slowly but surely going inside Earth. I was happy, but nervous because I could hear screams and cries on the outside. I knew that we were in big trouble. I saw the heart breaking its outer lawyer as it was halfway into Terramondetierra.

At last, Terramondetierra started to speak to me in its wordless ways. What it said to me terrified me. It showed me how the Phylmecs had already begun the harvest, and how those who weren't harvested were left scared and alone. I saw how people's eyes opened up to what was truly happening. The look of sadness and despair. I saw images of people being harvested all over the world; from the tip of China to streets in Paris, France.

I cried silently. Then Terramondetierra "told me" something truly awful. Out of the 9 billion humans on the planet 5.5 billion were capable of being harvested and 3 billion were currently being harvested. That means 2.5 billion humans that are capable of being harvested were left on earth. Plus the 4 billion whom the Phylmecs have no use for. That meant that Earth only had 6.5 billion humans left down from 9 billion just a couple of days ago.

So much terror and pain is already happening. We had to stop this now. I started losing connection with Terramondetierra because I kept getting shaken to the ground. The battle outside was getting out of control. Someone or something had knocked me down to my knees. I put my hands over my head and focused hard. I saw in horror how Terramondetierra's heart was still only halfway in. It was struggling to open. What was happening?

Was someone blocking the sun out, or was one soul sacrifice not enough? My connection with the people had been severed. Something was wrong. I knew at that very moment that Terramondetierra would not have enough energy to put the entire heart back into its chest. It would not be able to release its energy storage.

I was doing everything I could to help it release its energy, and then it "spoke" to me and showed me everything that was happening. The Phylmecs had found Terramondeteirra's "physical body," because of the high energy being released. They were attacking Earth's body. Beams were being blasted at the mysterious being of golden white light. Earth could not hold on much longer.

Unfortunately, the only way for the energy storage to be released was to have Terramondetierra in its original sentient form. Terrarmondetierra! I yelled in agony. You have to return to your planetary form. Your body cannot handle blasting anymore. I felt tears running down my cheeks. It would have to leave or be killed. My heart sank to the floor. Earth would not be able to expel the Phylmecs out of itself.

Terramondetierra reached for my soul as it was being blasted, and touched it. As it was being blasted it showed me that it had opened part of its heart. Some of its life-giving energy had been expelled. This meant that it had destroyed all Phylmec ships on Earth and in orbit. It was also able to destroy all Phylmec technology, including the beam used from the mother ship to aid in the harvesting. All harvesting would reduce drastically.

Earth was doing everything it could to show me what was going on. I felt nervous and terrified, as I felt a strong Phylmecs presence near me. Terramondetierra, please tell me is there anything else I can do to save you, and all life on this beautiful planet? Terramondetierra could not keep communication much longer. I felt it press its entire being around me. I closed my eyes harder and focused. Earth "said" my name, **"Daniel."** That is when Terramondetierra showed me the very last way to rid humanity of these parasites.

I saw images of a raw blue substance. It looked like molten lava, but dark blue. Earth showed me how this blue material aided in space travel. I saw how it could be used to build advanced technology, and how it could also be used to help Earth put the rest of its heart in its body. I saw the location of the blue molten lava. It is hidden within the very core of Terramondetierra. Normally this blue liquid would not be important for the Phylmecs.

Every sentient planet has this blue molten liquid. The Phylmec home planet has plenty in fact, but there is no way for the Phylmecs to harvest it. Blue matter cannot travel through space without the proper manipulation, and this manipulation can only be done on a planet-level gravity, so not in space.

What does this mean, Earth? I yelled in frustration, but then it clicked. The Phylmecs will want Earth's blue matter. They cannot get it from their planet since it cannot travel to space. They need blue matter for survival to get their spacecraft, technological communication systems, and harvesting beams back to work.

Will retrieving your blue matter be enough to get your heart through your chest? I saw the simple answer as a smile. I was glad that it would be enough, but I also got a horrible feeling in my stomach because I knew this blue matter would be used to recommence all Phylmec technology. That is if they found it before we did.

Sadly, Terramondetierra could not retrieve the blue liquid by itself, since it had to be in its physical body to get to it, and its body was so badly beaten up that it would not take another Phylmec encounter again. Also, the energy surge of having Terramondetierra in a physical form would immediately notify the Phylmecs.

Earth then showed me rapid visuals in my mind. It felt like I was watching a movie, on fast forward. It was sending me more information on the blue matter, its whereabouts, and storage. I saw something translucent. I saw a cube. A cube that was jagged and looked as sharp as a knife. This cube was about the size of a normal-sized paint bucket, and it was completely transparent, except for the fact that it contained all of Earth's blue matter.

The blue matter was so powerful that one single gram of it could be used to build faster-than-light space travel. With only a couple of grams, an entire planet could be destroyed while in the wrong hands. Earth's blue matter was what helped Terramondetierra regulate life within itself. That is why it kept it safely locked in its core. Always moving within its own lava.

Earth showed me how it pushed the cube that contained its blue matter to the outer layer of its core. It was the only way to keep it undetectable from any alien eyes and make it reachable to us without causing instant death. The out layer was still a place as hot as the very sun. I did not understand how we would retrieve it, but I knew we would find a way. One way or another we would get it. We would find it and finish pushing it through TT's chest, so the Phylmec threat can be over once and for all.

Terramondetierra and all its children were low on time. My head was spinning in circles. How can I help Terramondtierra? How do I get to your core without burning up? Please show me how. Then everything went completely dark, and Terramondetierra was no longer there. It was pitch black, and I was confused. I suddenly started to hear a ringing in my ear. An intense ring as if someone had shot a gun near me. My body felt hurt. I felt like I had been hit by a car or something. Then I realized that my eyes were still closed, so I opened my eyes, and I saw that the sunset was starting to set. I was lying down, so I got all the energy I had and shakily stood up.

It was hard because every muscle, joint, and bone in my body hurt. When I finally managed to get up, what I saw horrified me beyond belief. There were thousands of dead bodies lying all over Chichen Itza. An image that I would never be able to remove from my head. A scene that would haunt my dreams. Have you ever seen the movie "Day of the Walking Dead?" That is what it looked like.

Deceased bodies all around the compound. What is going on I thought, as tears slid down my face. A cold chill ran down my spine. Where are my friends? Did the Phylmecs take control of the planet? Was it too late, and only a matter of time before Earth caved into itself?

Calm down, Daniel. First, think back to what happened. What did happen? Was it even the same day? I closed my eyes to focus on what exactly occurred on the shrine, and the sacrifice. What happened next? I remember Valerie creating that tough-as-nails tree armor to protect us. I looked down at my body, and I was still wearing half of it. The remains of bark were still covering my knees and feet. I touched my head and half a helmet of hard bark still covered it.

I rubbed my eyes to see clearer into the horizon, but the fog that Sevashkish had created was still everywhere, blurring my view. What had Javier done in the battle? I couldn't remember anything. I sat down to focus better, and then I remembered.

We had to fend off the Phylmecs for a few minutes so Earth could properly open the heart. The Phylmecs arrived shortly after when the people first saw Sevashkish land on the shrine. I remember hearing a voice yelling, "Take this heap of mountains you alien viruses!" It was Javier he had picked up every hill and mountain and rocks, (including every pyramid around,) and had single-handedly destroyed 6 Phylmec ships. I opened my eyes, and now understood what had played out to an extent, but had there been more Phylmec backups?

Maybe not by air, but by ground? Yes! The ground Phylmecs had come after, and Sevashkish and Valerie did what they had to do to stop them. It was too dark to even think about it. What then? I started to playback the strange interaction that I had with Terramondetierra. The Phylmecs could not harvest to their full capacity, nor could they leave Earth without the blue matter, so that meant we must have fended off the Phylmecs long enough for Terramondetierra to have slightly opened its heart. No more spaceships, no more advanced technology for the Phylmecs.

Okay, that is good I thought, they do not have usage of their spaceships right at the moment, or any advanced technology. Unfortunately, they sure had the billions of humans that they harvested, and all of Earth's resources to build new weapons, plus human weapons. They have the codes for every serious nuclear weapon on this planet. This is not good, we had to find Earth's core, but I needed my friends for that. I had to hurry and find them, but my entire body hurt so much. So much pain.

I had bruises all over myself, and I noticed that I had been bleeding from my nose and ears. They had dried blood. I did a self-check and everything else looked okay, well minus the big purple bruises that I had all around my body, at least nothing was broken. I started to yell my friends' names. No answer. Where are they? I had stayed by the shrine, but they hadn't. Where were they? Had the battle gone on for so long? Fear was sweeping through me. Calm down, I told myself. Don't lose your cool. Think Daniel, breathe and think. Where can you go to search for them?

I had no clue. I really didn't, but I knew one thing. The Phylmecs ships could not fly anymore, so they would not reach my location in five minutes, and I still had my powers. There was still some daylight, so I am going to assume I was not knocked out for more than an hour. I had to take the risk to find my friends. I had to call on any animal with a great sense of smell and eyesight to help me find them. I knew that the risk was low of using my powers and getting the Phylmec's attention, but I was still scared. Well Daniel, do like the old saying says, "Sometimes you gotta do what scares you."

Okay Daniel, time to focus; I would call for help and wish for the best. I closed my eyes and thought, "Animals with a good sense of smell and sight, please come to me." "Horses or any big animal that can support the weight of a human for a long period of time, please come to me too." I opened my eyes and waited, and then I noticed the first birds coming in around me. I sent them off to look for my friends. I gave them a description in my mind of how they looked, and then they were gone. I continued to walk down the steps from the shrine. Every step was like getting slapped in the face. I hoped nothing was broken inside of me.

As I waited for the animals to come, I slowly started to remember the rest of what had happened. I had gone unconscious when I tried to warn every person in this world about the Phylmec invasion and show them the truth. I sincerely hoped I had reached enough people.

That was our key to survival. Our key to the survival of our planet was that these people did not allow anyone near their heads. As stupid as it sounds, that was the key. Until we find the blue matter that was locked away in a jagged cube in the very core of Earth. The cube that helped Terramondetierra transfer its energy all around the world. All of its life energy.

I could do it, we could do it. We will win this, I thought, there's no other way around it. I finally made my way down from the shrine when out of the blue my parents came into my mind. Do not ask me how, but I saw them vividly. They were hiding in a cave. A cave not even an hour from my house. A cave that we used to go to when I was younger. Our secret location and escape from the world. They had transmitted their thoughts to me.

I was so overwhelmed. My parents were still alive! I had pushed my parents out of my mind so I would not be sad, but they were alive. They were alive! I closed my eyes and thought about them. I pictured them vividly in my mind, and said, "I am okay, this isn't over, please stay put." "I need you more than ever to stay safe." "We humans will win this, I love you." I felt warm tears rolling down my cheeks. My parents were alive and okay. I got a renewed sense of motivation.

The Phylmecs would not take over this world, and they would not take any more souls. Their time will be up like it was supposed to be over millions of years ago. We will find that cube. They will be stopped, and we will get rid of them once and for all.

Off in the distance, I saw a horse running back towards me, and it was carrying someone, someone big. It was carrying Javier! He looked beaten up. He had a deep wound on the bottom of his cheek, and he was bruised all over his body, but everything else looked to be in place. Javier, I am here! He looked like he was about to fall off the horse. I ran to help him get off the horse, but I was too weak to be of any help. He fell to the ground. I am so sorry!

<It is okay Daniel, you do not look too good yourself.> <What happened Daniel?> <Did we lose?> <Please tell me we didn't lose.> I spent the next 15 minutes explaining what was going on with Earth to Javier. While at the same time, we were still looking for Sevashkish and Valerie. <So we have to go to Earth's core and retrieve the cube?> <How long do we have to do this?>

I do not know how long we have. All I know is that the Phylmecs need the blue matter as well, in order to better execute their harvest. <Well at least they do not have their weapons anymore.> That is true, but let's not forget that the Phylmecs have control of Earth's technological forces.

That being said, you are right. At least they do not have their own weapons. <Unfortunately, they have plenty of weapons to last a lifetime here on Earth.> <More than enough to control the 2.5 billion humans, plus the 4 billion that they have no "use" for.> <We got to find the others, and fast.>

Javier, what happened to your cheek? <When the heart was put in place, and Pancheuto was sacrificed a huge energy surge occurred and six Phylmecs ships showed up within 30 seconds.> <It was a nasty battle.> <A barbaric battle.> <You opened a transmission in everyone's mind I believe and people started to come over to help us.> <They started throwing rocks, and sticks, and shooting bullets at the Phylmecs' ships in vain.>

<Daniel, innocent people were sliced and diced by the powerful rays.> <They were slowly burned alive.> <They felt their pain,

they screamed and yelled and cried.> <I was so mad that I picked up the very foundation that we are standing on, all but your part, and dropped it on 6 of the ships, and they were destroyed.>

<Sevashkish, saved my life.> <He used all the force he had to electrocute all the ground Phylmecs, but a bit of the ricochet of a ray by a ground Phylmec hit the side of my cheek.> <I guess I'll be getting a nice little battle scar there.> <Sevashkish used so much energy that he was swept away.> What do you mean? <He created a tornado to destroy the remaining ships that were coming as reinforcements, but the tornado was so powerful that it also swept him away.> I am sure he is okay. He is strong and smart.

What about Valerie? <Valerie went over to immediately help out the people.> <She created a thorn barrier that you can see over there across the forest.> I turned my head and it was hard to notice at first because it looked so natural, but I could see the edges of the unnatural hill now. Is she still there? <I do not think so, before I went unconscious they sent another ship, and the next thing I remember is the horse coming to me.> We got to start with the hill, Javier.

It took us about 15 minutes to get to the hill, but our search was in vain. There was nothing there. Absolutely nothing. I closed my eyes again, and thought "Powerful eyes, come help me find my friends again." "Strong sense of smell, good hearing." Help me find my friends again. <Should we go into the forest?> Yes, let's go!

We slowly walked into the forest, and something powerful, or some powerful things jumped down from the tree. It startled me and scared me a bit. It was two jaguars. Two powerful muscular animals. The only big cats that lived in the Americas came over to me.

I got on the back of one and held it tightly. Its sleek fur felt smooth on my skin. We climbed back up the tree. There in the middle of the tree surrounded by a fortress of leaves and twigs was Valerie. I was beyond happy to see her, but I was quite shocked by what I saw. Most of her long red hair that she once had was burned off. Her hair was up to her ears all around. I looked at her, and before I could say anything she hugged me. <Daniel!> <I am so glad that you are alive.>

<When I left to save the people, I saw you being blasted endlessly for a minute straight by a Phylmec ship.> Wait, I was being blasted? I thought Sevashkish and Javier took out all the ships. <Javier and Sevashkish took out all the ships that they could until they too disappeared.> <I did my best to help you, Daniel.> <I truly did, but the entire vegetation in your area was burned.> <There was nothing that I could do but sit and watch in agony.> She slowly turned her head away in shame.

Valerie do not worry about anything. I know you did everything in your power to save me, and I am alive. I am beaten up, but alive. <How did you survive that blast, Daniel?> Honestly, I do not have a clue. I didn't even know that I was being blasted. Do you know what happened to the other ship? <Yes, large and I mean large birds came and started bomb-diving the spaceship, and ultimately one got into the engine and destroyed the entire thing.> I suddenly realized what probably happened. Earth must have shown up in its physical form and protected me. Terramondetierra saved my life.

I knew that was it, and that was probably the reason why its physical body was so hurt. I felt a lump in my throat. Was I really that important to Earth's survival that it came in its physical form to save me? My thoughts were cut short when Valerie asked me a question. <Have you seen Javier or Sevashkish?> <Are they okay?> Javier is down the tree waiting for us, and I am still trying to find Sevashkish. Are you ready to go? <Yes I am ready to get out of here.>

Also, Valerie, where are the people that you saved? <When we got away I was about to tell them the entire story, when all of us got a sudden surge of images of the past two weeks of our lives, and then they understood.> <I told them to help spread the word, and to get ready for a fight if necessary.> <They fled as soon as it was safe.> <I hope they made it safely with their loved ones.>

I am sure of it, but let's get going. We both got on the majestic jaguar and he took us out of the tree to the bottom where Javier was waiting. Before Valerie, and Javier could even hug we all heard the voice in our heads. [Daniel, Valerie, Javier are you here?] [I am looking for you, please shout if you hear my call. I looked up to the sky past the canopy of trees and saw the purple figure with the golden wings flying across the forest. It was Sevashkish. He was alive and he was looking for us. We all shouted instantly at the same time. "WE ARE HERE."

Chapter 21
ASTRAL PROJECTING

Sevashkish flew down right in front of us. His massive wings slowly stopped flapping and he ran on all fours to greet us. He embraced us in a tight hug. [I had feared the worst.] [I am beyond happy that all of you are safe.] His eyes were filled with tears. It was emotional. We had just known Sevashkish for about two weeks, and yet we all felt like we knew him for a lifetime <I am glad you are okay, big boy.>

[I am glad that you are okay too, Javier.] After an emotional interaction, we began to speak about what had happened to each of us since we got separated. As I had already heard what occurred to Javier and Valerie, I was curious to hear what had happened to Sevashkish. Tell me Sevashkish, what happened to you when we got separated?

[As Javier stated the tornado was very powerful and took me with it, and I eventually crashed and landed on a canopy of trees.]

[I do not know how long I was out, but I awoke to the sound of helicopters flying around.] [I quickly got up and made sure nothing was broken and left the spot.] [I went down to the forest and hid until I was sure all the helicopters were gone.] [I also heard your message Daniel, and I believe most if not all sentient beings heard it too.] [The world now knows of the Phylmec threat, and that is a double-edged sword.] Why do you say that?

[Some people will not be able to handle this scary reality, and chaos will come.] [I should point out that chaos is already here, but it will grow out of control to mania levels.] Oh no, I hope that isn't the case. <Do you know where we can find the location of the blue matter?> [I am not sure Javier, but Tailfin may know where it is at.] <We have to go to Tailfin then!> <I hope Tailfin is okay.> Valerie, I am sure he is okay, and I am sure he is patiently waiting for us to return to him. I just hope he isn't worried sick about us. <Okay, so what do we do now, do we go find Tailfin now, or do we rest?> Javier asked.

They instinctively stared at me to see what I would decide. It felt weird becoming the "leader" in all of this, but the others for some reason or another saw me as someone who was a leader I guess. It was a double-edged sword for me. On one hand, it did make me feel a little happy and prideful that they saw me as a leader, but on the other hand what if I made the wrong call, or what if I got someone hurt? Having the lives of others hanging over your head is not something one wants.

The only thing that made me feel better was that I took everyone into account when making a decision, so in reality, everyone was partially the leader as well. I guess I would call myself more of a team-builder than a leader. That made me feel better, even though I knew deep down that I was the leader.

I felt everyone's eyes stare at me as I decided. They all looked scared and tired. <Hello, Daniel, so what's it going to be?> I blinked at Javier as he snapped his fingers in front of my face, oh sorry I said jumping back to reality. Sevashkish, how do we get to the hidden Cenote to find Tailfin? [He is right under the shrine.] [We must remove one brick from the base of the shrine and fall straight into the hole, right into the Cenote.] Javier went over to Sevashkish and gently tapped his shoulder, <Why does everything we do involve jumping into a black hole where we do not know what awaits us at the bottom?>

We all started laughing, and Valerie responded with, <Hey we know water and hopefully Tailfin will be down there this time!> <Yea let's hope that there's water there and not solid ground.> Only one way to find out. Let's head there now.

It took us about 30 minutes to walk back to the shrine. It was absolute torture. There were lifeless bodies all around the area. Kids so young, probably no more than 2 or 3 years old. Families hugging each other all over the floor. There was blood everywhere, and the smell was so strong that it made me feel nauseous. Our shoes were covered with fresh thick blood. It was like a scene from the worst horror movie imaginable. We had to be careful to not step on any remains as we walked. I couldn't even begin to fathom how bigger cities looked.

We eventually took flight with Sevashkish because there were way too many bodies to walk around. Also, Javier's injuries were getting to be too much for him to walk any longer. I hoped that he was okay. He kept huffing and puffing. It scared me, but thankfully we finally arrived at the shrine with no one falling over. We landed safely at the base of the shrine.

Okay, so how do we know which stone block to remove? [It will have a symbol of the Earth.] [A symbol that only you, Daniel, should be able to recognize.] Only me? How am I supposed to know? Then by mere luck, I stared at a stone that was just to my left. It looked like the birthmark that I have on my lower back. Shaped like a crescent moon. It is that one I said. They all looked at me in surprise. <You found it that fast Daniel?> <Are you sure?>

Yes, I am sure Valerie. It has the same mark that I have on my back. I lifted my shirt and showed them. They agreed, and Sevashkish removed the giant stone block. We looked down into the deep empty hole. [I will go in first since I am the least injured.] [I will check if Tailfin is down there, and if he is I will fly back up and carry you down to him.] That sounds great Sevashkish. You truly are Earth's hero, and when this is all over I want everyone to know that. I smiled at him, and he soon went down the hole.

After a couple of minutes, we all started to get nervous. <Okay guys, I am going in after him.> Valerie there is no way you are going after him. If it has taken him over twenty minutes to come back that means the fall is long, and a fall like that will kill you. Water or no water, at this height the water is as solid as the ground. <Well we just can't sit around here and do anything.> <She is right Daniel.> <We have to do something.> I agree with you all, but I have faith that he will be okay. He just needs time.

It is pitch black there, and we do not know how massive the Cenote is. Also, [I am coming back up everyone.] A wave of happiness swept over me, and I could tell the same happened to my friends when they heard Sevashkish's voice by the look on their faces. [I am sorry for having kept you waiting for so long.] [It is beyond dark, and quite massive under there.] [Also, there are many hidden caves that each contain small lakes, so it was hard to locate what cave Tailfin was in.]

Did you find Tailfin? [Yes, he is waiting for us, and he is quite content that we are all alive.] [He was starting to feel very scared, and feared the worst.] I am so glad that he is okay. Tailfin may not be able to go on land, but he has been part of the team from the very first moment. He is as important as any of us in all of this.

It took well over 5 minutes to reach the area where Tailfin was located within the cenote. Sevashkish was not lying when he said the place was pitch black, lucky he knew where to find Tailfin. We slowly landed on Tailfin. {I am so happy you are all here because I was starting to fear the worst.}

<Tailfin you really think we would be taken out that easily?> Um Javier have you looked at yourself I said with a smirk that no one saw. <Hey!> <Who shoved me?> <Oh, sorry Valerie, I thought you were Daniel.> We all started laughing. It felt great to be together again.

We quickly debriefed Tailfin on everything that had happened. He figured something like that had occurred since he heard my pleas for caution of the Phylmec threat. <What do we do now?> <Where do we go from here?> <How do we even search for the jagged cube?> <Do you think it will be before the Phylmecs find it?> [Valeire, I think the first thing we should do is get back to the original Mayan tribe with Kach'ma'o-k and her people.] I couldn't stare at anyone since it was too dark, but I shouted out, "Everyone okay with that?" They each agreed, so next came the hard part.

The thing we had never done since this whole thing started. We would have to climb inside Tailfin. We would have to dive deep into the water to get to the secret passageway. This meant being underwater under tremendous pressure. Tailfin was the only one who could get us there safely. It might not sound like a big deal, but it is.

When we first started this journey we had all agreed to strictly stay on Tailfin's back. It was a "respect" thing. None of us would want someone going inside our mouths, but times were different now. I am so sorry Tailfin, <so am I, me too,> [I am sorry.] {Do not worry, it is hopefully only a one-time thing.}

Out of all the craziness that we had been through these couple of weeks, going inside Tailfin was up there on the list. Have you ever heard of Jonah and the Whale? Well, that is exactly what we were doing. <Hey Tailman are you sure it is okay that we go inside of you?> <We can find a different way.> <I do not want to disrespect you.> {Thank you for asking Javier, but it is okay.}

{We are in a dangerous time and we have to do everything in our power to save the world.} {Besides I eat over 8000 pounds of food each day, so you guys weigh nothing for me.} <Wow this is a wake-up call for me.> <It took a 300,000-pound whale to make me feel skinny.> We all started laughing. Javier has a way of making us all smile even in the scariest of times.

Stepping on Tailfin's tongue felt like stepping on a newly made track. It felt foamy, but firm. His hot breath made it hard to breathe, like on a hot humid day in Miami. His breath smelled like dead fish, but that is something that I'll keep to myself. He closed his mouth and everything went dark. {Everyone, hang on tight, we should be there in 7 minutes.} We got there in six minutes. Tailfin resurfaced and we were back on the little island of the Mayan. The ride was not bad at all. It felt like riding on a high-speed rail; super fast, but barely noticeable. We did not move at all while inside of him. We all gently stepped out of Tailfin's mouth and onto the soft island sand. Our clothes were moist, but not wet, thankfully.

It was almost dark at this point, but still light enough to see everyone's faces well. We all looked like a mess. Javier looked and probably felt like a car ran him over, Valerie looked like she wrestled a bear. Sevashkish looked like what had happened to him exactly; taken by a tornado. I looked at myself closely, and I was just as equally a mess as everyone else. I was bruised in almost every location of my body, but at least nothing was broken. Javier on the other hand had his already broken arm swollen at least three times the size that it should be. I hope Kach'ma'o-k would be able to do something about that. {Before you guys go I want to let you know something important.}

I felt chills go through my body because something in the way that Tailfin said those words made me uneasy.} {I have gotten word that the Phylmecs are dynamiting every major city in the world.} {They do not have access to nuclear bombs since Earth was thankfully able to disable them, but dynamite is still accessible, and Earth has a lot of that.} [They are trying to cause as much chaos as they can.] [This will force people from their homes, and when people are scared they go back to basic instinct.]

<They come together in groups for security.> Bingo, they will be easy to find and harvest. <We have to find that translucent jagged cube, Daniel, before it is too late.> I nodded at Valerie and looked at the others. We were tired and bruised, but we wouldn't give up. Tailfin I will call for you once I know exactly what we will be doing,

please stay nearby. {Don't worry Daniel, and all of you I will be here right under all of you.}

We said goodbye to Tailfin and right as we started walking two native Mayans were already standing patiently by us, waiting to take us inside. We walked to the hidden passage, and soon enough we were going through the hollow tree that leads to the underground town. Kach'ma'o-k, stood eagerly by the edge of the slide waiting for us. It took us about 40 minutes to tell Kach'ma'o-k everything that had happened. She stood there looking at us. Her gaze went from anger and fury to sadness and even a hint of fear and empathy.

"We will have a feast to celebrate your victory because even though it may not seem like a victory, it is." "You have stopped these monsters from destroying our planet for now, and they cannot leave until they harvest the remaining 3 billion people or so, and I have faith that you will all succeed in finding Earth's blue matter" <Ma'am you have more faith in that then we do.>

"Young man you must believe in yourself, or all will truly be lost." Javier didn't look too convinced, but he didn't say anything to Kach'ma'o-k. He just rubbed the back of his head and smiled at her. "You will all sleep here tonight, and relax, and tomorrow we can decide where to start looking for this jagged box that contains Earth's blue matter."

At that very moment, I knew that Kach'ma'o-k was truly a good leader. She knew how to make her people feel safe even though I could tell she didn't believe what she was saying, at least not 100%. She knew what she had to do, and she did it. I respected her for that, and I felt inspired by her.

After dinner, we all went to our beds. As I lay on my bed I started to think of so many things, so many thoughts ran through my head. I couldn't even focus on one. I just kept seeing people dead all over the world. I replayed the images that Terramondetierra had shown me of Phylmecs harvesting as many people as they could. I imagined different scenarios in my mind. I imagined how some people would fight back, and how others would hide. That gave me hope and peace. I closed my eyes slowly, and I must have fallen asleep at some point because I started to dream.

I was in a brightly lit room with many older angry people yelling at each other. HOW COULD WE LET THESE MONKEYS BEAT US? THIS WAS OUR TICKET OUT FROM THE 3RD DIMENSION AND STRAIGHT INTO THE 7TH! HOW IS IT POSSIBLE THAT A LUKEN WAS ABLE TO STEP INTO THE 3RD DIMENSION WITHOUT CAUSING HARM TO HIS OWN DIMENSION? I looked around the room. There were 7 Phylmecs, and in the center sat a very young boy, no more than 5 years old. He stood up and everyone sat down immediately.

NEVER MIND ALL OF THESE QUESTIONS, THE THING IS TERRAMONDETIERRA FIGURED OUT A WAY TO GET ONE OF ITS MONKEYS TO HELP IT. THEY HAVE SUCCEEDED IN DISARMING ALL OUR SPACE

CRAFTS AND ALL OTHER REAL WEAPONS THAT WE HAVE. WE MUST ACT FAST. OUR FIRST GOAL IS TO FIND THE BLUE MATTER BEFORE EARTH'S MONKEYS FIND IT. OUR SECOND GOAL IS TO SEND OUR PEOPLE TO HARVEST ANYONE THAT THEY SEE. REGARDLESS OF WHEN AND WHERE. WE HAVE TO HARVEST ALMOST 3 BILLION PEOPLE TO MOVE TO THE 7 DIMENSIONS, AND THE CHERRY ON TOP; EARTH WILL DIE. WE WILL DO IT. WHY? WE ARE THE PHYLMECS. SMARTER THAN ANY SPECIES OUT THERE, AND WE WILL RULE THE COSMOS.

I stared at this little boy as he spoke. This must be their leader I thought. The original old man who gave his speech just weeks ago in all those languages. There was no way to deny it, this was Tindawnstong. He had a new body, he was revived. DO YOU ALL WANT TO KNOW HOW CLOSE I FEEL 7TH DIMENSION? They all stared at him with dead curiosity in their eyes. SOMEONE IS IN HERE. They all looked around the room. WHO? Tindawanstong looked straight at me. HE IS HERE.

DANIEL THE EARTH MONKEY IS HERE. I FEEL HIS PRESENCE. HE IS SPYING ON US NOW. All the Phylmecs turned around and stared at where their kid leader was pointing. FOCUS HARD AND CLEAR EVERYTHING FROM YOUR MIND AND YOU WILL SEE. YES! YES! YES! They all started to yell, "I CAN FEEL HIS PRESENCE." YOU SEE MY FELLOW

PHYLMECS WE ARE ALREADY GETTING STRONGER. AS FOR YOU DANIEL THERE IS NOTHING YOU CAN DO TO STOP US, AND I PROMISE I WILL PERSONALLY FIND YOU AND HARVEST YOU MYSELF!

He came towards me, and I ran. YOUR TIME IS RUNNING OUT DANIEL, YOU AND YOUR FELLOW MONKEYS WILL BE GONE WITHIN THE WEEK. AFTER KILLING YOUR MONKEY CLAUDE THERE IS NO WAY THAT YOU HUMANS CAN TELL WHO IS A PHYLMEC AND WHO ISN'T. I stopped running. He struck a nerve. You underestimate us, you parasite, and I promise you that it will be you who will perish. I looked the "kid" straight in the eyes, and before I could speak, I was out of their spaceship. I was suddenly on a mountain.

It took my eyes a few seconds to adjust to the calmer light, but I knew exactly where I was. I was in Honolulu, Hawaii. I was standing on the Koko Head Volcano. I knew why I was here. This was a volcano that had been dormant for years and years. Earth's blue matter had to be there. It had to be dead in the center of the mountain. Protected by layers of crusted lava that had become hard thick rocks.

I stood atop the Koko Head Volcano, and I looked down ahead. I saw all the continents. I saw all those who had died and became Phylmecs. In their billions. Then I saw the bright silhouette come towards me. It was Terramondetierra. Terramondetierra placed its hand on my chest, and I saw through its eyes. It was weak, very weak. Just imagine a person who is fighting for their life in an ICU, and that is how Terramondetierra looked and felt. It was dying, and with it every human who ever came to be.

Every human that was harvested was like a slap to the face to Terramondetierra. One can only take so many hits. It has no more than a couple of weeks left if we do not find that jagged box with the blue matter. It would have less time if the Phylmecs harvested the almost 3 billion capable of being harvested, humans.

I felt Earth's grief. It felt its sadness and its despair, but still with a shining glimmer of hope. Terramondetierra still had hope that we would succeed, so that new life would grow from the destruction. New life to keep the Phylmecs from ever ruling or hurting it again. I felt the hope it still had for all of us. I felt tears falling down my cheeks. I rubbed the tears away as they fogged my vision.

I will do all in my power to get to Hawaii and take care of this threat Terramondetierra. Terramondetierra came closer to whisper something in my ear, but before I could hear I heard my name being called. <Daniel, Daniel please wake up.> <We do not have more time.> <The Phylmecs are here, and we cannot keep so many at bay.> <They are here in the dozens.> <They have new young and very fit bodies with deadly human weapons.> <We must evacuate immediately.> Valerie was screaming desperately trying to wake me. <Javier please carry him because he is not even responding to my slaps or screams.>

[Tailfin is waiting for us, so we can retreat, and we must go now.] [The Native Mayans have sent 50 of their top soldiers onto the island to distract them, but even they cannot keep them at bay for too long.] I am not sure what it was in Sevashkish's voice, but that woke me up immediately. What I did next is something that would haunt my dreams for the rest of my life. I looked deep into myself and remembered all the bacteria and even viruses at the microscopic level that live within us, and I thought of one single word, kill. Kill slowly and painfully. I wanted them to suffer.

Within seconds all the Phylmecs were down on the ground screaming and dying in pain. Completely eaten alive from the inside. It was a scene of pure carnage. Valerie helped me to my feet and gave me a single nod. I had tears running down my cheeks. My face felt hot, and I was huffing and puffing. Javier came to me and hugged me. <You did what you had to do.> <You saved us and the ancient Mayans.>

<These people have been living in secrecy for thousands of years and deserve to stay that way.> [I am not sure how they figured out that we were here.] I think I know, I said while trying to calm down. Everyone stared at me instantly.

Kach'ma'o-k, came towards me, "You "astral projected," and they saw you, right?" I was shocked that Kach'ma'o-k had guessed correctly. I guess my face gave away my response to her too. "Yes, I see that I guess correctly." "Let me guess, the Phylmecs have developed to the point that they can see when someone or something is astral projecting, correct?" "Though they may not know how to control it yet, right?"

How did you know this? "I have astral-projected a few times, but only when someone was doing it at the same time as me." "This leads me to believe that the Phylmecs cannot astral project themselves unless you or someone else with that knowledge can do it first." "They then get an energy surge that allows them to tap into the astral-projecting field."

I did not know what to say to her. <Kach'ma'o-k, you are such a knowledgeable person.> Javier said. "It comes with years of experience, and knowledge passed down from generation to generation." "You all must leave now because you are no longer safe here."

Valerie came over to Kach'ma'o-k and looked her straight in the eyes. <We will not leave as long as they keep coming back to fight you.> Kach'ma'o-k smiled and got a tender look on her face, "Do not worry child, our underground village is safe." "They will think that we all fled and left the island." "We will not touch the bodies on the beach to not draw attention, so hurry now to your whale friend." I looked at her in shock. She knew that Tailfin was sentient. I don't know how, but she knew. She winked and gave me a gentle smile. "I wish you all the best of luck, and pray and hope that you find the jagged box with the blue matter."

Just like that, we left the little island of the Native Mayan. {Where are we off to now?} We must go to Honolulu, Hawaii. That is where the blue matter is located. In fact, it is in the center of

Koko Head Trail Mountain. <Cool, let's go.> Javier said. <I hope it is not too dangerous.> Valerie said. [Hawaii is a beautiful place.] I was taken a bit by surprise. This was the first time that my friends did not ask how I knew where something or someone was. They knew Earth had shown me the location, and they trusted me.

I felt them stare at me. I was no longer that boy who did not know what to do in college or life. I was now the person who knew that he was destined to save the world. I stared at my friends and gave them each a smile. I wanted them to know that they were just equally as important as me. <We will do this!> Javier yelled. <Let's get going.> Valerie said. Sevashkish smiled with his big eyes.

Well, let's get going. How far away are we from Hawaii, Tailfin? {By sea we are far away from Hawaii.} {That is over a 3 to 4-day journey even with the secret water highways that I know.} <Well this is hard huh?> <The longer we take the more people that these parasites will take, and then at that point, there will be no planet, or people to save.> Javier was staring extra hard at me while saying all of that, and I knew he had a plan that he wanted to tell me.

A plan that probably meant risking all our lives again. That is probably why he was hesitant to tell me right then and there. <Javier just tell us.> <Whatever it is just tell us.> <We are all in this together, and whatever it is, we will face together.> Good ole Valerie had sensed what I had sensed. She chose to be the bearer of bad news and take a load off my shoulders by being the one to ask

Javier. I felt guilty for being secretly relieved that it was not me this time.

Chapter 22
THE VOYAGE TO HAWAII

<Okay, so Daniel can speak to animals directly, and we know he can control animals.> <Humans are animals too, so he can control humans.> <Right?> [Yes, I believe you are on the right track Javier.] <Okay so here is my plan.> <The fastest way to get to Hawaii is not by land or sea, but by air.> <You want Sevashkish to fly all of us that distance?> Valerie gasped. <No of course not.> <I believe that we can go by plane, or some sort of military jet to Hawaii.>

<We can ask a pilot to take us, but if they do not want Daniel can "control" them and make them fly us.> <Also, we all know the Phylmecs technology is down for now, so they won't even notice if we use our powers.> You are right Javier. When I used my powers to call upon the animals to search for all of you, it went unnoticed

by the Phylmecs. <Okay that settles it then.> <We must find a plane and a pilot.>

[We must go to Miami and get a fighter jet.] We all turned around surprised to see that it was Sevaskhish who had answered. <Sevashkish my man, how do you know where to find a fighter jet?> [Javier when I was in the Luken version of elementary school we had to find a sentient species who had faster-than-sound aircraft but did not have faster-than-light-space travel, and my research led me to Earth.] [Researching this project also led me to love your planet, and all of its beauty.] We all stared at him wide-eyed.

<Are you telling me the Lukens became interested in Earth because we are so far behind that it was part of your elementary school project?> [Of course not, we Lukens knew of Terramondetierra because they were a target of the Phylmecs, but I on the other hand became interested in Earth because of my project.] [I thought it was funny how these aircraft were designed.]

I looked at Javier, Javier looked at Valerie, and Valerie looked at me, and we all started laughing. [What is so funny?] Oh nothing Sevashkish, but let's just say you gave all of us a much-needed laugh. [Well, you are all welcome, but now let's get going to Miami.] Are we close to Miami from here, Tailfin? {We should be there in two hours.}

Great, that means we will be in Miami by 9 am. Hopefully, that means we can also arrive in Hawaii when it is still early there. How far is Hawaii from Miami? Javier asked. <I am not sure, but when I took a trip to Hawaii from California it took us about 5 and a half hours to get there.> <That of course was on a regular plane.> Valerie said. <It would take us at least three more hours to get there now since we are further East.> <That is if we were on a regular plane.>

That makes sense Valerie. Sevashkish, how far is Hawaii from Miami on a fighter jet? [It depends on the type, but most fighter jets can fly up to one thousand miles an hour, so Hawaii is about 4500 miles away.] [That means we are still looking at around at least a 4-hour plane ride.] That isn't too bad. Plus, at least we know that the Phylmecs do not have access to their ships right now. They are equal to us now. We take a 4-hour plane ride, and so do they.

<Whooh, to human technology.> <Let's see who can get where the slowest.> Javier laughed. <On a serious note, are we 100% sure that their technology is useless right now? [Yes, Javier, they are only able to access Earth machinery, or that is until they start to build other machinery here on the planet.] [It has been two days since our battle, and I am sure they are already working on advancing their technological capabilities.] <Oh that is not good, because remember at times of war people produce in mass quantities.> <Maybe we should just destroy all major factories for now.> Valerie looked at Javier with a puzzled look.

<Why would we do that?> <Oh just one of my crazy ideas you know?> <No major factories then no adequate place where they

can build new weapons etc.> I looked at Javier and just smiled. I was happy he was here. He always thought outside of the box. He had just helped us level the playing field a little more.

<How will we destroy the factories, Javier?> <That is where Daniel comes in.> <He must communicate with those people who work in factories and warn them.> <Daniel, are you able to do that?> Valerie asked. I believe I may be able to. I just hope that there are still humans working in these places. I'll give it a try now. I closed my eyes and searched for those who worked in factories.

I started to see and feel those who were working in factories around the world. I saw through the eyes of some factory workers working away in China. I rapidly went through what they saw trying to find the people in charge. To my happiness, there were still a couple of humans in charge who had not been harvested. I had to work fast because some of the "people" around these humans, I could not penetrate their minds. They had to be Phylmecs. Okay, Daniel, you have to talk to them now.

"Ni Hao, Wo shi American, wo shi Daniel, and I am sorry that is the limit of my Chinese, but I am here to warn you all." "The Phylmecs will start to harvest all of you that work in factories." "You must burn down all factories because the Phylmecs will try to create more powerful weapons in mass production as theirs do not work anymore." "Also, I think 3 of your leaders are Phylmecs because I cannot penetrate their minds." "Please be careful, and just know that Earth is weak, but still fighting, and wants all of you to stay strong."

"Stay strong and resist when you can." "Do not go off killing anyone, unless you see them in the two-day transition of being harvested, or if you see them being harvested." "Remember once someone touches your head a little then it is officially over." I cut my transmission, and I continued to contact factory workers all around the world with the same message and warning. I was feeling proud of myself until I got to India. As I was communicating with a worker in Delhi, our conversation was cut short when someone began to harvest him. Right out of the blue. I could do nothing but stare in horror, and then I heard the child's voice. I heard the Phylmec leader.

SO YOU ARE TRYING TO WARN EVERYONE AGAIN I SEE. YOU DO KNOW THAT I CAN NOW ASTRAL PRO-JECT ANYTIME THAT YOU USE ANY OF YOUR POW-ERS, RIGHT? The small boy stared at me with his intense dark eyes, but I knew well that in his mind was the mind of an ancient Phylmec leader, Tindawnstong. Tindawnstong stared at me, laughing, laughing like a kid who was playing video games with his friend. His laugh was the laugh of the bully teasing someone at school.

I was bullied a lot, and his laugh triggered me. I lost my control and decided to tell him off. Do you think that we are simple-minded monkeys? Do you think that you will have this planet? You have no idea how wrong you are. We will stop your parasitic species. We monkeys as you call us will end the great Phylmecs and stop your havoc on earth. You will never get out of the third dimension.

We will kill each and… <You got to wake up Daniel, the Phylmecs are here.> I heard Valerie's voice cry from a distance, and I knew instantly that I had fallen for the trap that the Phylmec leader planted. He was purposely trying to get me mad to target where my energy surge was coming from. He may not have access to his advanced technology, but he was able to astral-project now. He had pinpointed my location and sent over the Phylmecs who were near our area.

Their technology might not be working but human technology was, and unfortunately, the Phylmecs had people all over the world now. They did not need their craft to get to us if they had people in every major city.

I opened my eyes and a battle was raging on. We were near the military base, and my body was covered with a hard bark material. That had to be Valerie. I saw Javier open the ground between us and the Phylmecs. They were shooting at us with machine guns and with flame throwers. The sound of bullets being shot was hurting my ears. The heat of the flames was making my face sweat. The more they shot, the weaker the large barrier of several hundred trees that Valerie had formed got. We had to get away fast or stop them.

Sevashkish was forming a tornado. He couldn't freeze anyone because of the humidity in the air, so he formed a tornado. I hoped he would be able to control it this time. <Daniel go off and find pilots that can take us.> <We will handle these guys here.> Okay, but please stay safe Javier. <We got these clowns.>

I left running towards the base, and I could see from a distance that there were maybe around 50 guys there. At that moment I wished more than ever that Claude was still alive. He was gifted with seeing the souls of people. If I had to see the souls of people then I had to shut my eyes to fully concentrate, and I did not have the time for that.

There was no other way. I had to take a risk. I ran to the fence with my hands in the air. Guns pointed at me, and then I took the ultimate risk and shut my eyes. "I am Daniel, and I am here because I need to borrow four of your pilots and four fighter jets." "It is crucial that I do this to save the world." I scanned every one of the men there, and out of the 50 men, three were Phylmecs. Vile Phylmecs, but at least they had no weapons, well at least visible to me.

"Those three men standing to the left are Phylmecs!" "Grab them, and don't let them get any weapons!" "Do not let them get close to your head!" The pilots did exactly what I told them, but they looked doubtful. The Phylmecs yelled in vain that they were not Phylmecs. I felt my stomach turn. Maybe they were right, maybe they had a gift for blocking others from seeing their thoughts.

Unfortunately, I could not take the risk. I pushed their pleas from my mind. The majority was more important than the minority. I felt horrible for saying that, but I could not let my emotions get the best of me. I would worry about that later. Okay, Daniel, it is time to focus. "I need the best four pilots to come to me now, and the rest of you get four planes ready for take off." "One more thing, the rest of the planes must be burned down, so the Phylmecs do not pursue us."

Slam, slam slam! I was pushed to the ground hard. I hit my head, but luckily on lush grass. One of the Phylmecs that had just seconds ago pleaded for his life had his forehead in contact with my forehead. I looked at him with intense anger. You know you can't turn me, right? He looked at me with eyes that looked like they wanted to kill me right then and there. Of course, he couldn't turn me, as long as I wore the necklace that the native Mayans gave me. I tried shoving the Phylmec off of me, but he had the human body of someone who was well over 6 feet and at least a solid 230 pounds of muscle.

The other soldiers ran to help me, but the two other Phylmecs were trying to block their path by locking the gate behind them. The Phylmec started to choke me with some sort of metal chain. I was losing consciousness, but I wouldn't go out like that, and that's when I felt the presence of a particular reptile near me.

"Alligators come get your meal." Within seconds two large alligators jumped out of the small pond near the military base. They came and each took hold of the Phylmec's arms and they carried him away. I quickly took the chain off my neck. I started coughing, but I was okay. The Phylmec on the other hand, would have a slow painful death.

I was upset at myself for being so careless. I would never let that happen to me again. Next time I was attacked I would kill them from within their own bodies. I would never be caught off guard like that again. I've had enough. It was a war to save Earth and I had to be vigilant. I could not make any more amateur mistakes. I dusted myself, and I slowly walked back to the gate, by this point, the other two Phylmecs were tied by the soldiers.

We are so happy that you are okay, Daniel. We are sorry for ever doubting you. What can we do to help? Did you find the four pilots and four jets? *Yes, we have your four pilots here, including me, and we are currently fueling the jets. They should be ready in ten minutes.* [We are on our way Daniel, but we must hurry because more Phylmecs can arrive at any minute, through sea or land.] [Tailfin has found a secret highway passage to Hawaii, but it will still take him twenty hours to get here, sixteen hours after us.]

Thank you all. My friends should be here soon, and there are a few things I need to tell you. First, when we leave, you all must leave as well. I suggest you take what you can from this facility. Any weapons or food. Things may get really hard for a long time, but please try to help as many people as you can. Just remember to trust no one, but spread the word.

Do not let anyone near your head, because once they touch you, your literal soul dies. You won't have a chance of an afterlife without your soul. You will be dead. I noticed that a few of the soldiers were tearful as I told them all of this. I could only imagine the people that they had lost. I felt bad, but they had to know the truth of what was going on. This was war.

I was about to tell them more, but at that very moment, Sevashkish started to land right in between the men and me, with Javier and Valerie on his back. It still amazed me to see how massive his wings were, and especially the big golden swords he had attached to them. It astonished me even more when he stood on two legs and saluted the soldiers. Usually, Sevashkish stayed on all fours, but when he stood on his two legs he was well over 7ft tall. All the soldiers including the pilots ran to meet my friends. They stared at Sevashkish with great intensity.

The pilot who had introduced himself to me went over to greet Sevashkish. He saluted him and said, *"It is a great honor to meet a real-life alien and an alien who is defending a world that needs his help."* [I am glad to do my best to help Earth.] [Earth is an amazing world that cannot be lost to these vile creatures.] [I am grateful for all of you helping us too, but now we should get going.] The pilot nodded and led us to the four jets.

<If anyone cares I am Javier, and this is Valerie.> Javier looked at me while saying that. He could not keep a straight face. <I guess when you see an alien for the first time, well an alien that doesn't look human all of your attention kind of goes toward them, right?> <You got that right, Javier.>

We headed toward the fighter jets and surprisingly, they were not as big as they looked on TV. They were probably the size of a semi-truck. That made me nervous to get on them. I once read that smaller planes get in accidents more than larger planes. To make matters worse, we had to wear the fighter jet masks, and let me tell you if you have never put on a fighter jet mask then consider yourself lucky. It is the tightest thing imaginable, and highly uncomfortable.

I felt super bad for Sevashkish because even he had to wear one, and he doesn't exactly have a human face. Thankfully, his head was similar enough to a human's that a large mask was able to fit him. *We are ready.* The lead pilot, who I assume was the captain, looked at us and instructed each pilot to get into their fighter jet. I stared at the other soldiers as they waved bye to us. I stopped and stared at them.

Everything was moving faster now. It was getting overwhelming. I took a deep breath to ground myself, and I took one last stare at the soldiers. Half of them were burning down the remaining jets and removing things from the facility. It was a shame to be doing that, but it was the only way we could assure that the Phylmecs would not follow us. *We leave in 3 minutes.* The captain's voice brought me back to the attention of the jets. I watched as the others got inside their jets, and then I got into mine. I was in the captain's jet, and through the audio speaker he said, "*Have you ever been on the Superman ride at Six Flags?*" I answered him, "Yes."

Good, because the takeoff from this is a lot like that, here we go! He was not lying about the takeoff being incredibly fast. Before I could probably blink we were up in the air. I couldn't breathe properly for about ten seconds, but then my body adjusted. When we got to cruising speed the captain began to talk to me. He was extremely talkative, which was bittersweet for me. I wanted my personal space, but I also wanted a distraction from my reality.

The captain who indeed was the captain was named Hank Gomez, and he has been in the service for 15 years. He joined when he was 18. He is married and has a daughter. *Do you want to know something interesting that my three-year-old daughter said?* Sure, what did she tell you? *When the Phylmecs first arrived she said,* "Daddy they are evil." *I told her,* "No mama, they are nice and here to help us have a better life," *but she kept telling me,* "No Daddy see there is no one inside them." *We eventually convinced her to stop saying they were evil, but when the news reports came out of you and your friends, she looked me directly in the eye and said,* "They are nice." We lost a good friend who could see the souls of people through their eyes, maybe your daughter is like that. She must be a very special person. *Yes, you have no idea how special she is.*

Captain Hank asked me about every question he could think of and was surprised to find out that I was just a regular college student until about a month ago. *I'm so sorry that you and your friends have gone through all of this. I cannot even imagine the responsibility that you all must bear. You all are brave and amazing.* It was honestly nice to hear that coming from someone, especially since the entire planet hated us less than 3 days ago. Thank you, Captain Hank.

I appreciate it. *No problem, we are about 40 minutes from Honolulu, but it seems that no one is working at the airport since there are no airplanes that are showing up on radar around the island. This is strange.* To me, it didn't sound strange considering the circumstances. I would have to use my powers to see what was truly happening. I would do my best to not engage with anyone while using my powers. I think my engagement with others is what allows the Phylmecs to Astral Project and discover our location. It's just a theory, but a theory that I felt strongly about.

I closed my eyes and focused on Hawaii and the people there. I only saw a few human souls on the island. Sadly, I just saw black empty spaces on the majority of the "people" there. They were now Phylmecs. Phylmec after Phylmec only. This is horrible. I know I shouldn't engage, but I have to warn at least the humans that are still there. "To anyone listening to this, please hide as the majority of Hawaiians are now Phylmecs." I was about to say more, but I cut the communication short. Hopefully, my engagement wasn't long enough to be traced.

Captain Hank, they have all been harvested by the Phylmecs. *What, are you sure?* I am beyond sure. Also, we cannot land there. If we land it will be a nasty battle. Do you have enough fuel to go back home? *Yes.* Good, you all need to return now. *Then how will we drop all of you off?* I stayed quiet, and let the silence be my answer. *You want me to eject you, don't you?* Yes, please contact the other fighters and tell them to explain to my friends what is going on. Please leave us as close as possible to Koko Head Mountain, and do not communicate with anyone from ground control. *You got that? Yes, I understand Daniel.* We started to descend.

Daniel, I do not think it is wise to drop you off on the island of Honolulu. Why, Captain Hank? *As I was getting closer to an appropriate altitude to eject you I noticed what looked like spears all over the island. Big long dangerous spears. You all would be impaled.* I instantly thought of the two Phylmecs back in the station in Miami. They must have gotten out somehow or were able to communicate with the Phylmecs. The point is, they warned the Phylmecs that we were headed to Hawaii.

It made sense as to why there were almost no humans on the island. The Phylmecs discovered that we were coming and harvested everyone. I was beyond mad and also scared. Something in my gut told me that they suspected the reason for our trip. It is the only explanation as to why they would harvest so many people, and put their people at risk.

Captain Hank, you must eject us at least 50 miles away from Honolulu. That way we can guarantee no Phylmec eyes see us. *Eject you in the water? How will you swim that far? It is almost impossible!* Do not worry Captain Hank, we will be fine. Earth has given me the power to control every being on this planet. I will call on sea creatures to help us. Sorry for rushing, but we have to get moving and there is no time to waste. Captain Hank nodded. He radioed the other jets, and then I thanked him for all his help and wished him the best. *It was an honor to be part of your journey, Daniel. The greatest honor of my life. Defending planet Earth.*

A minute later I was in the air with a parachute slowly flying down to the ocean. I turned my head and saw my friends falling next to me. Even though the circumstances were dire, the experience was amazing. I saw the beauty of the world from a different perspective. Sadly, I could not enjoy it the way I would have wanted to. I had to call on a big sea creature to help us.

I closed my eyes and pictured whales and dolphins, or any creature that wouldn't cut us with its skin. Unfortunately, the last time that I had called upon a shark, its skin had cut some of the others. Turns out sharks have razor-sharp skin. Who would have known that, right?

The feeling of falling from the sky to the ground is something I will always treasure. No one knows how big the world is until they fall from the sky. <We must have been really high up, huh?> [Yes, Valerie we were at the threshold of breathable air and maintainable oxygen levels.] <I think I am going to be sick.> I turned around and saw Javier throw up. I felt bad for him. <I'm sorry guys I couldn't hold it in.>

Don't worry Javier, we should be landing in the water soon. As we were landing in the ocean I was relieved that the water was not cold. It was lukewarm. That was a nice surprise. <I am loving this water.> <So am I Javier!> Guys, I see the pod of sperm whales! We quickly each got on one. I felt the mind of the animal with my own.

Something that I have learned now is that I can physically control and manipulate the mind of the animal too. When I first used my powers I thought I could only tell them what to do, but that is not the case. I can physically change the way they think and feel, but I do not like doing that unless there is a cause for it. That being said, the most important thing that I have learned in the past few weeks about my power is that I can also speak to the animal and understand it. I truly love this

Of course, animals do not speak in ways that we humans consider speaking, but they do speak. The sperm whales felt that the Earth was different. They felt that the Earth was sick, but they did not know about the Phylmecs. I painted a picture of Tailfin for them, and they knew of powerful blue whales who rivaled even the land-walking apes in intelligence. [Daniel, do you have any idea how we will get to Koko Head Mountain?] Sevashkish's question awoke me from my trance. I was deeply in the mind of the sperm whale.

Sevashkish I think the only way of reaching Koko Head Mountain alive is with your help. <You want him to blanket the entire island with a dense fog, and you want dark clouds to cover the sky, so it can imitate the night, don't you?> Well Javier, yes the fog was correct, but nice touch with the dark clouds. That will be even better. <If it is super dark then there is no way we will be able to see our way to the mountain.>

<Valerie, that is easy, Daniel can just call upon nocturnal creatures like bats to guide us there.> <You got a point there Javier.> [That is something that I can do.] [I will create a dense fog that will blanket the entire island for miles, and I will call upon the darkest rain clouds imaginable.] [Once we reach the land I will fly us out there with the help of bats guiding us there.] [We cannot risk not even the smallest gap in light, or we can be detected by the Phylmecs.]

Okay, we have a plan, everyone. Does it sound good? <Sounds perfect to me,> Valerie said. <You got it, Daniel.> Javier said, and Sevashkish simply nodded. Perfect. Sevashkish, may I also ask you to lower the temperature to at least 60 degrees? This will hopefully prevent the Phylmecs from getting used to their stolen bodies. <That is a good idea, Daniel.> <They do not deserve to take over the body they stole.> [I agree with you, Javier.]

<Guys, I want to tell you something.> <What is it, Valerie? <This is the last battle we will have.> <Either we win or we lose, but this is our last battle.> <This invasion has changed all of us, and every single person in this world.> <I have learned that life is so important and precious, and I want to tell you all that I love you.> <I would give my life for any one of you.> I felt my eyes get watery as Valerie spoke. <I would do the same for each of you,> Javier said. [As would I.] You guys should never doubt that I would too. We are all family, including Tailfin, but let's not think that way. We have to win, but I will be honest.

I am beyond scared of what will happen, but I will do my best to fight for Earth and every single organism on this planet. I would give my life for all of you, but I do not want to die. I want to have a future too. I want to become the best linguist that there ever was. I want to be more than the average linguist.

I will become an officer of linguistic cultures. <Did you just make that term up?> Yes, Javier I did, and I quite like the sound of it. I smiled at my friends. I will be someone who is not just a soldier, but a teacher of languages and cultures. Not just humans anymore, but aliens and animals. I now know who I am and my purpose.

<My boy Daniel there you go.> <I always knew you would do amazing things.> Javier looked at me with a huge smile. <We are in this together.> Valerie said with a smile. [One for all and all for

one.] <Whatever happens there we will give it our all.> Javier said. So let's get moving! It was time for the last dance.

Chapter 23
THE BATTLE AT KOKO HEAD MOUNTAIN

<If there are Phylmecs in Koko Head Mountain what do we do?> <I think you know the answer to that Javier.> Javier looked at Valerie with a shocked expression. I don't think Javier understood how much Valerie had changed since all of this started. He looked at her for a brief second and then just shrugged his shoulders. <You are right, we fight and we give it all we have.>

[Remember do not let them capture you or turn you.] [It is better to die a quick and painless death with your soul intact than to be harvested and lose your soul.] We all agreed that we would help kill the other if there was no way to save that person. Horrible things to talk about, but that was the way that it had to be. The stakes were higher than ever before.

Okay guys, before we go in we should talk about how exactly we will retrieve the blue matter. How will we retrieve the jagged cubed box and survive, I said to myself silently. <I will form a barrier of plant life all around us.> <This is Hawaii so we should have enough protection to last a while.> <When you give the command I will open up Koko Head Mountain and you can retrieve the cube.> <Also, I will use the parts of the mountains as defense as needed.> Javier added.

[I will do my best to use the dark clouds to cause lightning and strike as many Phylmecs as I can.] [I will freeze as many as I can as well.] I looked at my friends as we each talked about the plan. It surprised me how easily we were talking about killing now. We would seriously need professional help after this. A wave of sadness flushed through me, but I had to shake it off. I have to push these emotions out of my mind for now. I cannot afford to be distracted right now. There are more important things to worry about, like getting the blue matter and saving the world.

Guys, I sense a lot of animals on the island. I will send every animal that I can to retrieve the box. Also, I know that there are some zoos on the island of Honolulu, and they have few apex predators there. I will call upon them, and I will show them how to escape from their enclosures. <That is a smart idea because we will need firepower.> Javier said. I closed my eyes and I told all the animals that I could, to hide near Koko Head Mountain. They will help us if things get rough.

<Seems like we are all set.> <Everyone ready?> Javier looked at each of us. No one said a word, but we all nodded in agreement. Before we left I instructed the sperm whale to stay in the general area until Tailfin was able to arrive. We would be needing him, and he wouldn't be here for another few hours, unfortunately.

[I will start to form the clouds over the island now.] [I will do it slowly to not raise suspicion.] <Does that really matter though?> <I mean they know that we are here.> [That is true Javier, but also it will have them doubting if it is regular island weather or us.] <Hmm I don't know, but whatever you feel is best Sevashkish.>

It took Sevashkish about twenty minutes to properly coat all the islands with dark rain clouds and some fog. It was only around 2 pm island time and it looked like it was evening. That was perfect for us. [I am ready to go when all of you are ready] [I have slowly started to dense the fog as well, so in five minutes it will be very thick.]

I stared at my friends one last time before saying "Let's go," and they looked so tired and beaten down. I looked at Javier and felt bad for just noticing how blue his arm was still. It had not healed at all, and at this point, I was sure that it was infected. I glanced at Valerie. She looked tough as nails. Especially with her new hairstyle, but I knew that inside she was broken. It was only a matter of time before they both broke down.

As for Sevashkish, he just looked tired and ready to go back to his planet. He was in a different dimension. I am sure it was taking a toll on him physically. Plus if Terramondetierra died Sevashkish would never be able to go back to the 7th dimension. <Daniel, are you there?> I turned around and saw Javier snapping his fingers to my face. Yes of course! <Well you've been daydreaming.> Javier gave me a push. <Come on let's go.> I quickly got on Sevashkish's back with Valerie, and Sevashkish grabbed Javier.

[Daniel please call on the bats to be our eyes and ears.] I was getting confident with my powers now and this time I did not have to close my eyes to call upon the bats. I simply thought of the word bat, and within a minute well over a hundred bats came flying to sea. I now saw through an animal's eyes. I could see what the bats saw. It felt like I was in a big room staring at over a hundred different tvs. I decided I would focus on just four, or else my mind would be too confused. I am ready now Sevashkish, and just like that, we took off towards Koko Head Mountain.

It took us about one hour to reach the top of Koko Head Mountain because flying blind is incredibly hard when you can't see anything but weird sketches. I found out that bats can "see" in complete blindness but only through echolocation which comes in weird sketches back into the bat's brain. It is not a clear image, more of a black-and-white image. Regardless it was clear enough to get us where we needed to be.

During our slow-hour flight we "saw" several Phylmecs stationed all over Honolulu, and there were some at the base of Koko Head Trail. We had no indication that the Phylmecs knew where we were going which was a good thing. If we worked fast we should be able to retrieve Earth's blue matter before they found out. As long as we didn't take too long I hoped. <I guess it is my turn now right?> No, not yet Javier. Valerie, may you please form the biggest barrier that you can over and around us? <I am on it.>

The trees around us started taking shape around our bodies. The bark gently scraped my skin, but still caused me to bleed. Within a minute we had a full suit of "armor." We were like knights, but instead of shiny armor, we had hard bark. Soon after, there was a thick wooden barrier surrounding us at the top of Koko Head. Valerie would not close the barrier until Javier opened up Koko Head Mountain. Javier my boy it is your time to shine. <Please give me some space guys.> <I need to get this right.>

I stared at Javier and he raised his good arm high into the air. The middle of Koko Head Mountain started to open. Right where the lava would escape from. A hole the size of two people split right through the mountain. The ground shook, but we were ready and hugged the floor.

I hoped that it wasn't felt down at the base of the mountain. It is my turn now. The animals that I had called for were near us, hiding. I felt the apex predators near, but now I needed small animals. Rats, snakes, birds, everything. Come to me, and find this box. In a matter of seconds a fury of animals came running into the open space Javier had made in the mountain's head.

Most were going to be burned alive, but I knew that by sending a lot it would form sort of a bridge for the one lucky animal to go down there and retrieve the jagged box. I felt awful doing this, but there was no other way. <I hope they find the box soon because I am getting a really bad feeling about this.> <Don't worry Javier I will close the top of the barrier to give us safety.>

Just as those words slipped out of Valerie's mouth Javier's infected arm fell to the floor. I stared in horror at the stump. His arm was fidgeting on the dirt, and as I stood there in shock, I soon heard the silent humming of a drone. I looked up and saw the lever on the drone that had shot Javier's arm off. I was furious. Before I could react Sevashkish froze the drone in midair and it came crashing down on the ground. It broke into a million pieces. I ran to Javier's side. He was in shock, but Sevashkish came over and touched the gaping wound where his arm was, and froze it tight.

There was blood all over Sevashkish's face (Javier's blood.) [This should keep you safe until we can get out of here.] [We must find the cube now!] [They will be here in seconds.] <I have closed the top of the shield.> <Let us go find this cube.> I searched the animal's eyes, and to my happiness, the box had been found. It was being carried up by ten rats.

Guys, the cube has been found. The rats are carrying it back up. They should be here within the next 30 seconds, and that is when the first dynamite explosion hit the shield. It threw me off my balance, but I quickly got back up. Then I heard machine guns hitting the shield. The sound was unbearably loud. They would destroy this place within a minute. Hurry please, bring me the cube, I thought silently in my head.

<They shot off my arm.> <They shot off my arm.> <They shot off MY ARM!> Javier, I can't even imagine what you are feeling right now, but we have to get that box to stop them once and for all. Is there a way that you can open the terrain to separate them for us? <I will do more than that.> The rats would be here in 15 seconds. Come on I thought, so close, and then I heard his voice. I heard Tindawnstong. JAVIER, I AM SORRY WE GOT OFF ON THE WRONG FOOT, AND I AM SORRY FOR YOUR ARM, BUT TO MAKE IT UP TO YOU I BROUGHT YOUR DAD. <What?>

Javier, it's dad. I love you so much but do not do anything to save my life. My life has meaning through you. Save the world, and don't develop a dark soul. You have always been special to me and your mom, and know that your mom is safe. They only found me before you and your friends disabled their technological system. They are just disgusting viruses, Javier. The rats jumped up out of the hole and came with the cube towards me.

The ground violently shook again, knocking me off balance once more, and then the ground opened up again and I started to fall. We were all falling. Rocks were falling like crazy. Valerie's shield was broken. I saw Phylmecs falling to their death. I saw some heading towards the lava, and others falling towards the ocean. I was falling towards the ocean myself, and then I saw Tindawnstong, the "little boy." He was falling towards the box. Oh no you don't I thought. Eat him alive. Eat them all alive, I thought, but to my horror, they were not twitching in pain as I had expected.

They must have taken something to temporarily neutralize the bacteria in their vital organs. Still, I called upon my animals and mosquitos and small insects to come to my defense. The insects started flying into their stolen eyes. I was about to hit the ground when Sevashkish came over and grabbed me. Thankfully he had Valerie and Javier with him, and unconscious Javier, but an alive one.

[I believe Javier lost control of his powers.] We need to get the box it landed over there by the entrance of the forest at the base of the mountain! Hurry, the Phylmec leader is heading that way. I looked towards the ground and before Tindawnstong hit, he pressed a button on the backpack he was carrying, and an engine-powered suit kind of like Iron Man's suit quickly covered his body. It looked medieval, but effective. I saw the Phylmec leader land with four of his men who each had a similar suit to his. <Trees form a barrier to protect the box, and weeds and grass wrap around these evil alien invaders.>

Immediately, the Phylmecs were wrapped tightly around with twigs and roots and everything you could think of. The four Phylmecs instantly went unconscious, but the leader simply burned the plants off. Tindawnstong must have small weapons installed into his suit or something. [I will freeze him and strike him with lightning.] Sevashkish did just that. He simply froze the Phylmec leader and struck him with a bright ray of lightning, but then the Phylmec simply started to walk faster toward the jagged box.

ARE YOU ALL WONDERING HOW THIS SUIT IS DOING SO WELL? WELL LET ME TELL YOU ALL. I DID NOT GET TO BE THE LEADER OF THE GREAT PHYLMEC SOCIETY WITHOUT BEING INCREDIBLY SMART. WE MAY BE POWERFUL, BUT I NEVER UNDERESTIMATE AN ENEMY, EVEN IF THEY'RE JUST MONKEYS. I ALWAYS CARRY THIS OMPHNITE SUIT WITH ME. YOU MONKEYS DO NOT KNOW THAT OMPHNITE IS AN ELEMENT THAT PLANETS USE TO FORM, RIGHT? SO TERRAMONDETIERRA'S TRICKS CAN'T AFFECT THE SUIT.

[That suit works to defend our attacks, but he isn't attacking us.] [I believe that we have to be at close range for him to attack us.] [Also, we must attack his exposed skin for us to have any effect on this parasite.] Thanks, that is all I need to know, Sevashkish. Animals come to me now I yelled in pure anger. YOU REALLY THINK YOUR PUNY EARTH ANIMALS WILL HAVE ANY EFFECT ON ME?

Two big leopards came down from the trees and started to swipe at the Phylmec's exposed face and legs. He went down hard. I ran for the jagged blue cube, but then I fell to my knees when I heard two gunshots. I turned my head and Valerie had been shot in the leg. Before I could see who or what had shot. Sevashkish simply swiped his massive wing over the arm that shot the gun. The stump bounced as it hit the flood. Valerie already had formed a bandage over her leg, so the bleeding had temporarily stopped.

I continued running and then saw that my two leopards were dead. They had gotten too close to Tindawnstong and he simply killed them. He ran for the gun that was still attached to the stump and grabbed it. YOU ARE NOW GOING TO DIE NOW EARTH MONKEY. AGHH. YOU HUMAN FILTH. THE PHYLMEC STARED AT HIS BLOODY HAND. A Hawaiian Hawk hand yanked the gun out of his hands with its massive claws. Birds started diving out from the sky attacking the Phylmec. I heard helicopters nearby. Suddenly vines and trees started to form a sort of dome around us.

I knew it was Valerie sealing up the perimeter. She would trap Tindawnstong with us. [They will start shooting at us soon.] More animals come to me. Attack these Phylmecs. Do what you need to do to destroy them. It had suddenly gotten a lot hotter. I had a feeling that Sevashkish was purposely trying to burn Tindawnstong in his suit, but he couldn't make it too hot, or it would affect us as well. I heard the machine guns up ahead.

I heard the bullets hitting the shield that Valerie had created. We did not have much time. I saw the way Sevashkish added an extra layer of solid ice around the fortress that Valerie had made. Hopefully, that would deflect the bullets.

Tindawnstong pointed another gun he had pulled out from his suit towards me and he fired. He hit every shot he fired. Birds fell to their death. The squirrels, the mice, the chickens of Hawaii. All the animals that I called for sacrificed themselves for me. They were all killed. He must have shot 80 rounds by the time he ran out of ammunition. Tindawnstong stared at us in disbelief as Sevashkish came toward him and dropped him to the floor with a slap of his wings. It was weird to see since he had the body of a child.

I dove down to reach the jagged box that carried Earth's blue matter. I grabbed it. I put it by my chest and the next thing I remember is hearing a ringing inside my ear. I felt the cold rush of air slap my face. I felt strong powerful arms carrying me out of the sight of pure massacre. I felt sudden coldness too. I tried to open my eyes, but they were just so heavy with sleep.

<Let's not wake him.> <He needs to rest.> <He is the one who got us out of that mess alive.> I opened my eyes and it was pitch black. I heard the waves crashing into the sand. I instantly got up and looked around. No one was there. Where am I? I silently called out. {Daniel, I am so happy that you are awake.} Tailfin, you are here? {I am here Daniel, do not worry.} How did I get here, and where is everyone? {You do not remember anything that happened Daniel?} The last thing that I remember is putting the blue box next to my chest.

Then everything else is completely blank. {When you placed the cube by your chest Terramondetierra was only able to partially use it.} When Sevashkish slapped Tindawnstong to the floor he knew it was too late for himself, so he took his omphnite suit off. He took it off and threw it toward the jagged blue box.} {He destroyed most of it with the suit} Where are the Phylmecs now?

Where is Tindawnstong {You killed him.} {You were able to bypass whatever they took to block the viruses and bacteria from their vital organs, and you destroyed him.} {You destroyed over 115 Phylmecs who were secretly hiding there.} {Not only did you save yourself, but you also saved Sevashkish, Valerie, and Javier as they were outnumbered beyond belief.} Where are they now? I felt so confused and afraid.

Chapter 24
THE DEATH OF TERRAMONDETIERRA

{ Valerie is now in the Amazon rainforest.} {Sevashkish is located on an island in the middle of the ocean.} {Javier is in the Himalayas.} What? Where am I Tailfin? {You are currently in Santa Monica, California.} California? {Yes, Santa Monica, California.} What, why? Why did we all get separated? {You were able to give Terramondetierra a bit of the blue matter before it was destroyed.} {You were able to keep the "world, the physical planet" from completely dying, but Terramondetierra.} {Terramondetierra is no longer with us.}

{Terramondetierra used the last of its strength to separate everyone throughout the four corners of the world.} {The Phylmecs are still here, and there are over 4 billion strong on Earth.} {There are only 5.5 billion humans left.} {Two billion are still capable of being harvested.} {Unfortunately, planet Earth has no more life to give.} What do you mean, Tailfin? {Humans, animals, plants, and any living thing on this planet for that matter will grow old but never produce life again.} This couldn't be happening.

How is it possible that our planet is still standing if Terramondetierra is gone? {Terramondetierra's life force is still "alive," but super weakened so it went into a coma.} {Before Terramondetierra went into this state it told me that the only way it can be revived and bring life back into the planet is to remove every single Phylmec from existence in it.} {The mere fact the Phylmecs are here makes it impossible for it to ever awake from its coma.} How will I, I mean how will we do this? {Terramondetierra split all of us up to help distribute what little power it still had over the Earth to help balance it.}

{It is up to us to tell people the truth, and to somehow figure out who the Phylmecs are, and to get rid of them.} That is impossible. We need more help and information than just that. {I am sure we will get it, Daniel.} {I am sure we will, but we must prepare.} {There will be times of great hardships.} {Our herbivores will be the first to go because vegetation will not grow anymore.}

What do you mean vegetation will not grow anymore? {I mean that new plants, grasses, shrubs, and everything that nature has to offer will no longer grow unless we drive the Phylmecs out of Earth, or find a way to stop them here.} I looked at Tailfin and I felt lightheaded. Everything he was telling me was awful.

First, Terramondetierra may be gone, and now we would not have access to plants. No plants mean no herbivores, which means no carnivores, which means starvation.

I knew that some countries had food and water reserves for up to ten years, but that was only in the most developed countries, and even in those developed countries the rations were small. I felt my adrenaline begin to flow throughout my body. I was getting panicky. {Daniel, you are not looking well.} {I am here with you, don't forget that, okay?} Tailfin was right. I was no use to anyone being accelerated and anxious. I took in smaller breaths and calmed myself down a bit.

Thank you Tailfin for reminding me that I am not alone. {You are welcome, Daniel.} Tailfin we must get to those food reserves now. We must get to them before the Phylmecs even know what happened. How long was I asleep? {You were asleep for 5 hours Daniel.} Do you know if the Phylmecs know that the jagged box is destroyed and that their leader is killed? {Earth told me that if they do not hear from their leader for seven hours then they get a new leader and assume the worst.}

So that leaves us with one hour to find the food reserves, but where do we even start to look for them? {That is another reason why we are in Santa Monica Daniel.} {Santa Monica is home to one of the biggest ration warehouses on the West Coast.} Perfect! Now we need people to help take as many rations as we can to a safe location.

I closed my eyes and searched in my mind for people. I searched for those who were not Phylmecs, and to my horror, there were only about 300,000 humans left in Los Angeles. Los Angeles had a population of almost 5 million people. Almost 5 million! Tailfin these monsters not only harvested most of Los Angeles, but they must have killed those they could not harvest. They are not playing around anymore. {They have been throwing the dead bodies into the oceans, and it is pure madness.}

They will pay for this. I was starting to get overwhelmed with anger, but that would cause me more harm than good. Okay, calm down, I reminded myself. I had to stay focused. I continued to look for what I was searching for, and within 5 minutes I found ten people who were truck drivers. These ten trucker drivers also only lived about forty minutes away from the warehouse.

I spoke to each of them, and I told them where to meet me, and why I needed their help. I tried to communicate as quickly as I could. The last thing I wanted was Phylmecs to know of my location. I had my fingers crossed that the truckers would show up, so we could hide as much food as we could before the Phylmecs discovered what was happening. Tailfin the Phylmecs do not know about this food warehouse, correct?

{They do not know that this warehouse exists.} {This warehouse was owned by a wealthy older woman who unfortunately passed away from the shock of seeing her niece being harvested.} Her hard work will not go in vain. Tailfin where should we meet after this? {We should not stay in California, and I strongly believe that we should head towards Alaska, but for tonight let us meet in San Francisco.} I don't know why Tailfin suggested Alaska, but I knew it was something that he felt, and I trusted him.

There may be something there that could help us. I was going to ask him to elaborate more, but there wasn't enough time. We had to get moving. Well Tailfin, let's hope it's not too cold there! {I can't make any promises.} Tailfin, what time is it now? {It is 6 am right now, so let's meet at 6 pm in San Francisco.} {Does that sound good?} That sounds perfect, but I suggest we should meet up in a town right before San Francisco.

There is a lake that directly flows into the ocean by the Amtrak station in Emeryville, CA. Does that work? {I will see you there.} Tailfin, do the others know about the food reserves? {Yes, that is also a reason why Earth sent them to their destinations.} {Each destination has food reserves for five-plus years} {What is even better is that those food reserves are in hidden locations, so they won't have to relocate them.}

I breathed a sigh of relief. That was one less thing I had to worry about. {Also, Daniel do not worry, they all know what is going on.} {Terramondetierra explained everything to them as it did to me.} Hearing Tailfin explain all this to me made me feel slightly better. At least I knew my friends were safe for now.

As I waited for the truckers to come, I wondered in my mind whether or not I should take away the powers Terramondetierra gave to my friends. Sevashkish had told me that I could do that. Maybe I should take away their powers and just let all the responsibility and destruction fall on my head. Haven't they done enough? Shouldn't they stay with their families at this time?

{Daniel, whatever you are thinking just know that you should not make any sudden decisions right now.} {Let's get to Alaska first and just rest.} {I have word that there is not too much Phylmec activity there just yet since it is so cold.} Then what should I do, just sit and wait for the world to end?

{The best you can do now is to warn everyone as to what is happening.} {Let them know that the Phylmecs will still harvest them, and they will do everything to get off this planet.} {I know this will be hard, but you must warn everyone about the reality of things.} {It is only fair that everyone has the chance to stock up on food.}

Tailfin! I cannot do that! I yelled at him with pure frustration. There will be destruction and chaos. {Daniel, every person needs a fighting chance.} Something in the way he said "Everyone needs a fighting chance," brought me back to reality. I was no God, I was just a person. I had to let others know everything that I knew.

I am sorry for snapping at you, Tailfin. I will warn everyone. {Do not sweat it, Daniel.} {We are in this together.} I will go ahead and warn everyone in the world that I can reach at noon California time. I think this is the time to warn the world because most time zones around the world are up. {That sounds like a plan.} Tailfin, I need to contact my parents before I go. I need to know that they're okay. {Of course, I understand.} I closed my eyes and looked for my parents. They had been hiding up in Sequoia National Park. They had been up there for 3 weeks.

I am sure that they were tired and scared for not only me but for the entire world. I prayed and hoped that they were still alive and well. Thankfully, my prayers were answered and I found my mother. I was looking through her eyes. She was just waking up. I could see her mind looking at the waterfalls, and where was my father? My mother turned her head and I saw my father sleeping. He was alive too. I was beyond happy. I would quickly communicate with them.

"Mom, Dad you must get to Emeryville by 6 pm today." "The world is dying and will not produce any food or plant life anymore." "The Phylmecs have done destruction beyond belief. They are not doing too well themselves, but they still have hope." "They have hope that by taking the 2 billion harvestable humans left they will be automatically moved from the 3rd dimension directly into the 7th." "I am not sure how, but we have to stop them." "We must get rid of them to save ourselves and our planet."

It was a mix of emotions. I felt my mother's happiness when she heard me speaking to her, but I felt the sudden fear when I explained what was happening. She couldn't answer me, but I knew she understood the severity of the situation. I wished her a safe journey to Emeryville, and I prayed to God that my parents would make it there safely. Tailfin, my friend I will see you at the lake at 6 pm. Thank you for everything, my friend. You should get going and settle everything up with your people too. {Thank you, Daniel, I will see you there.} Promise me that you will get there safely, Tailfin, please. {I promise I will get there safely.}

Talking to Tailfin had grounded me back to the mission. He has a special way of making us feel better. Weirdly, he made me feel connected to Earth, and I was once again reassured why Earth had not just given me all the powers. It was all about connection. It was all about how we are all beings of Earth, and Earth is a being for us. We are all connected. That made me smile a bit. Maybe the connection between all of us was the way to get the Phylmecs out of our planet, or at least eliminate them. The question was, how could we use the connection in our favor?

Too much to think about for now, but I would come back to that thought once I was in Alaska. Besides, I had to get to the warehouse. I decided to go running to the warehouse. It was a short run. It was only two miles from where I woke up, but it made me feel re-energized. It felt good for my mind and body. Feeling my heart rate accelerate for something other than my anxiety felt right. Feeling the runner's "high" flow through my body was soothing. By the time I arrived at the warehouse, the ten truckers were all there waiting for me. Each was standing by their big semi-trucks.

All the warehouse was emptied into the trucks by the time I got there. The ten drivers came to me, and each thanked me for "saving" the planet. I couldn't save it quite yet I explained to them. Nothing will grow and we will all disappear slowly. *You may not know this but we all have faith in your Daniel. Faith in you and your friends. We will do everything we can to help you drive those parasites out of here once and for all.* I smiled at each of the drivers until I got to one in particular. Honestly, I cannot explain how I knew without using my powers, but I knew in my heart that the kid who was standing next to the lady that I just smiled at was a Phylmec.

The kid who could be no other than her child. There was no shine in the kid's eye. Then I knew it was Claude. I felt his presence with me at that very moment, and it told me that the kid was a Phylmec. I had to act fast because I knew what would happen next. The kid would grab her mother's phone and communicate with whatever new leader the Phylmecs had chosen to replace their last. I went towards the woman, ma'am I am sorry to tell you that your child is unfortunately gone, and that person standing next to you is a Phylmec.

What that can't be? Why would you say that my child is one of them? How dare you! After helping you load all these rations into my truck. Everyone was staring at us at this point. Has your child been sick as of late? Can your child walk or talk correctly? *No, that is why I brought them here!* When did this start? *It started yesterday after he had a playdate at a friend's birthday party at Six Flags Magic Mountain.*

Let me guess, all the children came down with the same bug after the trip? She fell to her knees, and her child did its best to run, but it takes about 2 days for a Phylmec to fully take control of a body. One of the other truckers simply picked the child up and sat her down on a chair. I stared at the mom and gave her one of the biggest hugs that I could muster. This is exactly why the Phylmecs need to be stopped. They are evil. They are vile. They are cruel.

They live off stealing the life force of other people. *What will happen to my child?* Well, I will let you decide what to do with her body, but your child ma'am she is gone. This sounds cruel and it is not fair, but your child is gone. You must get the courage to fight for your child. What you decide to do with her body and this Phylmec creature is up to you, but you must decide now because we have to get going.

I do not want to mention what happened next, but ten minutes after that conversation we were on our way to Emeryville Cali-fornia, and as much as I hate to say this I had one less thing to worry about. I decided to ride with the mother of the child that the Phylmec had taken over. She was very adamant that she wanted to be directly involved to give her child's life meaning. I appreciated that. Thank you for coming to help us, ma'am. What is your name? *My name is Teresa and I am from Utah. Born and raised in Utah.* I smiled at Teresa. She had a sweet twang to her voice.

I wanted to keep her talking to try to distract her mind a bit from what had just happened to her child, even though I knew I was just putting a bandage over a bullet wound. What brought you all the way to California? *Well, back home a lot of the people thought the Phylmecs were the ones here to take us to the promised land, and they were actively choosing people to get harvested.*

I felt like the whole thing was wrong. The entire thing seemed off, and when you all had that battle in Mexico a couple of days ago I knew I had to get out of here. I took my things, and Chrissy (my girl), and we left for California where I knew there was a lot of work for me.

I felt like my stomach just dropped out of my body. I had been moving so much and doing so much that I never really saw how this genocide would affect others on an individual level. There are so many humans that you tend to forget that we are all unique. That we all have a unique story; animals included. *Daniel, Daniel what do we do?* Huh, what? I had been so focused on my thoughts that I did not notice that Teresa had been calling my name. *The road is closed and there are military trucks everywhere!*

This snapped me back into reality. I looked around and there were maybe twenty big military trucks blocking the road. I knew they were primarily Phylmec-controlled without using my powers, but still, some may be innocent humans. One thing was certain, the Phylmecs could not know that I was here, nor what my plans were, so I had to make a drastic decision.

They had to be removed. I wish Claude were here to tell me who was a Phylmec and who wasn't. I would have to find out for myself.

I decided to quickly close my eyes and use my powers. I searched for any human souls. I saw two human souls, and from the looks of it, there were about 38 Phylmecs. At least I hope I was right. Claude, you are missed. I had to warn these humans what I would do even if it meant getting noticed by the Phylmecs.

I took the risk and spoke to the humans, and I said "run." *We were now visible to the military trucks.* Teresa slammed the brakes on the truck and we both flew forward. The Phylmecs came toward our door, and sadly neither of the humans that I had warned were running. I didn't have much of a choice. I did not have time to control my powers and not harm the two humans. The Phylmecs would recognize me instantly. I did what I had to do. All the 38 Phylmecs were eliminated, and unfortunately the two humans as well.

Teresa, I need two brave people to move the two main trucks out of the way, so we can get through. Let them know that there were Phylmecs in those trucks, please. Within minutes we had passed the barricade of trucks, and we were on the freeway. I never in my entire life had seen the freeway so empty. I was used to the traffic in Los Angeles, and this almost felt like traffic you would have in a small town. It felt unnerving being the only few trucks on the road.

Would the Phylmecs know? Would they follow us? I only hoped that they had better things to worry about than following ten semi-trucks on the freeway. The good thing about having no traffic was that we were practically sailing to our destination. We would reach Emeryville in about 5 hours. *Have you contacted your other friends? Is there a way to contact them?*

Teresa's question caught me off guard. I hadn't thought about contacting the others. In fact, I needed the alone time to think. The others are my family now too, but sometimes you need that space to evaluate what you need to do as a person, and I am sure they all felt the same. Valerie needed the space to properly grieve the loss of her sister, and Javier needed more space. He lost his dad and his arm.

Sevashkish was lost in a different dimension and had no time to even accept any of this. Lost in a different time never to see his own kind. That is something extremely hard. Teresa looked at me waiting for an answer. I smiled at her and said, "I will soon." Teresa, may you tell me your perspective on how people reacted when the Phylmecs first arrived, and throughout the entire journey?

Well pretty much like I said before in my town in Utah they were treated like Gods and immediately worshiped. While driving through Nevada things were a bit different there. There were people on the streets carrying signs saying that the Phylmecs were not real aliens, that they were a government cover-up to take control of the people etc. People quit going to school. At first, everyone was active on the net, and right before the second week, everything went dark.

There was a worldwide ban on social media and video-watching places like YouTube. The looting got out of control. Crime went through the roof, and after the battle in Mexico, some stability came back due to fear. A lot of people were conflicted as to what was going on, but one thing was clear: a lot of individuals went into hiding. One thing I heard a lot though was, "Were you the real hero, or the villain that the media portrayed you to be?"

I arrived in California, and you are pretty much caught up with everything now. The people now know that the Phylmecs are parasites, and they kill people. Everyone is scared and hiding now, at least that is what I see. No news has been running for over a few days now, but you can be certain that your message has reached the people.

Chapter 25
HELLO MOM

After hearing Teresa share more of her story we both didn't say anything for over two hours. We just drove on. We were left with our thoughts. I think she figured that I kind of wanted to be alone in my mind for a while. I may have drifted off to sleep here and there, but after three and a half hours of driving, I finally noticed the sign that read Emeryville 65 miles away.

We are just an hour away now. I radioed the other truckers to the exact location that I wanted us to stop at. I was starting to feel happy. I was going to see my parents. I hadn't seen them in an entire month at this point. I hope they will be there. Unfortunately, my excitement died down when we were just twenty miles away from our destination.

There was another barricade of military-style trucks blocking the exit of the freeway. They were, of course, under Phylmec's control. Three military trucks were blocking the road. In front of each truck, there was a row of at least 30 people kneeling on their arms. There was also a pile of about ten dead bodies in the middle of the street. I felt my heart beating faster in anger. I didn't even have to close my eyes to use my powers this time.

I simply thought the word "die," and I made all the Phylmecs spasm and get eaten alive by the viruses and bacteria in "their" body. To the humans, I said, " Grab the guns and get out of here." "Hide and warn others of what is going on, defend yourselves against them, and remember we are all children of the Earth, unlike those parasites." Do not stop Teresa. Keep going.

Won't the Phylmecs know it was us? Teresa was right. Only one person could kill Phylmecs that way, and that was me. I had done the same thing in Santa Monica, but that was hundreds of miles away. I couldn't make the same mistake here. I was too close to my destination to risk them tracking us to San Francisco.

"Those of you with guns please shoot the Phylmecs so their leaders do not know that it was me." They shot them without hesitation. I didn't even bother to dive into the morality of what I had just sent the people to do, but to Tresea I said no. "No," they will think it was just people standing up to the Phylmecs.

That is why they shot them. *I'm sorry you have gone through all this Daniel. I can only imagine having to bear so much responsibility at such a young age. I have decided that I will give my daughter's death meaning. I will do my best to help others. I will let others know the truth, and share your journey if you allow me of course.* Thank you, Teresa, your words mean a lot to me. *I am glad and look, we are only ten miles away from the destination you wanted us to be in.*

Ten minutes later we were at the Amtrak station in Emeryville, and it was completely run down and deserted. Not a single car, not a single person. Trash was thrown everywhere, and two trains were abandoned on the tracks. It was 5:45 pm by the time we all parked and got out. One of the other drivers came to me and asked, *so what now?* I was just about to answer him when one of the doors to the train nearest to me opened. I couldn't believe my eyes. It was my mom.

My mom looked like she lost at least ten pounds since I last saw her. She cautiously stepped out of the train. Her hair was messy; her roots were showing. Her clothes looked like they hadn't been washed in weeks. Which I am sure was the case, but she was alive. She was alive and healthy! Mom! I yelled. I ran to her and we gave each other a giant hug. It felt amazing. She had tears rolling down her face, and I guess I did too since my lips tasted salt. Mom, I am so glad to finally see you again.

Daniel, I am so proud of you. You do not understand how proud I am of you. You are such a brave boy. My son, my light. The one saving the world. I pray for you every single moment that I get. I dream of you and wish you the best. I cry at night hoping that nothing will happen to you. My mom was talking a million words per second, yet I understood most of what she was saying. I was just so happy to see her here.

She was here with me in person. Alive and well. I wanted to savor every moment of this meeting, but I couldn't. Mom, we must head to Alaska. Where is Dad? She suddenly stopped talking and gave me a blank stare. A stare that revealed everything and nothing all at once. I felt like my insides were turning, did something happen to Dad? *No son, your father is doing well, but he couldn't join me on this journey.* Why not?

He is one of the leaders of the people that we have been saving since you first contacted us to leave our home. After your last contact with us, we decided to share the news with everyone to give them hope, but it scared some people. You know your dad has a way of calming others down. We both agreed that he would not leave. Mom, but how will he meet us in Alaska? We must get away, the more we wait the more time the Phylmecs have to follow our trails. My mom grabbed my hand and looked at me with tearful eyes. *Son, I am not coming with you to Alaska, and your father isn't either.*

We would compromise the entire mission for you. We know you would risk your life for us, and that is not something that we can do. You are much too valuable for the human race, and all of the life in it. I felt the eyes of the drivers staring at me. My vision had become blurry. I guess I was trying to hold back the tears. I wanted to blink, but I knew if I did the tears would instantly come rolling out. My heart sank to my feet. My mother was crying. Hugging me. She was telling me how proud she was of me, and everything that I had accomplished. She was praying that she would see me again, and hopefully, one day that this would truly be over. I couldn't hold back the tears anymore.

They came running down my face as I hugged my mother. I promise you Mom we will see each other again. I am so proud of you and Dad. I will do my best to always communicate with you both. Please make me proud too. I felt guilty telling my mother that because I didn't truly believe what I was saying. I was a mix of emotions and I felt disoriented.

During the time that my mom and I talked, the tuckers had filled up five cars worth of food on the train. I guess they realized that I planned to take the train as far north to Alaska as I could. They had fueled the train up and started it up. Fortunately one of the ten truckers knew how to drive a train, so he would stay back to drive it. I remember vaguely telling the others if they wanted to come. They all said no, including Teresa.

They took enough supplies to last a year, and then I said bye to them. Finally, it was my mom who left. She took a few supplies in three large hiking bags. I do not even remember how we hugged goodbye. All I know is I ended up by the edge of the river near the station.

{Daniel you will see her again you know that right?} Tailfin you are here! You startled me. I am so glad you are here my friend. I needed someone. {You may not know this Daniel, but you have the whole world with you now.} {Those people who came with you, they are with you.}

{I am with you, and so are Javier, Sevashkish, Valerie, and even Claude.} Thanks Tailfin I guess it doesn't feel like that at the moment. But don't worry, I have more motivation than ever to save our planet, our home, our species, and our creatures. You know what scares me, Tailfin? {What scares you, Daniel?}

I haven't been able to feel Terramondetierra. In some distant way, I always felt Earth. I felt connected to Terramondetierra, but now I haven't been able to feel it. I am scared that TT is truly gone. It scares me to believe that our planet will die a slow painful death. {I do not believe Terramondetierra is gone, Daniel.} {TT must rest, and that is what it is doing.} {It is up to you, and all of us to make sure TT comes back stronger than ever.} {I do not have a clue how that will happen, but I know we will all find out soon.} {I can't explain it, but I know that you must go to Alaska, and something tells me you will find out the reason soon, Daniel.}

{I know the pressure is the highest on you, but just know you are not alone.} {Javier, Valerie, Sevashkish and I are all doing our part to save every living being on this planet.} {We need you at your strongest Daniel because if you fall we all fall.} {Every single person on this planet that has good in their heart is doing their part to defend their home.}

You are right, Tailfin. Like those truck drivers, like my mom and dad. Everyone is doing their part to save the Earth. I got a sudden renewed sense of a small glimmer of hope. We must just find a way for everyone on this planet to connect because the Phylmecs will continue to harvest us if we don't. {Let us hope that people work together to keep the Phylmecs from harvesting any more of humanity.}

I want to ask, Tailfin, are you assigned any particular place on earth? {Yes, the ocean.} {I and 4 other sentient whales are swimming around the world now.} Okay, that is perfect. Tailfin, can you meet me in Alaska in three days? {I will be there, do not worry Daniel.} *The train is ready, and I am ready to go, are you?* I stared at the truck driver and with a smile, I said "Yes sir. " Tailfin I must go now, please be careful. Don't let anyone hurt you. {Don't worry Daniel, I will be on guard.}

{I wish you the best of luck and I will see you in three days, Daniel.} {Just remember, please be near the ocean that way I can find you.} You got it, Tailfin. Thank you for everything you do, and you truly mean a lot to me. I waved at Tailfin as he dove under the water.

Sorry about that, I told the man. Thank you for taking me on my journey. What is your name? *My name is Drew, and the pleasure is all mine Daniel. What you are doing is something that most people would not even dare to do. You are strong and a hero to all of us.*

Thanks, Drew. Which car shall I go in? *You may go on the first cart and we can head out right away.* I smiled and said thank you. I quickly went inside the train cart and headed for the back seats. I felt bad for not engaging more in conversation with Drew. He looked like a nice guy. I just did not want to talk to anyone at that moment.

Once we got going I made my announcement to everyone that I could reach. I let everyone know what was going on. I had been so tired on the way to Emeryville that it had slipped my mind to make an announcement at noon California time. The important thing was that I did it now.

At around 10 pm Drew came over and told me he would stop the train so we could get some rest, and he did. I had no clue where we were, but I was pretty sure we had left California by that point. I had been staring out the window for hours and not focusing. I needed a break, and I still felt tired. I closed my eyes and drifted to sleep.

Sevashkish? Sevashkish is that you? Yes, he was there. I saw him so clearly. He was on a tiny island near the Bermuda Triangle. A hidden island that is usually covered in water, but comes up over the water every 180 years. It only stays above water for 5 years. I don't know how I knew that, but I knew that was the case. He was there! He looked tired. His large wings were crouched down. His humanoid body was more hunched over than normal, and his face seemed sad. Sevashkish, can you hear me?

He jerked his head around searching for the sound. It is me, Daniel. [Daniel is that you, where are you?] [Are you Astral Projecting again?] Oh my gosh, I had forgotten the danger of Astral projection. The last Phylmec leader was able to track me the last time I did this. I must have been so tired that I did not realize what I was doing. My only hope was that the new Phylmec leader was not as keen on its environment yet, as the last one. Sevashkish, you are amazing.

We will figure this out. Please don't lose hope. With that, I was in the Amazon. I saw Valerie. She was with a group of people. She was sleeping soundly while two others took guard. Valerie, Valerie I called. I saw her rub her eyes. Don't get up Valerie. It is me, Daniel. Of course, that shot her straight up. <Daniel?> <Where are you?> Don't worry I am Astral Projecting, and I just wanted to say, stay strong. We will find a way.

Before I heard her answer I was in the Himalayas. I was deep inside a cave, but this cave was not dark inside. This cave had bright light. I saw Javier. He was with a group of locals. Javier looked down and depressed, but he was trying to keep up appearances with a smile. Javier, I called. <Daniel?>

He turned his head in all directions. Yes, friend, it's me. <Where are you?> I am astral projecting, but I don't have much time. Javier, you are amazing. You are a brave person. I am honored to be your best friend. Remember to not lose hope. We have this. I am sorry about your arm and about your father. You are a soldier.

You are fighting not only for a country, but a world, and with that, I left. I only prayed that my mistake and choice of continuing my astral projecting wouldn't lead the Phylmecs to track me. Thankfully, we were not tracked and I woke up a few hours later and felt rejuvenated. I woke up an hour before Drew. I went over to the conductor area and saw that we were about 45 minutes outside of Portland, Oregon.

I was glad Drew was smart and had decided to stop before getting to a major city. I wonder what dangers awaited us when we started our ride again. I had the bad feeling that every time we would pass a major city it was going to be a difficult task. That was one of the reasons why I wanted to start in Emeryville because the train did not go to San Francisco but around it. I took a glance at Drew and decided to not wake him because he would be driving the entire day.

I decided to explore the train a bit and headed towards the diner cart. To my surprise, it was still fully stocked with food. It was stocked with cereals and even non-perishable milk. There were a lot of canned foods and a lot of ready-to-make food items, but most I assume went bad because the refrigerator had been off for so long. I ate some cereal and waited for Drew to wake up. He woke up about thirty minutes later.

Hey Daniel, how are you doing? Are you ready to continue your journey? I'll be honest with you Drew, I just want to get away from any major city. Is there any way that we can get around Portland, Seattle, and Vancouver? I looked at him while he thought. I knew that these were the cities that we still had to get through. *Honestly, there is no way, but don't worry the train will pass the cities rather quickly.* Drew, there's a high chance that things could turn bad very, very quickly. I don't want to scare you, but I want to be honest. *I understand, Daniel. I am here to help in any way shape or form.* Perfect, I am ready to go when you are.

Just remember if I tell you to stop the train you must not hesitate. I saw Drew twitch his face a bit. He was scared, but he would not say anything. I felt bad for being so straightforward and a tad rude, but I could not sugarcoat anything to him. He had to know that we were in a life-and-death situation. I went over and patted his shoulder. He smiled and nodded. He then grabbed a bottle of water and a granola bar and headed to the conductor's car. I followed him out, and soon we were off again.

We are entering Portland in five minutes, Daniel. I felt my heart begin to beat faster. Portland is a city that borders a large forest, so I hoped people had escaped to the forest. As we started entering the city of Portland I began to see dead bodies all over the street. Hundreds of people piled up in corners. People who were not deemed fit enough to be harvested, or people who rather have died than be taken. I saw buildings that were burned to the ground. There were loose electrical wires everywhere, and then I saw people walking around normally as if there were no bodies around them; they must have been Phylmecs.

I closed my eyes and thought about humans. I could not find a single human soul in Portland. The first major city to be void of human life. I turned to look at Drew and his face was covered in tears. I turned away and headed back to my seat. Two hours later we crossed Seattle, and the same horrific plague had taken place in this city. Seattle was destroyed, but at least there was still human life around. I warned all those that I could, and then we left.

Vancouver would be the deadliest city in this short journey. Since we were leaving the USA and entering a new country there would be customs. We would be required to stop, but my plan was to drive through and not stop. I was not sure if that plan would work so we had to be ready and prepared. "Grizzlies, Moose, Raptors await in hiding for me at customs." I silently called out to them.

Daniel, I believe we should stop for an hour or so, to just clear our minds a little. Drew looked at me with his small dark eyes. He looked like he was going to be sick. I felt bad for him and felt guilty for avoiding him for most of the journey. What was becoming of me? I had to remind myself that emotions are important, and so are breaks. Drew, take the time you need. I'll be here waiting for you when you feel better, okay? He looked at me and gave me a faint smile. He stopped the train and got off.

He went to the other side of the tracks and sat down quietly. I got off the train and went outside too. I started walking and soon enough my mind was getting clearer. I had to remind myself that we were all suffering and we all deserved to grieve when possible.

I couldn't keep blocking my own emotions all the time. Sure, blocking my emotions when it was dangerous was sometimes good and necessary, but after the danger, I had to learn how to process my emotions. I couldn't let this war get the best of me. I was not going to let the Phylmecs turn me into them. They were the only true bloodthirsty killers. I have to stay true to who I am. A caring, compassionate, and brave person.

I headed towards Drew, and I stared at him. I hadn't even bothered to look at Drew at all. I had put a guard up to not get hurt when others died, but that was no way to live life. I wouldn't let the Phylmecs take that away from me again. I stared at Drew. He was somewhere between 23-30 years old.

He had dark long curly hair and dark eyes. He had brown olive skin, and he was around my height. I felt awful for being on this trip with him this entire time, and just now seeing him for who he was. Not a driver, but a person. I would not make that mistake again, with anyone.

Drew, how far are we from Vancouver? *We are about an hour's away, and once we cross Vancouver we should be pretty much in no man's land.* Vancouver is going to be the biggest hurdle that we have to cross. Drew, the train has to stop for a customs report. *Will Phylmecs be working there, or regular people, or even a mix of both?* I am hoping it is either just humans or just Phylmecs. Having the two at the same spot would be awful, and then a horrible decision would have to be made. That is why I had called upon my apex predators to await in hiding if needed. I said quietly to myself.

Okay, Daniel calm down, you still have at least an hour before you have to cross that bridge, relax. Hey Drew, sorry for not even being aware of your existence, but thank you so much for coming along with me on this journey. Just know that it means a lot to me and that you are such a brave person. I guess I caught Drew off guard because his face became flushed and he quickly said, "Thank you, thank you, mister Daniel." Just call me Daniel, so tell me a bit about yourself. I am sure you know enough about me, so tell me about you.

Honestly, there is not too much to say. I am an only child who was raised by my grandma. My parents died when I was ten. My grandma got sick when I was 17, so I took on a job as a truck driver and just stuck with it ever since. I love my grandma, and I love my parents. I had a fiance, who was sadly taken by the Phylmecs about a week ago. We were in New York City. I had proposed to her, and she had said yes. We were super happy. We were staying in a nice hotel right in the center of the Big Apple.

While I was sleeping, my fiance woke up early to buy me a New York Cheesecake to surprise me. I always wanted to have one, so she went out to get it for me. Did you get to try it? *No, I woke up to a frantic call from her. "Drew, the Phylmecs are here, they have everyone outside lined up, and they will harvest us." "They are shooting all the weak and those that are too young, or old." "Drew I love you, please get away, hide Drew." "I'm sorry I couldn't be there with you, but I came to get you your cake." "Don't feel bad, it is not your fault, please hide till they are gone, and live a life, fight for your life, fight for me, Drew." That was the last that I heard from her.*

Drew had tears falling down his face, and I felt that my cheeks were wet too. I wiped them away and hugged him. Drew, I promise you that I will take this world back. If you want to cry, cry, but also remember when push comes to shove we must be strong, and defeat these parasites. Drew looked at me with his dark eyes and nodded. Now let's get going.

We are thirty miles from arriving outside of Vancouver, Daniel. Thanks, Drew. It was time. I closed my eyes and searched for humans in the area. Empty, empty most of the Vancouver area was empty. My heart sank deeper into the hole that it was already in. I searched outside of Vancouver and thankfully there were humans scattered in various areas, and some in big numbers. Okay, so this means that more than likely the Phylmecs have taken over most if not all major cities throughout the world.

They have not taken over much of the smaller towns and natural areas yet because based on what I have seen those still have higher numbers of humans. Okay, Daniel, I thought to myself, after you get well away from Vancouver you must warn everyone to not hang out in big concentrations. Something told me that hanging out in smaller groups would help us better survive this massacre.

Daniel, we are ten minutes away from reaching the area where we need to stop for customs control. I heard Drew yell from a distance, but I was already busy, hard at work. I had already called upon a variety of animals after the break we had taken, and the animals were hiding near customs waiting for my command. "Cougars

attack, focus on neck bites, and move on to the next person."
"Grizzlies slam the back of the head with your powerful blows."
"Deers, elks, and mooses pierce their necks with your powerful antlers, and the rest of you get eaten alive by the very bacteria and viruses that your 'body' carries within."

I opened my eyes and felt pain and horror as I knew some innocent humans had gotten killed. I did not have time to concentrate on just the Phylmecs. I had to concentrate on who was there. Within a minute everyone working in customs was gone, human and Phylmec. I felt tired and wrong, but there was no other way.

I pulled out a lighter that I had found in the diner cart and threw it out the window. The customs building quickly caught on fire. I had to hide the evidence of the killing. The Phylmecs could not know it was me. The animals ran back to the forest.

Drew, do not stop and just keep going. *But what about the other trains that may be blocking the tracks?* There are none, Drew. My animals moved the one that was on the track. It is lying on its side now. I quickly closed the curtains to the window where I was sitting. I did not want to see what I already knew, pure destruction. Drew looked out the window as we passed Vancouver. He did not say anything for over an hour, and finally, he broke his silence.

Daniel, I am sorry that you are going through all of this. This is not your fault. Please know that this is not your fault. I gave him a grim smile. *Also, we will need to stop in about an hour. We can then head to a privately owned airport that is in that area.* Why do we need to stop, and why at an airport? I stared at him. *We need to stop because it is the end of the line.*

The train does not go further than this. This is back to wildlife. I felt my face getting red, but I started laughing. Well here I am trying to save the world, and I don't even know basic facts about it and its geography. Drew smiled back at me.

Drew, do you know how to fly a plane? *Yes, I do. This is another reason why I knew that I needed to come with you, Daniel. I grew up flying planes. My grandpa was a pilot, but I never myself wanted to be a pilot. The changing of the time zones is just too difficult for my taste.* You are full of surprises Drew!

An hour later we reached the end of the line which thankfully was only a twenty-five minute walk to the privately owned airport. We got off the train and headed toward the airport. The walk there was nice. It was nothing but wilderness. When we reached the airport it did not look at all like an airport. It looked more like a big farm. It even had a big old red barn right in the middle. There were two airplanes. Two very small airplanes, but they were big enough to carry our cargo. The only thing that made this "airport" look like it was an airport was the long narrow runway.

I am assuming that is what made it an "airport." "If you boys take one more step into my property you will both have a hole coming straight through your legs." I turned my head to the voice. It was an older man, maybe 70 years old. He wore rugged clothes and had a long Santa Clause beard. I stopped walking and closed my eyes. "Sir, I do not mean to cause you any harm." "I am here because I need to get to Alaska, and I need to borrow one of your planes."

I opened my eyes, and he was staring at me with amazement. What do you say, sir? Maybe you can come with us, but just remember that the Phylmecs cannot know where I am headed. They are currently harvesting the entire world, and I need to do something about it. The man put his gun down. "I am sorry for my aggression, but many people have been trying to take my planes." "They think that going to a third-world country will save them from the aliens that are taking us over." No, that will not save them.

"Why don't you boys come in and have dinner with me and my wife? "You can spend the night and have a good night's rest here." I looked at Drew, and he looked very tired. I nodded and headed in with the older man, as he unlocked his gate.

Chapter 26
WHEN WILL THIS TRULY END?

As we made our way into the man's home I could hear a woman crying. I scanned the brightly lit-green-colored house and saw that it was an older lady. "This is my wife Jane." "Rudy, you didn't tell me you would have guests." She said while rubbing her tears away. "Jane these are not just any guests, this is Daniel himself, and I'm sorry what is your name son?" *My name is Drew, and it is a pleasure to make your acquaintance.* Jane ran towards me and started to shake me. She started to yell at me. I was caught by surprise. "Why couldn't you save my daughter and grandson?" She yelled in agony.

"My daughter and grandson are dead because you couldn't save them!" Rudy came over and pulled his wife away. "Jane, stop this." "This young man is the only thing keeping this world going." "If you want to be angry, be angry at the Phylmecs and not with him." Jane sat down on the couch. "I am so sorry Daniel, please truly I am sorry." "I have lost my only daughter and my only grandson." "I am broken, and I took it out on you."

Don't apologize for what you are going through. I can see and feel your pain, so do not apologize. I looked at her sympathetically and then at Rudy. I need to tell both of you one important thing, and I know it will sound awful, but hear me out. We have to turn our pain into our strength right now. We must grieve our losses, but we have to be strong too. If we do not stop the Phylmecs the entire planet will be dead. All of us will be dead. I walked towards Jane and looked into her pale gray eyes.

You owe it to your daughter and grandson to stop these creatures. To save the planet for future life. To give your daughter and your grandson their legacy. It is awful to ask, but can I count on you, Jane? She wiped away her tears. "You can count on me, what can I do?" I need to borrow your plane to make it to Alaska. I need to get there as soon as possible.

Second, I need both of you to take in anyone that needs you. I looked directly at Jane and Rudy while speaking. I wanted them to know the gravity of the situation. The Earth is dying. No new plants will grow anymore. No more births. Earth is in a coma state, and the Phylmecs know this.

They will harvest as many humans as they possibly can before we start to die in masses. "How will the Phylmecs feed themselves?"

They have food supplies to last a few weeks on their ships, but they will also locate all available food sources on Earth. They have already begun killing those that they cannot harvest. This will prevent food competition.

We have to stop them fast. We are almost certain if they take at least 2 billion more humans they will evolve to the 7th dimension and will not need Earth anymore. They will destroy it before leaving it. Rudy stared at me blankly, and Drew just stared intensely. Jane on the other hand had a look of determination on her face. She looked at me and asked, "How will people know to come here?"

"Also, we can host about 100 people for about 3 months." "My husband is one of the conspiracy theorists who always thought the world was going to end." "I guess you were right, Rudy." Rudy got up and simply said "Yup."

I closed my eyes and focused. I saw people but most were far away. They felt at least 50 to 100 miles away. I decided to send out my message to only 60 people. I did not want to overwhelm Rudy and Jane. "If you hear this message, please come to the "airport" 25 minutes south of the end of the tracks." "We have some food reserves for up to three months." "Do not bring any more people only yourself and your family.

Okay, Jane and Rudy, I let 60 people know. That will give you guys a wiggle room if more come along. "Thank you, Daniel." You are welcome, Rudy. If more people than that come, or try causing issues you do not need to worry. I will send out a few grizzly bears to come be your guards. They will protect you. Rudy and Jane both came over and hugged me.

We ended up having a nice dinner. We had meatloaf and potato salad with a slice of moist red velvet cake. It was delicious. After dinner, Rudy and Jane were generous enough to give me a luggage full of warm winter clothing. They also gave me a large blanket with some other supplies. It took a lot of convincing on my part, but Drew agreed to simply drop me off and head back to Canada with Rudy and Jane. He would help them with the people coming in.

That night I slept well. I don't remember any dreams that I had, but I remember falling asleep as soon as my head hit the pillow. I woke up to Jane gently telling me that it was time to go. Sorry, Jane. I'll be out in a minute. She nodded and left the room. I got out of bed, and I went to the restroom. I washed my face and noticed that I looked different, yet again. Maybe it was the bright light, or maybe it wasn't. But my face looked older. It is not like I had wrinkles or anything, but it looked more "mature." The face of war.

I guess stress does age a person. I once read that presidents tend to age much faster than the average person. I guess that was true. Well, at least people would see me as being 17 and not 15. I said to myself jokingly. As I headed out the door I took one long deep breath and stared at the farmhouse. I hoped that I would be able to come back and visit this place one day. I said bye to Rudy and Jane, and we took off. A plane stocked with enough food for a small army, and a guy who was meant to save the world.

The flight went relatively slow. I could not talk to Drew at all because the cockpit only had room for one person, so I just stayed with myself and my thoughts. That was tough. I kept thinking of Sevashkish, Valerie, and Javier. I prayed for their safety. I wondered if my mom made it back safely. So many things to think about, and I was feeling overwhelmed again. I decided to close my eyes to clear my mind, but before I knew it I was asleep. It felt cold, so cold, and it was dark, but I knew it was there. I knew it. Fossilized for billions of years. The one thing that would destroy the Phylmecs, but unfortunately it would destroy most of life on Earth including mankind.

Buried under dirt, rocks, and ice was the Trof. One of the deadliest weapons to have ever been created. Left on Earth by an ancient alien race. A race that had visited Terramondetierra billions of years ago when Earth was just starting to seed life. This ancient alien race loved how Earth was seeding life, and they never wanted it to end.

This alien race knew of the danger of the universe, so they wanted to leave Terramondetierra with something to protect itself, "the Trof." They did not tell Terramondetierra about the Trof. They simply hid it on earth. Terramondetierra never knew of its existence. For billions of years, Earth was left alone, so the Trof was buried deeper and deeper within Earth, and it fossilized. Terramondetierra was never able to detect it, let alone use it, and the reasons why are unknown.

Now that Earth is beyond weak the power that this weapon emits is more detectable. Thankfully the Phylmecs do not have the technology at the moment to detect it, and even if they did they would not be able to use it. The Trof is so powerful that only a living planet can use its power. Terramondtierra is the only one who can handle the Trof.

Once it is used Earth would become void of almost all life. The Trof will cause a fire in every part of the planet, including the oceans. The fire will only last a week, but almost everything that is not single-celled will die. This was the only "sure way" of saving Earth and giving future generations a fighting chance. Terramondetierra would get a chance to "seed life" again as the Trof would re-energize the planet. I was floating at this point. Who is telling me all of this? Show yourself. Who are you? What are you?

WE ARE NO MORE IF YOU ARE HEARING THIS MESSAGE. WE WERE THE FIRST ANCIENT CIVILIZATION THAT CAME TO EARTH. IF YOU ARE HEARING THIS MESSAGE IT MEANS YOUR PLANET IS ON THE VERGE OF DEATH. YOU MUST MAKE THE ULTIMATE SACRIFICE. END ALL LIFE ON YOUR PLANET TO GIVE FUTURE CREATURES A CHANCE TO BE. WE BID YOU THE GREATEST LUCK, BRAVE SOLDIER. YOUR PLANET NEEDS YOU!

I felt shivers running through my body. Who was this mysterious force speaking to me? Where are they now? Do they even exist anymore? What in the world is a Trof? Who am I to decide whether I use it or not? *Daniel, Daniel wake up, we are here. We made it to Alaska.* I opened my eyes and we were no longer in the air. The airplane was docked and parked in an empty airport garage. *Don't worry there has not been a single person in this airport for a few days now. There have been no reports of anything coming in or out.*

I quickly got up. How could I have been so stupid? I let Drew park the airplane without checking if anything or anyone was there. I shut my eyes and scanned for any life around this area. Thankfully Drew was correct, only animal life, no humans or Phylmecs in the area. *We are 40 minutes south of Anchorage in a privately owned airport that has been abandoned I suspect. I walked around the airport, and thankfully one airplane was fully fueled and could take me back to Canada. That means we don't have to remove any of the food cargo from Rudy's plane. Plus this airplane is newer than his, so I am sure he will be quite happy.*

I feel like we should move this plane somewhere safe and try to hide it. As Drew was talking I nodded and smiled, but I was not paying attention whatsoever, and I did not even notice when he left. I kept thinking of the "dream" that I had just had. Was it real? Had I imagined it? Who and what had contacted me? *Daniel, I was able to hide the plane three miles from the airport near the mountains, let me take you there.*

I was so lost in analyzing my dream that I didn't even notice that Drew had been gone for almost an hour and a half. It took us about an hour to get to the place where he had hidden the plane. Thank you Drew for everything that you have done for me and our world. You must get back to Canada before the evening. I appreciate you. I closed my eyes and scanned the area for any large animal that could take Drew back to the airport, and I saw several caribou near the area.

Come to me Caribou. I need you. A minute later a large caribou came in. Drew, this caribou will bring you to the airport. Go now, my friend. Go save some people.

Drew looked at me with sorrow on his face. *I can stay here with you to help you, Daniel. Just give me the word and I will stay here.* You are needed more in Canada Drew, but just be ready if I call you, okay? *How will you call me?* I pointed at my head and smiled. Drew smiled and just like that he was gone.

I waited for an hour to pass before I did anything, and then I pulled up a map from the computer panel on the plane. The GPS showed me that I was only five miles from the ocean. "Tailfin if you can hear me I am coming to you now." I hoped that he would be there. Even though I knew that it was highly unlikely.

I grabbed a large jacket and put a beanie on. I went to the back of the plane to grab a snack for the road. My heart started to flutter when I saw the box of burritos. The same ones that I used to have for breakfast. A tear rolled down my cheek. The last time I had eaten one was the last day my life was "normal." I decided against eating it. I would not eat one till I knew Terramondetierra was safe. I headed for the exit on the plane, and I hopped off. On my way to the ocean. Only time will tell what will happen.

About the Author

E.R. Ayon was born and raised in a small town in California. He has lived and studied both in the USA and France. He is an educator and holds a Master's degree in TESOL Linguistics. E.R. Ayon developed a passion for reading science fiction and horror books from a young age. He loved how those genres of books took him to places so different from his own world. E.R. Ayon hopes his book PHYLMECS can help someone let go of their problems and divine into a fun, exciting universe he's created. E.R. Ayon can be found on two social media sites.

@ayonrunner is his Snapchat @howdoI15 is his Twitter.